www.totallyrandombooks.co.uk

Also by Victoria Lamb:

For adults
The Queen's Secret

Witchstruck

✣

VICTORIA LAMB

CORGI BOOKS

WITCHSTRUCK
A CORGI BOOK 978 0 552 56611 7

Published in Great Britain by Corgi Books,
an imprint of Random House Children's Publishers UK
A Random House Group Company

This edition published 2012

1 3 5 7 9 10 8 6 4 2

RANDOM HOUSE CHILDREN'S PUBLISHERS UK
61–63 Uxbridge Road, London W5 5SA

www.**kidsatrandomhouse**.co.uk
www.**totallyrandombooks**.co.uk
www.**randomhouse**.co.uk

Addresses for companies within The Random House Group Limited can be found at: www.**randomhouse**.co.uk/offices.htm

THE RANDOM HOUSE GROUP Limited Reg. No. 954009

A CIP catalogue record for this book is available from the British Library.

Printed and bound in Great Britain by CPI Group (UK) Ltd, Croydon CRD 4YY

For my daughter Becki,
whom I hold entirely responsible
for turning me to the dark side.

✠

Contents

Much suspected of me,
Nothing proved can be:
Quoth Elizabeth, prisoner

Reputedly scratched on a window
at Woodstock Palace, 1554

ONE
Full Moon

When the power falls on me, it buzzes in the warm, dark spaces of my skull. It stings like nettles at the tips of my fingers. The power is a fever I have felt since early childhood, a heat in the blood that leaves me flushed and unsteady, dreaming in daylight. My aunt once told me the power came from being born on the spring equinox under the martial sign of the Ram, with baleful Saturn rising. And truly my power is often strongest when Mars and Saturn clash in the heavens, as they did the day I was sent to serve the imprisoned Princess Elizabeth. Yet on that occasion I was unable to influence my own fate.

I felt the power that evening of the full moon in June though, sitting cross-legged in the ruins of the old palace at Woodstock. I stared across the candlelit circle at my aunt's narrow, slant-eyed face and *hungered* to be a witch, just like her.

Aunt Jane leaned forward, her fair hair wild and unbound about her shoulders. With her witch's dagger, a black-handled athame, she cut a jagged gash across a dead lamb's belly.

'By Hecate,' she chanted under her breath, widening the gash with her fingers until the lamb's entrails began to spill bloodily onto the floor, 'by our Lady of the Forest, strengthen our spell tonight. Let this dumb creature answer the question: *Shall the Princess Elizabeth be Queen?*'

Beside me, Elizabeth shuddered. The lamb had been dead three days and the smell from its innards was disgusting. Her pale, bejewelled hand gripped mine compulsively.

Though the princess was five years my senior, tonight I knew more than her, for this was her first attendance at a moon ritual. Elizabeth looked younger than her twenty years, even if the dark shadows under her eyes suggested otherwise. Yet she held herself very regally considering her recent stay in the grim Tower of London, accused of conspiring with the rebels against Queen Mary. Half-sister to the Queen, Elizabeth always looked as though she were holding court in one of her own great houses, when in truth she was little better than a prisoner in this ruined old palace in the middle of nowhere. Her gown of black velvet, no doubt splendid when new, looked worn and dowdy as she kneeled in the dust beside me. Yet the princess did draw the eye with the elegant length of her neck, and her hair – fair, though with a strong reddish glint – which peeped out from under her hood.

Her small dark eyes, hooded like a hawk's, were staring fixedly at my aunt through the smoke. Her mouth was also small, pinched at the corners, and her high forehead spoke of tremendous learning, though she knew little of the witch's craft her own mother had been accused of practising.

'Is the magick not working?' the princess demanded, her voice sharp with frustration.

'Hush, my lady, give it time.' I looked back at my aunt, the fine hairs on my neck rising in horror. My head was spinning in the fragrant smoke from the candles, my mouth uncomfortably dry. Already I could see the blank stare of my aunt's eyes as the spell worked its magick on her. Soon Aunt Jane would fall into a trance and there would be no chance of questioning her after that. The princess squeezed my hand again and I spoke, catching her urgency. 'What do you see in the lamb's innards, Aunt Jane?'

'I see a coronation,' my aunt replied in her hoarse voice. Slowly, with delicate, bloodied fingers, she probed the slimy coiled intestines of the lamb. Its liver glistened in her hand and she bent over it, staring. 'I see good fortune following bad, and a reward for long years of patience. I see the Lady Elizabeth walking through a great doorway with a crown on her head, and all the people on their knees.'

'But what of my sister?' Elizabeth demanded. The exiled princess sat back on her heels, her face pale and tense, her usual caution abandoned. 'Is the Queen going to die? When will my coronation come to pass?'

My aunt did not reply. She trembled, swaying where she sat, lost in the grip of prophecy.

'There is danger for all of us,' she managed at last. Her voice grated in the silence. 'No one is to be trusted. Beware a traveller who comes over water, over land.'

Elizabeth and I both stared at her in horror, unable to move. Danger for us all? Then something tugged at the far edges of my hearing and I stiffened.

Turning my head, I caught the echo and scrape of booted footsteps downstairs in the old palace. Then the sound of a man whistling to keep away the spirits of the dead.

The Lady Elizabeth had heard him too. She looked round at me apprehensively, her eyes darker than ever. 'It must be one of Bedingfield's guards, making his patrol. We must leave at once. I can't be seen here.'

'Better to wait until he's gone, my lady.'

'The fire!' My aunt suddenly gasped, terrifying me. 'The fire . . . it burns me!'

The vision in her head must have changed, for her thin face had contorted with horror. My aunt's watery blue eyes were no longer staring at the bloody coiled innards, but over my head. She lifted her shaking finger to point, as though someone were standing behind me in the shadows. I glanced back over my shoulder, unnerved. But the three of us were alone in the dusty room.

Then my aunt gave a sudden, high-pitched cry and fell backwards on the soiled floorboards. She began flailing about and shaking as violently as the village idiot in one of his fits.

I gawped at her like an idiot myself, momentarily lost for what should be done.

'Keep her quiet!' the Lady Elizabeth urged me, her eyes wide with panic. 'The guard will hear us!'

Tripping on the hem of my gown, I scrabbled round to where my aunt still lay thrashing, spittle on her lips, her eyes almost white in the shadows.

'Hush, Aunt Jane, for pity's sake,' I told her urgently, my heart thundering at the possibility that we might be discovered. I stroked the hair back from her face, hoping to comfort her, and leaned close to her ear. 'One of the princess's guards is downstairs. He may hear you.'

For a moment I despaired of silencing her. But some grain of sense must have filtered through, for Aunt Jane's wild tossing gradually slowed and then ceased altogether. Her body lapsed into a kind of restless unconsciousness in my arms.

Shivering now, I stared about the old palace chamber. If we were caught here tonight, with these unholy instruments strewn about, we would be accused of witchcraft. And rightly so, for we were far from innocent. Even the princess would face execution if discovered like this, as her poor mother had gone to the block when Elizabeth was but a small child. Being the Queen had not saved Anne Boleyn from an accusation of witchcraft, any more than being of royal blood would save her daughter now.

I looked at the Lady Elizabeth. She was still on her knees, frozen in shock.

'My lady,' I said softly, 'these candles must be put out

and all traces of the circle rubbed away before we leave. Will you help me?'

Elizabeth nodded, though I could see she was badly frightened. She leaned forward and began frantically rubbing at the circle my aunt had drawn in the dust, her hands soon filthy.

Ignoring the foul stench, I dragged the bloodied lamb back to the sack and pushed it inside, along with its entrails. My aunt's soiled knife lay on the floorboards beside her. The cup of ceremonial wine we had shared was empty now but its dregs were still potent if anyone should think to taste them.

Downstairs, the whistling had stopped. I listened intently for a while, but could hear nothing.

'Meg?' my aunt moaned, stirring as she came back slowly to herself.

I looked down into that white, drawn face. What had caused Aunt Jane to lose control like that? I had never seen her so wild. Perhaps she was growing too old to control the spirits we had invoked. I rubbed her hands gently between my own to warm them, as though she were the child and I her guardian.

'Better now?' I asked my aunt softly. 'Are you able to walk? We must get out of the palace.'

'No,' she groaned, pushing me away. 'Not yet. The spell was not finished in proper fashion.'

Struggling weakly to her knees, my aunt cast about for her instruments. Then she saw the circle erased and the candles extinguished.

'Why have the candles been put out?' she demanded. 'Where is my sacred knife? Help me, we must appease the spirits.'

'Aunt, there is no time to relight the candles. We must return to the lodge before they discover that the Lady Elizabeth is missing. If anyone should find us with these' – and I indicated the remains of our magickal work – 'it will be we who burn. Don't forget the Lady Elizabeth is a prisoner under threat of death. If her sister the Queen should ever hear of this . . .'

Aunt Jane seemed to grasp the truth in what I said, the crazed light slowly fading from her face.

'Yes, you are right,' my aunt agreed reluctantly, and began to gather up her various tools instead. 'But the spirits will not be happy.'

I helped her tidy the last objects away, cleaning her ceremonial knife before wrapping it in its stained leather sheath.

Flashing me a weary smile, my aunt tucked the knife inside the bodice of her gown. 'You are a good girl, Meg,' she whispered. 'If only my sister could have been more like you. But she had no time for the power once she met your father, only for marriage. And look where that brought her. To an early grave, never to see her daughter grow up so gifted and fair.'

'I'm hardly fair, Aunt.'

She laughed then. 'Fair to me, Meg. And you do have beauty of a sort—'

I shushed her, holding up a hand. I shot a warning look at the Lady Elizabeth too, who had stood up now and was shaking the dust from her skirts. I had heard a faint sound from the other side of the thin wall. No whistling this time, but the quiet protesting creak of a floorboard.

My skin crept in warning. I felt certain that someone was outside the chamber, listening to our conversation. Yet when I crept to the door on tiptoe and looked out through a crack in the wood, there was nobody there. All I could see was the dark, empty corridor and the stairs down to the ruined great hall, lit with pale patches of moonlight.

Elizabeth came silently to my shoulder. 'What is it?'

'I thought I heard . . .' I shook my head. 'Nothing. It was just my imagination. We must return to the lodge without being seen. My aunt will walk home across the fields. Are you ready, my lady?'

Elizabeth nodded, but looked petulant. 'I wish we had not been interrupted tonight. I want to hear more of this vision of my coronation.'

'Perhaps we should wait a few months before meeting again, my lady, just to be sure we are not being watched. Sir Henry Bedingfield will be suspicious if we are caught out of bed at the full moon.'

'Bedingfield may be my gaoler,' Elizabeth snapped, 'but he's a round-faced fool and can prove nothing. Besides, why should I not seek knowledge through magick? To know the future is a mighty weapon for a princess.' She gave me a sharp stare. 'Your aunt will visit us again at the next full moon. I wish to hear more of her vision. Though we can meet in the forest behind Woodstock if you find the old palace too dangerous.'

I curtseyed, recognizing the determined note in the Lady Elizabeth's voice. 'Yes, my lady.'

Cautiously, I opened the door a few inches and peered out, listening for any signs that we were not alone.

The ruined palace was an eerie place to walk at night, room after empty room draped in deep shadows. My aunt carried her instruments and the blood-stained sack containing the dead lamb. I knew she would have to bury it in the forest before making her way home. We descended the staircase, the only sounds the swish of our skirts against the crumbling walls and the faint cooing of a wood pigeon in the rafters above us.

I thought of what my aunt had said about my mother. Catherine Canley had been a beautiful lady of the court, my aunt had always told me, who had given up her power as a witch to marry my father and bury herself alive in this remote corner of Oxfordshire. My unmarried aunt had come to live with her and my father as a companion, and had stayed on after her death to care for me. I could not remember much about my mother, for Catherine Canley had died of pneumonia when I was only five years old. Whenever I thought of her, I had a vision of laughing blue eyes and a rustle of silk as a woman bent to pick me up. But

I could not even be sure that was a true memory of her.

There were no portraits of my mother in our house, or none that I had seen. It hurt me to think I could not even remember her face. However, I have never been a girl to cry, but rather to nurse hurts deep inside in silence. Besides, I had my dear Aunt Jane to love and hold, and thought of her as my mother instead, the woman who had cared for me and secretly taught me her craft once I was old enough to cast a spell.

I parted with my aunt at the side entrance, kissing her fondly, and we met no more guards on our way back to our dilapidated rooms in the old palace lodge. The lodge was where the princess had been installed on her arrival at Woodstock, for the palace itself was deemed too ramshackle to be inhabited, with part of the roof missing in places and the whole building unsafe. The lodge itself was little better though, a damp heap of stones barely warmed by the fire-places which smoked incessantly, bats living in the eaves, the rooms dark and cramped with most of the narrow windows open to the wind and rain. Though at least the weather had been good to us this past month. The summer night was still and warm now, a fleeting hint of lavender on the air from the kitchen courtyard.

At the back door to the lodge, I caught Elizabeth glancing round at the ruined palace, her face pale and wide-eyed. Yet despite her fear, there was always a calmness about Elizabeth, as though she stood constantly at the centre of a storm.

I was a little scared myself, truth be told. But I was accustomed to fear. Ever since I had first discovered my power, I had wanted to be a witch – just as other girls my age wanted to be wives and mothers – and not even the threat of death could deter me from that path, now that I was finally beginning to test the extent of my powers.

When I was seven years old, out on a walk with my older brother, our nurse had given us a scolding for hiding among the bushes. Suddenly, a rook had swooped down, screaming and flapping great black wings, and begun to peck at her eyes. We all ran back to the house, pursued by the furious bird, and no one was hurt. But my nurse avoided scolding me after that, even crossing herself whenever I looked at her sideways.

That was when I first knew that I was different from other girls, and over the years I grew determined to discover just how much power I possessed. I could never forget that the punishment for witchcraft was the most painful of deaths. Yet it seemed like death to me to own a gift and never use it out of fear.

TWO

The Red Cross Knight

The Lady Elizabeth had not liked me when my father first brought me to the old palace of Woodstock from our home at Lytton Park, perhaps sensing with her inherited gift for magick that I was not like other girls.

But as the Queen's prisoner, forbidden all her ladies except Mistress Parry, Elizabeth had not been given much choice in the matter. She had looked on frostily as my father and I were introduced by her gaoler, Sir Henry Bedingfield, who had promised my ambitious father that, in exchange for my services, I would be allowed to accompany the princess back to court if she was ever found innocent of the accusations levelled against her.

I had not wanted to leave Lytton Park, not least because I would miss my beloved aunt and also my brother William, with whom I had been close before he left for university.

But serving Elizabeth would at least help me to escape the unwanted attentions of my suitor, Marcus Dent, whose fits of temper and reputation for cruelty frightened me. Not only was he far older than me, but he was also the local witchfinder, which made it both ironic and desperately uncomfortable that he should have fixed his interest on me as a possible bride. Though Marcus had travelled to

Germany that spring, I knew he would want to see me on his return. And he was not a man who could easily be rejected.

Much to my father's relief, the Lady Elizabeth spoke of how my long-dead mother, Catherine Canley, had been kind to her at court after Anne Boleyn had been executed, and gestured me to step forward.

Standing by the crumbling fireplace with a mildewed book in her hand – I later learned that she had been allowed to bring none of her own books to this prison – the young Lady Elizabeth considered me in silence.

I curtseyed, waiting for her verdict. It was hard not to feel uncomfortable under the princess's penetrating stare. Had I forgotten to lace up my gown? Or perhaps my best cap was on askew?

'I shall take the daughter for the mother's sake,' the princess decided, and signalled me to rise from my curtsey, as regally as though she were the Queen herself.

Soon after I arrived at Woodstock, I tried to influence Elizabeth into sending me home. All my life, I had been able to persuade others to do my bidding with only the power of my voice, sending my brother to steal sweetmeats from the cook's pantry for us to gorge on, or persuading my nurse to bark like a dog to amuse me in an idle hour. It was a gift, my aunt had said, that could become a power if strengthened by witchcraft. Yet however many spells I tried on the Lady Elizabeth, from a simple charm muttered behind her back to a ritual incantation with candles and a black mirror, it was no use. My power had no effect on the princess, and I had a good idea why.

My aunt had told me once that a witch is often proof against another witch's spells, which is one of the mysteries of witchcraft and nature's way of limiting a witch's power in this universe. I did not believe that the Lady Elizabeth was a witch. She showed none of the signs of it, though she had a power of sorts – I knew that from her face alone. But her mother, the executed Queen Anne, had been a powerful witch to the end, everyone was agreed on that. And it seemed this latent power from her mother's magick was what prevented me from influencing her, even though the gift lay dormant in the young princess.

So it was that I found myself put into service at Woodstock and was unable to magick my way out of it. Much of the work was drearily menial: darning holes in the Lady Elizabeth's stockings, washing out her underclothes, even fetching and carrying her food. Some days were more entertaining though, such as when she talked of her life at court, or played word games in the evenings. When the sun was not too hot, we were even permitted to take rambling walks about the boundaries of the ancient estate, listening to the distant shrieks of peacocks, once bred there as ornamental birds, now living wild amidst the tumbledown buildings.

Elizabeth was never allowed to forget that she was a prisoner though. A guard would accompany her everywhere, even out in the summer sunshine – keeping his distance out of respect for her rank but always watchful.

'I have done nothing to merit my imprisonment here,' the Lady Elizabeth complained bitterly to me one day, having been refused permission yet again to send for books from her library at Hatfield. 'Nothing – do you hear me? Yes, that fool Wyatt led a rebellion against my sister the Queen, and it was rumoured that I had agreed to take the throne if his rebels were successful. But it is all lies! There is no proof whatsoever. No letters exist with my signature on them that might confirm my involvement, and Wyatt himself admitted on the scaffold that I was innocent. Yet still I am held against my will in this dark, gloomy ruin, where I shall probably die of a fever – or some poison administered by my enemies!'

'Hush, my lady,' Blanche Parry warned her, and hurried to the door to make sure no one was listening. 'You must say nothing that could be taken for treason. That is what they watch for.'

Frustrated, Elizabeth scratched out these words on her chamber window:

Much suspected of me,
Nothing proved can be:
Quoth Elizabeth, prisoner

Elizabeth was a difficult mistress to serve, especially in my first weeks as her maid. Sometimes she would toss a heavy book at my head for not fetching her meals quickly enough, or pinch my arm cruelly if I dozed off during Holy Mass – which took place every day at Woodstock, and often very early in the morning. Yet the princess often overlooked faults in her servants that another mistress might have punished severely.

I discovered this when I had been at Woodstock only a week.

Blanche Parry came across me secretly reading one of my aunt's books on witchcraft, and dragged me before the princess.

I was terrified. I had been caught with a forbidden book on the dark arts in my hand. I fell on my knees, expecting to be condemned as a witch there and then.

Instead, to my astonishment and huge relief, the Lady Elizabeth had asked me searching questions on the craft: which spells and rituals I had performed, and whether I possessed any special magickal powers. She seemed a little disappointed when I admitted to being only a novice, but asked instead to meet my aunt, who had been training me in the ways of witchcraft for the past few years.

'For there is much in the world of darkness that could bring me light in this prison,' the princess had whispered in my ear.

That was how our sabats at each full moon had begun, with the two of us creeping out to meet my aunt in the ruined palace. There we would light the four candles and sit within a circle to work out spells. We did not perform dark magicks though, for my aunt followed the path of the hearth fire and refused to work any of the unmentionable spells that are found in the charmbooks of dark witches. But she allowed the Lady Elizabeth to learn a harmless spell of white magick – to extinguish and relight the candles in our circle, one by one – and this she was able to do with a little practice.

My aunt clapped as Elizabeth relit the last candle, giving the princess one of her rare smiles. 'You have a gift, though I cannot be sure how strong it is,' she told Elizabeth. 'Only remember your mother and beware how you use it. Witches work best alone and in darkness. To be a witch in the light is to invite enemies.'

It was a strange, isolated life at Woodstock. But as I listened to Elizabeth's whispered tales of how potential Catholic husbands had been presented to her regularly since her sister had ascended the throne, I felt an even greater relief that I was beyond the reach of my own persistent suitor, Marcus Dent.

It seemed almost comical that I should have attracted a man like Marcus, whose passion in life was exposing and executing witches. Marcus was about thirty years of age, a wealthy and influential man in Oxfordshire with a vast library of books. He was always travelling abroad, searching for arcane tomes on the subject of witchcraft. Indeed, I am sure that if Marcus had been at home more often, rather than off hunting books and witches in far-off countries like Germany, I would have been forced into matrimony with him at the age of fourteen when he first began to take a special interest in me. For although my father hated and feared the witchfinder, who had been known to laugh out loud at the sight of proven witches twitching on the gallows, I suspected he did not wish to cross Marcus either.

I had watched Marcus Dent preach to an eager crowd once, while a young witch was led out from the courthouse to the gallows, barely fifteen years of age, thin as a cat in her white cotton shift, her face terrified and streaked with tears. Marcus had called on God for her damned soul to be cast into the smouldering pits of Hell, then encouraged the crowd to shower the poor girl with rotten fruit and stinking cabbage as she shivered, waiting for the noose to be placed about her neck, not even allowed the dignity of a hood to conceal her last throes of agony from the crowd. I had seen men hanged as thieves or murderers before, but this was my first experience of a woman's execution. I turned away in horror when the girl's body twisted and rocked, her legs flailing helplessly as the rope strangled her. But Marcus strolled over afterwards to check that she was dead, then coolly asked the executioner to cut off a few locks of her hair as a trophy for his collection. Watching secretly from under my hood, it was hard not to imagine the witchfinder triumphing over my own corpse one day.

I knew Marcus Dent was desperate for an heir. His first

two wives had died horribly in childbirth, and their poor babies with them. But I had no intention of becoming dead wife number three. A witchfinder for a husband would be a very poor choice indeed for a young witch. For even if I did not die giving birth to Marcus's child, I would almost certainly dangle at the end of a noose myself if he ever discovered my powers.

Much to my relief though, the witchfinder did not ride over to visit me at Woodstock, no doubt too busy hunting witches to pursue his hopes of matrimony. Indeed, it was such a quiet life we led there, at times I almost forgot my aunt's vision of approaching danger.

One scorching day in the month of July, the Lady Elizabeth decided we should take a walk about the grounds of the estate. She had been unwell for several weeks, barely able to rise from her bed. This was a sickness she had suffered since a child, according to Blanche Parry, which struck hardest when her nerves were stretched to their limit. So when at last Elizabeth felt strong enough to leave her bedchamber, she insisted that we escape the confines of the lodge and take a walk around the boundary of Woodstock.

It was a sunny morning, and the birds were singing gloriously in the leafy green trees about the estate. Elizabeth stood at the window, chafing to be out in the fresh air.

'You will make yourself unwell again,' Blanche Parry warned her, wrapping a cotton neckerchief about the princess's exposed throat. 'The sun is too strong today, and there are stinging cattle flies everywhere.'

'Oh, don't fuss!' Elizabeth snapped irritably. 'You may stay here, if that's your wish, and I shall take only Meg. We do not need your company if you are going to be a sour-faced puss.'

'Now, my lady,' Blanche replied comfortably, 'you're talking nonsense now, and you know it. Young Meg is not a suitable companion for a walk in the countryside. Would she know what to do if you took a tumble down a rabbit-hole, or if a great cow tried to attack you?'

'It is you who is talking nonsense. Of course she knows such things. She is a country girl.' Elizabeth looked at me sharply. 'Are you not, Meg?'

I curtseyed low to the princess, nodding my agreement without speaking. I had learned early on not to get involved in these arguments, for I knew better than to waste my time trying to influence the princess.

Blanche Parry was less of a problem, thankfully. She would slap me and speak harshly behind Elizabeth's back, cursing what she called my 'evil eye'. For that, I sometimes took my revenge.

I would make sure Blanche was a little clumsier than usual, once spilling the bowl of heated water for the princess's morning ablutions. Another time, Blanche tripped over some invisible obstacle, the clean linen in her arms ending up on the dirty rushes, much to Elizabeth's annoyance.

Mischievous rather than harmful, these little tricks made Blanche Parry's cruelty easier to bear.

That day, we took a track we did not commonly follow, for it was narrow and overgrown in places, and we crossed the river at a shallow fording-place downstream from the palace, leaving our shoes and skirts damp.

Elizabeth was in a difficult mood, bored and restless, and determined to make her guard sweat. A thick-set man, he was approaching his middle years, and none too athletic. Her small mouth pursed in a tight smile, Elizabeth encouraged us to walk at a brisk pace, leaving the poor man to puff after the three of us in the hot sunshine, his heavy leather jerkin weighing him down.

Despite our good speed, it was late morning before we came back round to the River Glyme, which sank at that point to a swift but shallow race across a rocky bed, the marshy banks on either side thick with clustered brown rushes and the sunny yellow flags of irises.

Elizabeth paused to look back over her shoulder, her expression calculating.

The guard was nowhere in sight, perhaps having mistaken the path we had taken on descending the slope, and thinking we were making for the old stone bridge across the river. Indeed, we could see the bridge from the riverbank, not five minutes' walk upstream.

Elizabeth clapped her hands in delight. 'We lost him!'

'Sir Bedingfield will find us at fault for this, my lady,'

Blanche Parry warned her without any heat, and did not bother to restrain a chuckle. 'Still, it is good to walk without a spy constantly on watch.'

'It is good indeed,' Elizabeth agreed with a gurgle of laughter, and whirled in a circle, spinning out her skirts so that the grasses on either side of the path trembled, sending up bees and butterflies above our heads.

Then the princess darted forward to the water's edge, slim and graceful in her simple gown. The path across the river was made of stepping stones, some set further apart than others, and it took some skill to be able to cross without a foot or a hem slipping into the water.

'The water is a little high for fording, my lady.' Her lady-in-waiting stood uncertain on the bank, eyeing the swirl of water about the rocks. 'If we keep walking, the bridge is not far. See?'

'But the bridge is not as much of a challenge,' Elizabeth countered, and set her foot experimentally on the first stepping stone. It rocked slightly, unsteady on its glistening bed of pebbles. Blanche tut-tutted at her back, though she rarely tried to curb Elizabeth's wild behaviour, and her charge tossed her head defiantly. 'You take the bridge then, old fusspot. Meg and I will cross here. Won't we, Meg?'

I looked at the river dubiously. 'Yes, my lady.'

'Don't forget you have not been well, my lady,' Blanche reminded her, but it was clear from her tone that she was resigned to Elizabeth using the stepping stones. 'If you should miss your footing—'

'Then I shall get wet, and you may crow about it all the way back to the house.'

Without waiting for further arguments, Elizabeth began to hop from stone to stone, light as a butterfly across the sunlit water. Blanche and I both watched her progress in silent apprehension, afraid the princess would slip, or turn her ankle and be hurt.

She had almost reached the other side when one of the stones wobbled furiously beneath her, and Elizabeth cried out, casting her arms wide for balance. A tiny glint of light spun away like a jewelled bee and fell with a splash into the middle of the river.

'Oh no! My ring!'

Elizabeth reached the other bank and jumped onto the grass, turning back with a horrified expression. She raised her eyes from the dazzling water to our faces.

'I must get it back. My father gave it to me.'

Blanche Parry made an anxious noise under her breath, and turned to stare at me.

I stared back. 'But it fell right in the middle,' I pointed out resentfully. 'I shall be soaked!'

She gave me a sturdy push towards the first stepping stone. 'Better you than me.'

Elizabeth, watching this exchange but perhaps unable to

hear us above the noisy rushing of the current, called out, 'Be careful, Meg. The water is deep there.'

As if I couldn't see that with my own eyes!

Gingerly, I placed my foot on the first stepping stone, and was not reassured when it wobbled violently beneath me. Though it mattered little if I slipped now and got my feet wet; I would soon be soaked to the skin, retrieving the ring for her. So I ignored the perilous movement below my foot and stepped onto the next stone, then the next, until I stood at the heart of the river, gazing out across the bright water.

There was nothing for it but to walk through the water, cold or not. The sun beat down on my back as I lowered my foot into the swift current, gasping with shock. I moved my other foot and sank fully into the river. The pebbles, slippery with green weed, grated under my thin-soled shoes. Now the hem of my best gown was sodden with water, even held up above my ankles.

Reaching the spot where I guessed the gold ring must have fallen, I whispered, 'Gold from the earth, no longer hide your light but show yourself.'

At first I thought nothing was going to happen. Then there was a rippling shift at the bottom of the river, and a sudden glint of gold as the ring tugged itself free of the muddy silt.

I smiled, exultant that my simple summoning spell had worked. But there was still a problem. To reach down for the ring would mean relinquishing my hold on one side of my skirts, unless I was to tuck them up over my belt.

If anyone should happen along and catch me in such an indecorous position . . .

Well, there was no choice for it. I hooked my skirts up into my belt and bent forward, hot-faced and embarrassed, my soaked woollen stockings on show.

The golden ring lay glinting at the bottom. As I straightened up, the ring in my hand, I lost my balance and fell backwards into the water.

For a moment, I could do nothing but sit and gasp, my legs and behind thoroughly immersed in cold water, then I struggled back to my feet, dripping and close to tears.

But at least I had the Lady Elizabeth's ring.

That was when I looked up and realized we were no longer alone at the river.

Shame flooded my cheeks.

Three figures were staring down at me from the stone bridge. It was too far for me to be able to see them properly, but I knew they had seen me and were no doubt enjoying the spectacle immensely: a girl standing in the middle of the river, gown tucked almost up to her waist and dripping with weeds.

One of the strangers was fully armoured and on horseback. Another lay in an elaborate, covered horse litter which the third man was driving, this one standing up to see me better and gesturing insolently with his long-handled whip.

Slowly, red-faced and shivering, I waded to the marshy river bank, scrambled out through the waist-high sticks of reeds and handed the ring back to my mistress with a curtsey.

The man on horseback reached us first, approaching at a steady trot across the field. As he drew nearer, I realized he was younger than he had looked from a distance; I guessed he must be a year or so older than me, maybe seventeen years of age.

He sat tall and relaxed in the saddle, wearing a fine suit of armour with a white surcoat decorated with a red cross over the top, its fine silk rippling in the breeze. He wore a black velvet cap with a feather instead of a helmet, and the jewelled hilt of his sword suggested nobility – though he was clearly not of English descent. His skin was deeply bronzed, as though he was constantly in the sun, his hair black and his eyes too, lowered to examine our faces as we examined his.

His mouth unsmiling, his look sombre, the young man reined in his horse. He glanced at my sodden skirts, and then at Elizabeth's plain gown and cap.

'Well met, ladies,' he addressed us at last, inclining his head. From his accent it was clear he was a foreigner, though his English was perfect. 'I was told on the gate that this was the road to Woodstock. But I fear we may have taken the wrong turn, for it has been half a mile at least and still no sign of the palace.'

'This is the road to Woodstock, sir,' Elizabeth replied, standing straight before him, her chin slightly lifted. 'You will see the palace towers beyond those trees. But you would do well to turn back now, before you are seen by one of Bedingfield's guards. Indeed, I am surprised you were allowed to pass through the gate. Visitors are not allowed here, by order of the Queen.'

He studied her face again, more slowly, his gaze lingering on her reddish hair under the plain cap.

'Forgive my intrusion, madam. My name is Alejandro de Castillo, and I have been sent by the Queen's Majesty as a servant and companion to my holy master here' – he indicated the old man lying on scarlet cushions in the horse litter, which was approaching more slowly over the bumpy ground – 'on a visit of instruction to her sister, the Lady Elizabeth.'

'Instruction in what, sir?' Elizabeth demanded, her voice a little shrill, though still not revealing her name.

Alejandro de Castillo regarded her steadily. 'In the tenets of the Holy Catholic faith, Your Highness.'

Astonished, I looked again at his splendid Spanish armour, the red cross on his white surcoat and the serious expression on thc young man's facc.

He was a priest?

Elizabeth flushed then, as it became clear that he had guessed her identity. Almost invariably polite in company, she pulled herself together with an effort.

'I need no religious instruction, sir, from your master or anyone. I'm sorry you have had a wasted journey. But you must not address me so royally. After my mother's death, my father King Henry decreed that I was no longer to be known as the Princess Elizabeth, but the Lady Elizabeth.'

He swung down from the saddle, landing lightly before us. 'I beg your pardon, my lady,' he murmured. 'I had forgotten.'

Then his head turned, and his eyes finally met mine.

I felt an odd shock, as though the power had suddenly descended upon me. My legs began to tingle, and my lips itched and burned as though I had been kissing nettles. I clutched at the sodden folds of my skirts, unpleasantly faint.

Perhaps I had been in the sun too long.

'Madam,' he said, turning back to Elizabeth as though he had examined and dismissed me as unworthy of his attention, 'I understand your frustration. But we are under orders not to leave this place until my master is satisfied with the state of your immortal soul.'

'Father—'

The young man interrupted her with a shake of his head, his bearing suddenly a little stiffer, his Spanish accent more pronounced.

'I am not yet a priest, madam. I am a novice in the Holy Order of Santiago de Compostela.'

'I see.' Elizabeth looked past him at the elderly man in

the litter, his dark robes and heavy silver cross proclaiming him a Catholic cleric of some importance. 'And your master has travelled all the way from Spain to see me?'

'My master attends you here at the Queen's personal request,' Alejandro corrected her swiftly, and I wondered if he considered Elizabeth suspect in some way. 'You must know that Prince Philip of Spain is due to arrive on English soil within the next few weeks, when he will be joined in holy matrimony to your sister.'

Elizabeth said nothing for a moment, though her lips worked silently. She seemed a shade paler than usual. 'I knew they were to marry this year. I did not know it would be so soon.'

'They are to wed at Winchester Cathedral at the end of this month, madam. We sailed to England ahead of Prince Philip and his entourage, on his express orders, to bring spiritual sustenance to his bride. And the Queen sent my master to you here, so that her sister might also benefit from his wisdom.' Suddenly the cleric in the litter signalled impatiently to the young man. Alejandro removed the cap from his head and swept a bow, low and graceful, his Spanish armour glinting in the sun. 'My Lady Elizabeth, I have the honour to present to you my master, His Excellency Father Vasco Fernandez de Aragon.'

'Your Excellency,' Elizabeth murmured to the man in the litter, and sank into a curtsey, her head bowed.

I too curtseyed, as did the plump and breathless Blanche

Parry, who had finally caught up with us, her face flushed with exertion and dismay.

'I was told that a letter had been sent ahead of us, advising you of our arrival,' the elderly Spanish cleric remarked, sitting up against his cushions to stare unpleasantly at Elizabeth. I was shocked by the acidity of his tone. 'Yet you seem unaware of our mission here. I trust there will be comfortable rooms prepared for myself and my novice at the palace. We had expected better hospitality of the Queen's sister, even if you are a prisoner and suspected of treason.'

'I received no such letter, sir,' Elizabeth replied, and I could tell that she was angry by the curtness of her voice.

'Well, that is vexing news indeed,' Father Vasco commented, his thin lips pursed. His disapproving gaze swept across us, lingering on Elizabeth's simple gown and my own dishevelled appearance. 'Nonetheless, Her Grace the Queen informed us that you had agreed to take into your household any priests who came to you in faith.'

I glanced at Elizabeth. She was biting her lip. 'It is true,' she muttered reluctantly. 'I did make such a promise to my sister.'

Alejandro looked at the princess encouragingly, his smile a sharp contrast to the cold gaze of his master. 'So you will receive us into your household, my lady?'

The princess looked almost disdainful. 'Do I have a choice?'

'You have our thanks, my lady.' Alejandro de Castillo bowed at this, as though Elizabeth had graciously welcomed him into her home. He had not looked in my direction again since I had first waddled out of the river. For this I was deeply grateful, as my wet skirts were now steaming in the midday sun like a cow's droppings, and I was sure there must be strands of green river weed in my hair. 'The Queen has generously provided for our needs and comforts while under your roof, including those of our servant.'

'You seem very sure of yourself, sir.'

This time the bite in her voice was unmistakable. This was Elizabeth standing tall, at her most icy.

Still the young man did not flinch. 'Forgive me if my words were insolent, my lady,' he said solemnly. 'I am here to serve my holy master, and by request of Her Grace the Queen.' His dark eyes flitted to mine again, and I felt a shudder run through me at that contact. 'Might I suggest we adjourn to the manor and continue our discussion there, so this lady may make herself more comfortable?'

For a moment, I did not grasp that the Spaniard was talking about me. Then I felt everyone's gaze turn towards me and my steaming wet skirts.

Oh, he would pay for this humiliation.

I saw his eyes narrow, and suddenly realized that he had noticed my birthmark, a small clover-shaped blotch just above my left breast. I tugged at my bodice, which had gone awry in my struggle to climb out of the river, and hid the offending mark, which I knew a superstitious priest might consider a sign of the Devil's favour. A flush came into my cheeks as I bowed my head and stared at my sodden feet instead.

'Very well,' Elizabeth agreed tightly.

'Will you take my mount, my lady, to rest your feet? Your lady-in-waiting may take a seat in the litter,' Alejandro added, glancing at Blanche Parry and then at me. 'There is only room for one, I am afraid.'

'The girl can walk,' Blanche responded with a snap, and accepted his hand up onto the driver's seat of the litter.

The sturdy man with the whip made room for her, his weatherbeaten face crinkling into a half-smile, half-grimace, though Mistress Parry barely acknowledged his presence, pulling her skirts tight about herself as though she did not wish to brush against him.

Alejandro de Castillo lifted Elizabeth up onto the high stallion's back, then wheeled the animal in a careful circle. He glanced back at me over his shoulder, an odd little frown on his face, then the small procession started off across the sunlit park towards the woodlands, beyond which stood the ancient Palace of Woodstock and the lodge.

I followed on foot, my feet squelching at every step in the river-clogged shoes, my sodden gown clinging to my body. The dizzy, tingling sensation I had experienced under his gaze seemed to have spread all over my body now. Had the Spaniard put some kind of foreign spell on me?

If so, he would soon taste plain English magick, a[illegible]
sorry for it.

Yet I was uneasy.

Beware a traveller who comes over water, over land.

Perhaps it was the arrival of Alejandro de Castillo that my aunt had seen in the lamb's entrails.

THREE

At the Sign of the Bull

Just before supper was laid out for us that evening, I received a note from my older brother, William.

His unexpected message came to my hand via one of the groundsmen, a servant who often sneaked in messages, food and other tokens when Sir Henry Bedingfield was occupied with other matters, expecting a small coin at least in return for his troubles.

I hid my brother's note in my gown during our meagre supper of bread, cheese and salted ham, then ducked into the gloomy stairwell with a candle to read it.

M., I'm up from Oxford for the summer. Come and see me at the Bull tonight. I have news you must hear. Your ever-loving, W.

Shocked, I read this message several times, not quite able to believe it.

Did my brother William seriously expect me to trudge nearly a mile cross-country at night to the notorious Bull Inn, at risk of being caught by Bedingfield's guards and suspected of seditious leanings?

I have news you must hear.

I bit my lip, staring down at the hurriedly scrawled note. My brother might be irresponsible and foolhardy, but he would not endanger me lightly. There must be something urgent he needed to tell me. Something that could not be put in a letter, for fear it might be seized and read by the wrong person.

For all I knew, it was news of my father or my aunt. Though why such news needed to be kept secret was beyond my comprehension.

I was just turning away from the unlit stairwell when I bumped into someone, and was so startled I almost dropped my candle.

I stared up, dismayed, into the face of the young Spaniard, Alejandro de Castillo.

Had he been standing there in darkness the whole time, watching while I read my letter?

Fury choked me. 'What are you doing, lurking about down here?' I demanded, momentarily forgetting the courtesy due to a guest, particularly one who had come to Woodstock on the orders of the Queen herself.

His dark eyes glittered at me in the candlelight.

'I was not "lurking" down here,' Alejandro countered smoothly. 'I have just come in from the stables. My servant Juan has been quartered there, for want of a bed in the house. I merely wanted to assure myself that he was *comfortable*.'

Incredulity made my voice high. 'You were checking that your servant was comfortable?'

Though unsmiling, his face seemed to mock me. 'Juan has served my family loyally since I was a young child.

What kind of master does not look after his servants' needs?'

I could not answer that, and the candle was beginning to burn low, so I turned to climb the stairs. But Alejandro de Castillo had not finished with me. He caught at my left hand, in which I had hurriedly crumpled the note from my brother, and held me fast by the wrist.

'Wait,' he said, his tone unhurried and all the more sinister for that. 'What are you hiding in your hand there?'

'Let me go!'

Mercilessly, Alejandro unpeeled the clenched fingers of my left hand to reveal the tiny, crumpled piece of paper there.

My heart was thundering under my ribs. I was afraid, yet furious too at his arrogant interference. It was all I could do not to call on my power right there on the stairs, make the young Spaniard gibber incoherently, oink like a pig, or bark and chase his own tail.

His eyebrows rose and he looked at me assessingly, no doubt seeing the anger in my face.

'What's this? A letter?'

'It's nothing!'

'If it is nothing,' Alejandro replied coolly, 'then you will not mind if I read it.'

He removed the paper from my grasp, smoothed it out and read William's message by the light of my candle.

Alejandro frowned, then met my eyes directly.

'Who is this . . . *W*?'

'That's none of your business.'

'Is it not?'

'The letter is addressed to me.' I straightened my back, glaring at him. 'Not to you, priest. Give it back to me at once and let me go to my bed.'

I had hoped to influence him with those words, all my witch's power thrown behind them like a man's shoulder pressed to a cart stuck in the mud.

But, like the Lady Elizabeth, Alejandro de Castillo seemed infuriatingly oblivious to my gift. Ignoring my command, he lowered his head and read through my brother's note again, this time aloud.

I stared, speechless and dumbfounded. I understood why the Lady Elizabeth would be able to resist my spells – but a priest? Surely it was impossible that he could possess magickal powers to rival my own. After all, could there be a more unlikely warlock than a priest? Then Alejandro surprised me by folding the note carefully and handing it back to me.

'This letter comes from a lover, I think. You should be more careful where you open such intimate messages, mistress,' he said, his face expressionless. 'But you forget. I am not yet a priest.'

'Thank you for your advice,' I snapped, and thrust the incriminating note back into the folds of my gown. 'But you should not call me mistress either. Just plain Meg will do.'

'*Plain* Meg?' he repeated. His gaze moved slowly across

my face before dropping to examine my figure. 'No. Such a word does not suit you.'

I thought he would say something else then. But suddenly Alejandro bowed and left me without another word, climbing the stairs until he was lost in the shadows above.

I stood a while after he had gone, my eyes narrowed, staring up at the empty stairway.

So Alejandro de Castillo dared to lift his eyes to me as a man, did he? Even priests in training were expected to practise strict chastity and keep themselves only for God. To do otherwise would be to commit a mortal sin, I was sure of it, for he would be committing that sin in the full knowledge of its wickedness.

I wondered what his priestly master would say to such a look. Did Catholic initiates still have to scourge themselves for impure thoughts?

I reached the Bull Inn without incident, though my gown was now almost as soiled as the previous one. I had been forced to cross the narrow stream that skirted the village and had slipped on the muddy bank. But there had been no other way to reach the inn if I wished to avoid the guards on the gate. At least the moon helped me find the stream in darkness, its pale light gleaming on the water.

The public taproom at the Bull was lively and well-lit. The men were delighted to see a woman enter the place, sending up whoops of excitement as I elbowed my way through the crowd.

Some hurried words with the landlord led me to the snug, a quieter room at the back of the inn. A small fire was burning in the hearth, filling the room with a harsh smoke that made my eyes sting. I found my brother playing dice with two young men I didn't recognize.

At sight of me, William leaped up and embraced me, knocking the dice table to the floor. 'Dearest Meg, I knew you would not fail me!'

We had not been in each other's company more than twice in the past few years, since my brother had left to study in Oxford, making a home for himself there. Will looked more mature, his shoulders broader now, his narrow face filled out, with a full beard instead of the stubbly chin I remembered.

'You've changed,' I said, kissing him on the cheek.

'So have you, little sister. Though by the Rood, you are not so little as you once were. Perhaps I was wrong to ask you here tonight.' Will eyed my tight bodice as I swung the cloak off my shoulders. He frowned, glancing around at his friends' faces in the firelight. 'Don't look at her like that. She is too young for either of you.'

I suddenly realized that one of the young men was my cousin, who had sailed from England to the distant Low Countries when I was barely twelve years old.

'Malcolm?'

My cousin kissed me enthusiastically, though with much muttering from my brother, who accused him of being over-friendly and of putting his hand on my hip, at which all three men laughed.

Malcolm too had sprouted a beard since I'd last seen him, and had shaved his hair close to his head, a style which became him rather better than his previous boyish curls. I realized that he must be in his early twenties now, no longer a youthful student like my brother.

'It is good to see you again after all these years, Meg,' my cousin said soberly, pulling out a seat for me at the table. 'Though Will is right. He should not have asked you here tonight. It is too dangerous.'

I sat down and looked searchingly at my brother. Now that the initial greetings were over, I could see that he was frightened, constantly glancing towards the door as though he expected men to burst in at any moment and arrest us all.

'Why *did* you ask to meet me tonight?' I asked Will suspiciously. 'Your note said you had news for me.'

'That was a ruse,' he admitted, turning back to me with a sheepish expression, 'to get you out of the house without drawing unwanted attention to us. It's hard to know who to trust these days. The servant who carried the message may be loyal to the Queen for all we know.'

'So what am I doing here?'

My brother clasped my hand, his grip warm and damp. 'Malcolm and I need to ask a favour from you.' He indicated the third young man with a nod. 'And Tom there, who's an Oxford man too and another with no love for the Catholics.'

I was frightened now as well. I could smell a Protestant conspiracy in the air here, and knew my brother and cousin would not easily be dissuaded from whatever mad plan they were hatching. I was also uncertain of their friend, Tom, who had said nothing but was watching us closely, his watery blue eyes reflecting the firelight.

'What kind of favour?'

My brother hesitated. 'We need you to help us get into Woodstock. We have to speak to the Lady Elizabeth. In person and in private.'

I stared. 'Are you mad?'

Malcolm leaned in, shaking his head. His voice was low and earnest. 'It's the only way we can be sure of our path ahead, to speak to Her Grace alone, without her watchers present.'

'It will never be permitted.'

'Of course not.' My brother was impatient now. 'That is why we need your help.'

'But what can I do?' I stared at them all in turn. 'I am nobody.'

Will drained his tankard compulsively, then set it down on the table with a crash.

'Don't you care what is happening to this country, Meg?' he demanded, ignoring his cousin's hurried gesture to lower his voice. 'In a short space of time, Queen Mary will marry

Philip, and these green hills will no longer be ours. Philip is already King of Naples. Soon he will be King of Spain too. Then England will belong to Spain and we must become Catholics, living under Spanish law. The Inquisition will come into every house in the country to search for Protestants and will have no mercy when they find them. They will torture and burn those who refuse to take Mass, and will set up their Catholic idols in every church in the land.'

Malcolm hushed him, glancing anxiously at the open doorway into the taproom. He pushed his own full tankard towards my brother, who picked it up and began to drink without even a word of thanks.

I realized then that Will must have been drinking most of the evening, and no longer cared what he said or who might be listening.

My cousin turned to me. 'All we ask,' he told me quietly, 'is five minutes' private speech with the Lady Elizabeth. There are those who do not want this marriage between England and Spain to happen, and who plan to put a stop to it. But first we must know if Elizabeth will lend her support to such an uprising, and also whether she would accept the crown herself if her sister were no longer wearing it.'

'But it was just such a conspiracy that brought her to this prison,' I hissed, angry both for Elizabeth and for my impulsive brother, whom I had never known to be so interested in politics before. I suspected William had been infected by my cousin's old obsession with ridding the country of Catholics.

'Yes, and this new plot will release Elizabeth Tudor from her unjust prison and elevate her to the throne of England.'

'It is more likely to land her back in the Tower of London,' I pointed out to my cousin crossly, 'and the rest of us with her. If you cannot see sense and drop this ridiculous conspiracy, none of us will live beyond the summer.'

I stood up, pulling on my cloak again.

'The Queen will marry her Spanish prince at the end of this month,' I continued, keeping my voice pitched low. 'Two Catholic priests have been sent to stay with us, to ensure Elizabeth does not slip back to Protestantism. Though I cannot see why her faith matters so much. Once Mary has a child, Elizabeth will no longer be heir to the throne.'

'Yes, *if* Mary has a child.' With a shy glance in my direction, Tom joined our conversation at last, speaking low and hurriedly. 'But if she should prove barren, and Elizabeth can be shown to be down on her knees, worshipping the Holy Virgin, then she can be married off to some Catholic prince, keeping the English line of succession within the Papist fold.'

I shivered at the thought of Elizabeth being married off to a foreigner without her consent, but had to acknowledge that Tom was probably right.

'Once the marriage goes ahead, England will be a very

different country,' I agreed unhappily. 'It is not what any of us want. But there is nothing we can do to prevent it. The sooner you three accept Catholicism and get yourself to church with the rest of us, the better your chances of survival when the Inquisition do come knocking.'

'I cannot believe you are saying this, Meg,' my brother exclaimed, jumping to his feet, 'when a few words in the wrong ear would be enough to condemn you as a witch. Aye, and our aunt too.'

I blanched at his cruelty, but could not weaken now. To allow them into the lodge to speak to Elizabeth alone would be beyond dangerous. It would be an act of madness that would endanger my mistress's life as well as my own.

I should never have come to the Bull tonight, drawn into discussing rebellion openly in this public place. My brother was too drunk to realize the danger he was running, and my cousin was too reckless to care. Who knew what ears these walls might have? It was already considered an offence to follow the Protestant faith. The country was full of Catholic informers, and even to think such things could be seen as treasonous.

'We have ways of protecting ourselves,' I told him.

'Yes, I heard that the witchfinder Marcus Dent holds a special place in his heart for you.' My brother Will was sneering at me now. 'Does he know you practise the dark arts?'

'You would not dare!'

'Oh, I would never betray my own sister, not even if a

whole host of Catholic torturers had me on the rack. But others would betray you for the price of a tankard of beer.' Turning his mood in an instant, Will grasped my arm as I made angrily for the door, almost pleading with me. 'I'm sorry, Meg. But you do not seem to realize the danger you are in. Remember that I am your brother and mean you no harm. Help us purge England of this Spanish disease. Give us five minutes alone with the Princess Elizabeth.'

'Elizabeth is no longer a princess, but a prisoner of the Queen,' I reminded him, and shook my head. 'And I cannot help you, Will. Please don't ask me again. Now let me go home.'

Malcolm stood up calmly, reaching for his woollen cap. 'Wait, you cannot go alone. Are you taking the back road? I'll walk with you as far as the old palace. It's not safe so late at night.'

I wanted to refuse, but knew he was right. It would be dangerous to return alone at this hour, even on the quieter path behind the village. Besides, my brother had sunk down onto his seat again, his head in his hands, and no longer seemed to care if I was leaving with our cousin.

Even his friend Tom would not meet my eyes, staring down into his beer.

I bent to whisper 'Farewell' in my brother's ear, wishing he would drop this madness before it proved his death, then let Malcolm guide me towards a back door so I would not have to pass through the noisy taproom again.

* * *

We took the streamside path that skirted the back of the village, only the moon was so bright now that we had to be careful not to be seen. Several times we had to wait in the shadows while a drunken man, staggering home from the Bull, stopped to relieve himself in the bubbling stream. Despite the lateness of the hour, the moon seemed to have kept the birds awake, for I heard what sounded like a song thrush high above us in the dark net of branches, and later, a white owl passed on broad wings, hooting softly into the night.

'I thought you were gone for good, Malcolm, that you had made yourself a home in the Low Countries. Why did you return to England?'

Malcolm smiled and helped me across the narrow stream, his arm about my waist. 'This is still my country. And it needs me.'

'You cannot truly believe there is anything you and Will can do to stop this Spanish marriage.'

'It is not just me and Will,' he told me quietly, setting me back on dry ground. 'There are many exiled nobles and gentlemen in the Low Countries who could be persuaded to return if they thought Elizabeth would support an uprising. But we hear so many rumours there, that the princess is now a Catholic like her sister, or that she contemplates a marriage to some Catholic prince, and people are nervous. All they need is a sign of Elizabeth's support, some secret token to give the Protestant cause new vigour.'

While he talked, we followed the path on the other side of the stream, striking out cross-country for the dark, unlit lurch of buildings that was the ruined palace of Woodstock. Beyond that, unseen behind trees, stood the old palace lodge where Elizabeth lay imprisoned and under constant guard.

'There are many who share a belief that this Spanish marriage is wrong for England. If you could only persuade the Lady Elizabeth to give us a sign, it will act as a rallying-point for other men like us. Trust me, many thousands will rise against Mary if they think Elizabeth would accept the throne after her sister's removal and restore England to a Protestant nation.'

'But why should she not accept the throne?' I asked daringly, testing out the question on the still night air.

'She is a woman,' he replied drily. 'And women are unpredictable, especially when offered power.'

I bit my tongue, not wanting to argue with my escort. It seemed to me that Elizabeth was not the kind of woman to refuse power.

At last we reached the edge of the silent, tumbledown palace with its gaping black casements and leaning turrets. I turned to thank him, knowing it was too dangerous for him to come any closer. Bedingfield's guards would be patrolling the old palace grounds every hour.

Nonetheless, Malcolm insisted on accompanying me to within sight of the lodge.

'I will see you safe inside before I leave,' Malcolm said stubbornly, waving aside my whispered protest.

In silence, we walked another quarter of a mile across the unkempt lawns and halted near the stables, in a cobbled, weed-infested yard overlooked by the back windows of the lodge. The kitchen door was near at hand, and although there was no key to secure it, I knew it was unguarded, for the hounds slept there at night and would soon bark if an intruder tried to gain entrance that way. Since I often fed them scraps when the cook wasn't looking, I knew the dogs would not bark at me. Though my cousin was a different matter.

Malcolm asked which was Elizabeth's bedchamber, and seemed disappointed when I told him it was on the other side of the building, where Bedingfield's guards tended to patrol most frequently.

'Promise you will try to get us into the lodge one day soon,' he whispered in my ear, 'and I will leave.'

'That's not fair.'

He lowered his head and kissed me lightly on the mouth. 'Promise me.'

I was flustered, remembering how much I had enjoyed his company as a child, following him about in a daze, my handsome older cousin.

'I promise to think about it,' I managed.

His smile was wolfish. 'Very well,' he said softly, and kissed me again, this time more lingeringly. Then he pulled back and told me goodnight before melting back into the shadows, hood drawn cautiously over his head.

I waited until Malcolm was out of sight, then turned to make my way across the yard to the kitchen door.

Catching a sudden movement at a casement window high above, I glanced up and recognized the dark profile at the glass.

Alejandro de Castillo, still awake at this late hour, had been watching me cross the yard.

What else had he seen?

Flushed and breathless, angry that the young Spaniard seemed to be spying on me, I pulled open the door and slipped into the kitchens with only a quiet word for the wolfhounds there.

Let him watch jealously from the shadows and report my loose behaviour back to the old priest, or even to Queen Mary herself in London. I did not care what the disapproving Alejandro de Castillo thought of me, so long as he believed me a loyal Catholic and no witch.

FOUR
Casting the Circle

Being kept busy with our new regime of daily prayers and meditations on the Catholic faith, it was another five days before I was able to send a note to my aunt, warning her of the arrival of the Spanish priests at Woodstock. Along with a coin from my meagre hoard, I gave it to the servant who had brought me William's message and asked him to ride over to Lytton Park with it as soon as he could find an excuse to leave the grounds.

Not entirely trusting the man, I worded the message with extreme caution in case it fell into the wrong hands, and hoped she would understand. Elizabeth had stubbornly refused to miss our next meeting with my aunt. But she had at least suggested we could hold the ritual somewhere safer, beyond the patrolled grounds of Woodstock. Now all that remained was for us to slip away for an hour or two at dusk, returning before the princess was missed at evening prayers.

On the appointed day, I took early morning Mass with the princess in the decaying palace chapel.

We kneeled on the flagstones under the steady gaze of Alejandro de Castillo, who seemed almost more interested in my faith than in that of my mistress. Just visible through the latticed rood screen, Father Vasco blessed the wine and raised the Host, his muttered Latin incomprehensible.

It was all I could do not to stick my tongue out at the dark-robed Alejandro when he turned solemnly to offer me the blood of Christ.

Instead, I restricted myself to a dutiful 'Amen' and saw his lips twitch.

Late that afternoon, Elizabeth took to her bed with one of her sick headaches. I was called away from mending some household linen to attend her, and found the princess at the barred window of her room, already wrapped in a dark cloak and itching to be off. Blanche Parry, though deeply disapproving of Elizabeth's interest in magick, played her part by distracting the guard outside the bedchamber with some pretence of hurting herself on the stairs. As soon as he had gone to help, Elizabeth and I hurried out of the bedchamber and into the small room opposite, whose window opened over a low-roofed outbuilding. I helped the princess through the window, then followed her, both of us climbing down to the ground as silently as we could. Then it was only a matter of slipping round the back of the ruined palace and into the woods.

We walked briskly through the chill of the dusk. Soon we came to the small copse known as Lady's Wood. There, I prepared the ground for our meeting while Elizabeth looked on, clearly fascinated by my gestures and muttered incantations. I set out the candles for the ritual, then burned a bundle of dried thyme and sage, using the smoke to clear the circle of evil influences. When the place was ready, I found a quiet spot for us to hide amongst the trees.

Shortly afterwards, I heard hooves approaching at a walk and waited impatiently for the rider to come into view.

It was my aunt, riding a broad-backed ass through a glowing patch of moonlight. Aunt Jane slowed to a halt in the middle of the wood and sat listening, no doubt fearful of pursuit.

I stepped out from my hiding place between the dark trees.

At the sight of me, she dismounted and hurriedly led the beast away from the track.

'I thought you were a ghost, standing there in the moonlight. You are sure you were not followed?' my aunt asked anxiously. Once I had reassured her that the three of us were alone in the woods, she dropped a curtsey to the Lady Elizabeth, then hugged me. 'I have missed you, my little Meg. Have you been well? Indeed, you look well enough. There's new colour in your cheeks and' – she pinched my arm playfully – 'more flesh on your bones.'

'We are expected to sit around all day at Woodstock, sewing or reading from the scriptures,' I complained, and led them both to the secret place I had prepared in the copse. 'Begging the Lady Elizabeth's pardon, but it is no wonder women grow so fat at court, with nothing to do but idle each day away at their samplers.'

Elizabeth, who was as slim as a willow wand, merely

smiled. She had heard my complaints before and I knew she sympathized, for the princess was an active young woman who loved nothing better in summer than to be out hunting or walking in the fresh air. Yet Sir Henry Bedingfield would not even permit Elizabeth to keep a horse at Woodstock.

We sat on the woodland floor in dappled moonlight, forming a rough kind of circle that I had marked with the four candles, and listened to the trees whispering above us, the rustle of small creatures in the undergrowth.

Quietly, I told my aunt of the old Spanish priest and his attendant, and the reason for their arrival at Woodstock, though I skirted any further discussion of Alejandro de Castillo. I did not want the listening princess to know how Alejandro made me feel whenever he raised his eyes to mine. I focused on my aunt instead, asking for news of my father – who was well, it seemed, and missing me more every day – and of my home, Lytton Park, where one of the chimneys had fallen in and would not be repaired until my impoverished father could find the money to pay for it.

I listened with interest to this talk of home, though Lytton Park already seemed a distant memory. I missed my father, but I had grown fond of the Lady Elizabeth, and the arrival of the Spanish priests had certainly changed the mundane routine of our lives.

My aunt was thinner than when I had last seen her a month ago. Her long yellow hair was wilder than ever, and there were ominous shadows like bruises under her eyes.

I had seen sick women look like that before they died, and wondered with a sudden fear if my aunt's health was failing. She would never tell me, of course, being the kind to suffer in silence, searching for a cure herself among her herbal remedies and magick arts.

'Did you say the three-fold charm before I arrived?' she asked.

I nodded. 'Though I only cast the circle on the air. I did not want to disturb the ground. Will it be enough?'

She did not answer but looked around at the trees, their gently moving branches in the dappled moonlight, her expression distracted.

'Did you hear that?' she asked in a whisper.

I glanced at the Lady Elizabeth across the circle, but the princess merely shook her head, her dark eyes wide.

I replied cautiously, 'I hear only the trees rustling and the rabbits in the undergrowth.'

'I thought I heard . . .' My aunt hesitated. 'Well, it does not matter. The candles have not gone out. The circle is good, it will hold.'

I sat uncertain, remembering how I had been unable to sway the Spaniard's will. When my aunt saw my hesitancy, she asked what was wrong. Briefly, I told her of my failure, leaving out everything I did not wish the Lady Elizabeth to hear.

'Sometimes it falls that a man or woman is beyond even the most skilled witch to influence,' Aunt Jane told me, and

I could see she was concerned by my story but trying to comfort me. 'In Spain, they know many ancient ways to avert magick. Does this priest bear a charm or talisman around his neck, or hidden about his person, that might weaken your powers or turn your spells aside?'

'I don't know. I've never . . .' I found myself stammering, and avoided the princess's curious gaze. 'I've never looked.'

My aunt thought for a moment, seeming not to have noticed my embarrassment. 'A gift, from one witch to another, is the strongest kind of magick. I shall give you something before you go that may help strengthen your magick.'

'Could Alejandro be the dangerous traveller you saw in your vision?' I pressed her.

'It is possible.' Aunt Jane drew her hair down about her face, hiding her expression. 'For now, cast the bones and let us see the future.'

Carefully, I took the bones out of their pouch. I rattled them in my cupped palms as I had often seen my aunt do, breathed my spirit over them and muttered a few words of power.

I had gathered the bones myself from the woods over the past few months – the spines, thighs and knuckle-bones of long-dead creatures – and hidden them under my bed at Woodstock. Cleaned and polished, the bones felt smooth in my hands, full of the creature-memories of their previous owners, the tiny scratchings and foragings among bracken, the constant fear of death.

'Hurry,' the Lady Elizabeth said impatiently. 'We cannot be gone long or they will send the guards out after us.'

I threw the bones down between us with a rattling clatter. We all huddled forward, looking for the omens in the moonlight.

'The arrow,' I whispered, pointing to the thigh-bone of a bird tipped with another, set cross-wise.

My aunt nodded, staring. Her finger trembled as she touched the nearest knuckle-bone. 'The singleton.'

'The eyes that watch,' I added.

'And the folded arms of death,' she interpreted the last placement, tracing the rabbit bones that had landed across each other.

I raised my head and stared at her. My breathing was rapid and shallow. This was my first time of reading the bones within a charmed circle, and it was hard to remain composed.

'Whose . . .' I felt the Lady Elizabeth's gaze on my face and struggled to sound calm. 'Whose death?'

'The singleton's,' my aunt replied, looking over to the princess, her voice matter-of-fact, and began to show us how the signs worked.

'The eyes that watch, over here, will send the arrow of Inquisition' – she indicated the first sign I had seen – 'to the heart of the singleton, and death will follow swiftly. See how close they lie? That means we do not have much time.'

'But who is the singleton?'

'One who walks alone.' She met my gaze, and I could see no fear in her eyes. 'The knuckle-bone points north. An unmarried woman.'

The Lady Elizabeth stiffened. She could not disguise the squeak in her voice. 'Me?'

'Or me,' my aunt told her drily, and gathered up the bones, handing them back to me. I noticed that her hands did not tremble. 'Or even young Meg.'

'What does it all mean?' the princess asked hoarsely. There was a fine sweat on her forehead.

Aunt Jane gave Elizabeth a half-smile, her thin lips just turning up at the corners. 'This young Spanish priest at Woodstock, his may be the eyes that watch. Or they could be those of our neighbour, Marcus Dent.'

'Marcus Dent?' I frowned, and a cold shudder ran down my spine at the suggestion that a man as cruel as Master Dent might be aware of our moon rituals. I slipped the bones back into their pouch and tucked it inside my gown. 'Why would he be watching us?'

My aunt gave a fierce bark of laughter without humour. 'Marcus Dent is a dedicated Catholic and a ruthless witch-hunter. He is dangerous, believe me. We work our magick under his nose, and so far he has not suspected us. His interest in you, Meg, is what keeps him distracted from the truth. But Master Dent is no fool and one day—'

I looked at her in surprise. My aunt had stopped, her face suddenly shuttered, her lips closed tight.

'One day, what?'

Aunt Jane shrugged, making a hurried gesture with her left hand to avert the sin of a heart-lie, and I knew she would never tell me what she had been going to say.

'One day you will either have to marry Marcus Dent or face the consequences of refusing him,' she finished flatly. 'That is all.'

I did not understand what she meant by 'face the consequences', and did not like to press the matter any further, for my aunt had a bitter temper when crossed. Besides, if the bones spoke truth and we were under suspicion, it would be wise to discontinue our full moon sabats for a while. Which meant that this might be our only meeting for months. It would be horrible to end it on an argument.

I let the moment pass and helped the Lady Elizabeth back to her feet. We cleared the circle with the ritual of our hands and voices, calling on the spirits to see us safely home. I said no more about Marcus Dent. There was more here than Aunt Jane was prepared to tell me.

It was the first time I could remember my aunt hiding something from me. I felt worried and uncomfortable as we kissed cheeks and left each other on the dark woodland track.

'Here,' she said, beyond the princess's hearing, swiftly pressing a wrapped bundle into my hand. 'The white stone is charmed. Keep it under your pillow, and it will help to avert the eyes that watch. There is also a dagger, so you may cast a full circle without me. Remember to honour the four points of the compass once the circle is closed.'

I unwrapped the bundle a little, feeling its weight, and gasped when I saw the knife she had given me.

'Aunt, this is your sacred dagger. Your athame. You cannot give it away. It has been consecrated for you alone.'

But Aunt Jane only shook her head and smiled when I tried to offer the knife back to her.

'I pass it to you now, Meg. I have no further need of it. It is my gift to you, from one witch to another. We may not be able to meet again this year. Use the athame to strengthen your skill.'

This close, I could feel her sickness, the dry heat of her bird-like wrist and forearm, narrow enough for me to encircle with my hand. I had been right to think her thinner than before. She had the wasting sickness – I could see the signs she had tried to hide from me under her long-sleeved gown and loose neck-cloth.

'You are not well, Aunt.'

'It does not matter,' she said, echoing her own words from earlier, when we had sat in the circle and listened to the birdsong high above in the green branches. 'Go now, before your absence is noted. And be careful.'

'Will you . . .' I hesitated, unable to speak the words. 'When will I see you again?'

'If you need help, speak to the spirits through the bones,' Aunt Jane whispered, close up against my ear, and there was something in her voice that sent a shiver down my spine.

Then my aunt kissed me one last time and was gone, scrambling up onto the broad back of the ass and turning its head the way she had come. Without waiting to see her ride away, I slipped back into the dappled shelter of the trees and waited there trembling until I could no longer hear the clop of hooves across stony grass.

My aunt was mortally sick, perhaps not far from death, and according to the bones one of us was under suspicion as a witch and a heretic.

If any who accused us could prove heresy, we would burn at the stake. Witchcraft would see us drowned or hanged.

Either way, one of us was doomed to die an agonizing death.

My immediate instinct was to run away, to leave Woodstock and never go back, hiding myself in some far-away place, perhaps over the sea. I could work as a laundress or a servant in some quiet town where they would not bother to search for me.

But that was cowardice, and nonsense too. If I were to leave Woodstock under suspicion of witchcraft, my aunt would be among those questioned, to see if she knew of my whereabouts, and if her room in my father's house was searched . . .

No, I must stay at Woodstock for now, and trust to my aunt's protective charm-stone to ward off discovery.

I shivered, and thought of the sinister 'eyes that watch'.

If the bones had spoken truly, we might soon discover by whom we were observed: the witchfinder Marcus Dent, as my aunt suspected, or perhaps the Spanish priests, who already felt like spies in our midst, constantly watching and reporting back to the Queen on her sister's lack of devotion to Catholicism.

One morning the household was set into uproar by the arrival of a letter from the Queen.

Elizabeth made a hissing noise and strode furiously from the room, knocking her chair to the floor, the letter clutched in her hand. 'My sister writes to tell me I cannot leave this vile old place, for her counsellors advise against it. Still no proof of my guilt, yet here I must remain, a prisoner of the Queen's whim!'

Blanche hurried after her, making comforting noises, but for hours we could hear the princess pacing her room and speaking in that harsh, angry voice we all dreaded. 'If the Privy Council cannot prove me guilty of any crime against the throne, I should be released from this uninhabitable prison. Feel this chill air, look at the smoking chimneys and the damp on the walls! My health suffers daily while my sister keeps me in this cramped Hell-hole on the strength of rumour alone. I am innocent and have proved it again and again. To keep me here under guard is an outrage. This is not English law!'

That evening, she ordered all the windows to be

shuttered, and took to her bed in 'great pain', according to Blanche Parry, who came scurrying back along the corridor, demanding candles, lavender water and warmed cloths dipped in a distillation of wormwood.

Sir Henry Bedingfield had gone hunting that day but was hurriedly summoned back to the lodge. He, in turn, called for a physician to be brought to the princess, only to discover there were none living nearer than Oxford who were learned and respected enough to attend royalty. Sir Henry wrote to several in the university there, but Elizabeth swore she would rather commend her soul to God than entrust her body to a stranger.

She would not even admit the old priest, Father Vasco, though he limped to her door several times a day to offer her the holy sacrament and even banged on the wood with his stick to attempt entry.

For days Elizabeth kept to her bed, just as she had done in June. It was a dreary time. We spoke in whispers, our conversation of little else but the letter from the Queen and Elizabeth's sickness. I wondered what my brother would think of this latest breach between the Tudor sisters. No doubt it would lend weight to his hatred of the Catholic Queen. Though since I had refused to communicate with him, or my scheming cousin Malcolm – despite their occasional notes that ended up on the fire – he was unlikely to know what was going on at Woodstock Lodge.

Amongst this chaos, I looked for a chance to slip away

and strengthen my skill as my aunt had suggested, casting a circle with my new dagger. No one would miss me while everyone was so intent on the closed door of Elizabeth's bedchamber. So long as I was back at the lodge before dusk, there should be no danger.

I decided to return to the ruined palace to work my spells. There would be no guards on the palace entrances after dark, for although Bedingfield had demanded they patrol there at night, the men were lazy and complained there was nothing inside worth stealing. The ornate wood panelling and all the old-fashioned furnishings were riddled with wormholes and little better than tinder. Even those wall tapestries still hanging were tattered and mouldering, beyond repair. Besides, many locals believed the old palace to be haunted and would not venture near it after dark – which made it the perfect place to practise casting the circle.

With my aunt's dagger strapped to my leg under my gown, which I wore loose over a russet-brown kirtle to conceal the bulge, I slipped out through the busy clatter of the kitchen. The broad-shouldered cook did not seem to have noticed me, and black-haired Joan – who shared my bedchamber – was whistling 'Robin of the Greenwood', a popular tune amongst the guards, as she scoured one of the iron pots.

I heard the cook curse the girl for whistling as I pulled the door shut behind me. Joan was simple-minded, and a happy enough soul, but she seemed unable to learn that whistling would only get her into trouble in that household, for Sir Henry – and indeed most men – considered it unlucky for a woman to whistle. Certainly, many believed a whistling woman was doomed to remain forever unmarried.

Just as I had hoped, there were no guards in sight as I approached the ancient palace buildings. Nonetheless, I kept to the deep shadows under the walls, schooling myself to be cautious. It was growing cool, the sun having already dipped below the level of the lodge, and there was an eerie silence to the place. It almost made me wish I had chosen to cast my circle in the woods after all.

I found an unlocked door and counted my way swiftly though the downstairs rooms and corridors, remembering the way we had come with Elizabeth. It was very dim inside and surprisingly chilly for a summer's evening, the air damp and thick with dust.

My thin-soled shoes echoed on the stone flags of the great entrance hall, the rushes that must once have lain there long since rotted away.

I paused at the base of the stone staircase, and gazed up into the shadows on the upstairs landing.

The last thing I wanted to do was go upstairs. The awareness of ghosts here seemed to press in on me, like a sick headache. But it was too dangerous to cast the circle down here, where it was more likely I would be seen or heard from outside. I did not wish to be caught, after all. The prospect of suffering a witch's death was too horrible to contemplate, yet I often dwelt on it when alone in my room. I had heard of witches drowned, hanged or even burned to death for daring to practise the craft. Once my aunt had whispered of a young witch in Scotland, accused of poisoning her neighbours' goats; she had been found guilty and rolled down a steep hill in a barrel filled with iron spikes. The mere thought of the agonies she must have endured left me shuddering and afraid.

Yet still I could not imagine a life without magick.

At that moment, a young housemartin, roosting somewhere amongst the rafters, burst into flight above me with a clatter of wings.

I was not the only creature on edge in the old palace.

I climbed the stairs, lifting my gown so it wouldn't brush against the dust and debris. I knew that if I did not hurry, night would fall before I was finished. Then I would have to come down again in complete darkness, and find my way back across the lower rooms without even the dying rays of the sun to guide me.

Even as I considered that possibility, I chided myself as a coward. What witch was afraid of the dark?

The third chamber I peeked into looked perfect. It was small and unswept, but the narrow windows had no glass, which meant there was more light here than elsewhere, and there was nothing on the floor except dust.

Quickly, I drew the dagger out from beneath my skirts, and stood in the centre of the shadowy room. Recalling my aunt's incantation for the casting, I spoke the spell as clearly as I dared in the silence. I lay down an oak twig for an altar, along with a few fragrant leaves and flowers, then stooped to draw a rough circle about myself in the dust. I did not dare burn any herbs this time to clear away evil influences, in case any escaping smoke was seen from outside. But I spoke the words of protection under my breath, hoping they would be enough.

The air stirred darkly at the spell, raising the dust as though a door had been opened somewhere. I listened, but heard nothing. It had probably been a sudden wind from the gardens below. The old palace was so draughty, with most of its bare windows unshuttered beyond the royal apartments.

Seating myself in the middle of my circle, I sat straight-backed and cross-legged, facing my little makeshift altar. I called on the four directions – north, south, east and west – and begged each one to look favourably on the magick I would work there.

The power began to come into me from the shadows, tingling at the tips of my fingers, a rush of blood to my head that left me momentarily dizzy.

I was just groping for the ritual that would open the dark magick of the moon for me, the women's magick that is best worked at twilight or in the hours of darkness, when a terrible scream shattered the stillness.

'Witch!'

I scrambled to my feet at that scream and spun in the fading light to face my accuser.

My breath was coming short and fast, and the sacred dagger was still clutched in my hand as though I intended to use it.

To my amazement, it was Joan who had screamed, the simple girl from the kitchen who shared my room and loved to follow me about my duties like a faithful dog. Tonight, she had followed me into the dark silences of the mouldering Palace of Woodstock. I don't know why. Perhaps she had thought I was playing a game, like hide and seek, and wanted to join in.

But what she'd seen here tonight must have terrified the poor simple girl instead.

Joan's mouth was agape as she stared at the ceremonial knife with its wicked blade, and the uneven circle drawn in the dust between us. Then her finger pointed at my face in dreadful accusation.

'Witch!'

FIVE

Witch

I took a step towards the girl, intending to calm her down, but instead Joan backed away as though I meant to come after her.

Stumbling, she fell backwards through the doorway into the deepening shadows on the landing. Joan yelped with hurt and fear. Then she jumped up and ran back to the staircase as though all the hounds in Hell were after her, still crying, 'Witch!'

The circle broken, the dagger forgotten in my hand, I stood horrified.

What had I done?

In my stupidity, I had thought it safe to work magick here in the old palace, casting the circle and never believing I might be caught. Now I had likely brought down the wrath of the Inquisition on my head, and led the witch-hunters straight to my family.

For a moment, I considered running away. Then I remembered my gift.

There was still a chance I might influence Joan into believing she had seen nothing but a girl exploring the ruined old palace. But only if I could catch her before she had a chance to tell anyone else. If I ran away, I would soon be caught and condemned. Nor would it be long before the witch-hunters wondered who could have taught me the craft, and began to ask questions of my aunt.

I could not have Aunt Jane's death on my conscience.

Hurriedly, I scuffed out the circle and concealed my aunt's dagger under a heap of mouldering rushes in one of the downstairs rooms. Then I picked up my skirts and ran back across the dark lawns to the gloomy buildings of the lodge.

The sun had finally set, and everywhere was steeped in the glimmering darkness of twilight. Birds still sang, and a bat flitted low past my head, its fleeting body almost brushing my hair.

I hurried across the cobbled yard to the kitchen door. There were shouts from inside, and the sound of Joan crying. I was too late.

I smelled of dust and dark magick and knew the remnants of my spell hung about me like tattered clouds around a mountain top. In this state, nothing but a miracle could save me from the witchfinder's noose.

On impulse, I stooped to the gnarled old rosemary bush growing at the back door and dragged my fingers through its fragrant leaves. With any luck it might confuse those who sought to accuse me of witchcraft.

The scent of the fresh rosemary was powerful and dizzying, like a blow to the head. For a few seconds, it threatened to overwhelm me. Then I pulled myself together, lifted the latch and stepped inside.

Up in the long, narrow room that overlooked the park, I found Joan on her knees, head bent almost to the floor, weeping noisily into her filthy apron. Guards and servants crowded about her, shocked and uncomprehending, arguing over the girl's head. It seemed the alarm had been raised immediately on her return to the lodge, for the room was crowded.

The thin-lipped old priest, Vasco Fernandez de Aragon, was standing at the window, staring out into the darkness as he muttered some prayer under his breath. Alejandro de Castillo stood by his side, his voice urgent in his master's ear. I could only imagine what he was saying about me. Red-faced and furious, Sir Henry Bedingfield was remonstrating with Blanche Parry, whose arms were folded staunchly across her chest.

Even the burly cook had ventured up from his pots and pans to comfort the kitchen maid, and one of the guards was fitting a bolt to his crossbow, with little success, for his fingers were shaking so much it kept slipping from the notch.

The Lady Elizabeth herself was nowhere to be seen. No doubt she was too sick to rise from her bed, even to discover the cause of all this commotion.

My appearance in the doorway brought them all to a sudden, prickling silence.

Then Bedingfield shouted an order. One of the guards seized my hands, dragging them painfully behind my back.

Perhaps the man feared I would work some spell that would reduce them all instantly to dust.

I stood, unresisting, my face reflecting both my shock and an innocence I did not possess.

'What is this we've been hearing, girl?' Bedingfield demanded harshly, coming closer – but not too close. He snapped his fingers at the guard. 'Bring the witch forward into the light!'

Alejandro had turned away from his master and was watching me now with sharp, intelligent eyes.

My face, ashen before, turned to uncomfortable heat under that gaze. If the Spanish novice had thought me a woman of loose morals before, receiving notes from my lover, slipping out to meet him at night, what must he think now that I had been caught practising witchcraft?

Bedingfield ordered one of the lanterns to be raised. He stared down into my face. 'Joan tells us she saw you in the old palace tonight, working some kind of spell. She claims you are a witch, that she caught you calling on your master the Devil.' He ignored the mutter that ran round the room. 'Is this true?'

I shook my head with fierce denial. 'No, sir, it is not true.'

Bedingfield was not a superstitious man, and I was counting on his sturdy, pragmatic nature to save me. But he was a clever man, and he could smell a lie when he heard one. He examined my face, then lowered his gaze to my gown and the kirtle underneath, the tell-tale streaks of dust along the hem of my skirts.

'But you were in the old palace tonight?'

'Y-yes, sir.'

'Then you had better explain what you were doing there, and how Joan could have made such a mistake. And do not bother to lie, for it will go badly for you if we search the palace and find any unholy instruments of witchcraft hidden there.'

Alejandro stirred. His hand dropped to his sword hilt, and for an awful moment I thought that the young Spaniard intended to kill me there and then.

But of course he would not dare. Not in Elizabeth's household, so openly, without even a formal trial having taken place. It would be impossible.

Yet still he gripped his sword hilt, his knuckles whitening with pressure.

I thought of the dagger I had hidden under the mouldering rushes. Night had fallen, and it would be too dark for the guards to search the old palace now, even armed with lanterns and torches. But come daylight, the dagger would be found and I would be thrown into prison to await my trial and execution.

Assuming the furious Alejandro de Castillo did not take the law into his own hands first.

I shivered, my mind working fast. 'Sir, as God is my witness, I am no witch. Please, you must believe me. Joan kept wanting to explore the old palace, but I told her no. That it was too dangerous. Tonight, she ran away there instead of finishing her chores, and I had no choice but to follow. I . . . I did not want her to go in there alone.'

The cook turned to Sir Henry Bedingfield, his florid face filled with excitement at these rare goings-on.

'That part is true, sir,' he told his master eagerly. 'Joan did slip away before she had finished her work. The lazy girl was there one minute, cleaning the pots from supper. Then the next, she was gone.'

Bedingfield gave a grunt, but I could tell he was still unconvinced. He looked back at me.

'Go on.'

I could have kissed the fat-paunched cook for his help. But it would not do to show anything but fear to these men. That was what they expected of me, and what they must see. The danger was not over yet, not by any means. I still had my neck to save.

'She ran upstairs, and I had to follow. I was afraid she would hurt herself up there. But it was so dark, and there were so many rooms, I couldn't find her at first.'

I saw Joan look up at this lie. I was sorry to land her in trouble for running away, but if everything went well, neither of us would suffer for this night's events.

'Then I heard Joan cry out that she had seen a ghost,' I continued, my voice gaining strength. 'I followed the sound of her weeping, and found her terrified, hiding behind a chair. I took her downstairs and tried to comfort the poor simple thing. But she must have caught some reflection in one of the windows that scared her, for she suddenly screamed that I was a witch, pushed me over, and ran back to the lodge.'

I had everybody's attention now. Even Joan was staring with her mouth open, no doubt trying to reconcile my fanciful account with her own memory of what she had seen.

'By the time I got back to my feet and ran after her, she had already told everyone in the house that I was a witch.' I injected a note of righteous anger into my voice. 'But it's not true, sir. I am a God-fearing girl and would never tamper with such evil.'

'No one would expect a witch to admit her wickedness.' Speaking for the first time, Father Vasco broke the silence that had fallen. Their heads turned to the old Spanish priest, listening to his suspicions with respect. 'And this girl may be simple, but she seems fairly certain of what she saw.'

'I swear on my mother's grave, I am no witch.'

Bedingfield shrugged. 'Well, I cannot uncover the truth in your account. But Father Vasco is right. Joan's story is not entirely to be dismissed, for all she is a simpleton. We must rouse the Lady Elizabeth. You are her maid, so she should hear the testimony on both sides and decide what is to be done.'

My heart sang when I heard those words. Elizabeth

might be angry with me for taking such an enormous risk, but at least she would save me from this accusation.

But the infuriating Blanche Parry would not allow Bedingfield to wake Elizabeth. Blanche stood her ground when he became angry, her arms folded stubbornly over her chest. 'I am sorry, sir, but I will not have my mistress disturbed over this nonsense. She is still unwell and must not be upset. Any small thing and her condition worsens.'

'Then I must send for the witchfinder, Marcus Dent. Witchcraft is a hanging offence, as you must know, and I would not be doing my duty as head of this household if I did not take Joan's accusation seriously.' Bedingfield paused, glancing at me. 'Master Dent knows this girl's family, and I've heard he has some skill in interrogation. Perhaps he will be able to uncover the truth behind these two contradictory accounts.'

My blood ran cold at the thought of being interrogated by Marcus Dent. His cold, sharp mind would leap straight to my aunt when he heard I had been accused of witchcraft, and although I felt sure I could handle Marcus, he had always disliked my aunt and would happily use this accusation as an excuse to investigate her too.

'Joan is a simpleton. She does not know what she is saying, sir,' I protested. 'This is all a terrible mistake—'

'Then Marcus Dent will be the man to clear it up for us, won't he?' Bedingfield thundered back at me, banging his fist on the table. 'Be silent, girl. It is no longer your turn to speak.'

I suddenly wondered how many days I had left to live. Not many more, if this man's belligerence was shared by the others who would examine me. My hands began to shake. Would Blanche even tell the Lady Elizabeth of the danger I was in?

Elizabeth's gaoler asked for pen, ink and paper to be brought, and scratched out a brief note for his messenger to carry to Dent's house, which lay just beyond Green Hanborough, a few hours' ride from Woodstock by road.

I stood and watched him write his letter, wondering if I could use my gift to influence the man into letting this matter drop. But there were too many people here as witnesses. I could not hope to influence them all, I was not skilled enough for such a powerful magick. Especially with the two Spanish priests present, who had stood listening to every word of my explanation with suspicion etched on their dark faces.

Alejandro de Castillo had finally lifted his hand from his sword hilt, though the expression in his eyes was still dangerous.

Did the Spaniard suspect and hate me so fiercely?

I shook the question aside. It did not matter what he or anyone else thought of me. It only mattered what Marcus Dent could prove.

'There,' Bedingfield said, and handed the note to his messenger. 'I have requested the witchfinder make his way here first thing in the morning. Meanwhile, you will both go straight to bed and not leave your bedchamber until called before Master Dent.'

'I won't sleep in the same room as the witch!' Joan sobbed, hiding her face in her apron again.

'There, there, silly girl,' Blanche Parry said comfortably, and gathered her up against her chest. 'You can sleep with me in the room next to the Lady Elizabeth.' She glared at Bedingfield over Joan's head, as though daring him to refuse permission. 'She'll be as well-guarded there as her ladyship, and I'll make sure she does not leave the house.'

'Very well.' Sir Henry nodded to one of the guards, who had just come back in. 'Have you searched her room? What did you find?'

'Nothing, sir,' the guard said, 'except this, which was under the Lytton girl's pillow.'

He was holding up the small white stone my aunt had given me to ward off those who were observing me.

Bedingfield looked at me. 'Explain.'

I managed a maidenly blush, which was not hard given the way the Spaniard had been glaring at me throughout Bedingfield's questioning, and hung my head.

''Tis a love stone, sir. Just a girl's trick, nothing more. You place it under your pillow for a se'ennight, and at the end, you . . . you dream of your husband-to-be.'

There was some muffled laughter around the room at this fanciful explanation. Even Bedingfield's usually stolid features held the faintest hint of a smile. I noticed that

Alejandro was not amused, however, but continued to watch me sternly from the window.

The guard looked down at the white stone dubiously, then hurried to set it on the table before Bedingfield, as though just touching the thing might mean he'd have to marry me.

Bedingfield picked up the stone and turned it over in his hand. But it was only, after all, a small white stone, with no markings or carvings to reveal its true purpose, and he could find nothing remarkable about it.

'I'll show the stone to Dent when he arrives. He's an expert in these matters and may be better able to tell us what it is.' He dismissed the guard with a wave of his hand. 'Take young Meg to her room, and make sure she stays there. I don't want her slipping away before the witchfinder arrives.'

I found myself being led away to my chamber and imprisoned there in the darkness, without even the comfort of a candle. While the young guard coughed and shuffled his feet outside my door, I lay fully clothed on my straw mattress and tried not to imagine how it would feel to dance in agony at the end of a rope.

It was almost dawn when I heard the door creak open and someone come in.

In the gloomy half-light of my chamber, it was hard to tell who had come to visit me, though I could see that it was a man. One of the guards, perhaps, eager to torment me before I was taken away for good? I sat up groggily, ready to shout for help, but the man was too quick for me.

He kneeled on the edge of my mattress and clapped a hand to my mouth. 'Hush, little witch,' said a now familiar voice, heavily accented. 'You don't want to wake the whole household, do you? I've paid good coin for five minutes' speech with you, and I'd like to get my money's worth.'

I stared into Alejandro de Castillo's dark eyes.

Slowly and cautiously, he removed his hand. I threw myself back against the pillow. 'Five minutes' speech? Or five minutes' pleasure?'

Alejandro raised his brows, seeming to consider this question seriously. His gaze moved down and settled on my stockinged feet. I drew them up at once, hiding my feet beneath the folds of my gown.

'If that had been my intention, *mi alma*,' he replied coolly, 'I should have asked for longer than five minutes.'

I was not sure what the words in Spanish meant, but the look in his eyes was unnerving.

'Perhaps five minutes was all you could afford?'

Alejandro sat down beside me on the mattress, though I could see he was careful not to allow our bodies to touch, even briefly.

'You are a cat, Meg Lytton. You like to draw blood with those vicious claws of yours. But you do not have nine lives to lose, I think. So I have come to see what I can do to help you avoid the noose. If you wish to avoid it, that is.'

I stared up at him through narrowed eyes, wondering what to make of this. Why would a Catholic novice help an accused witch avoid torture and execution?

'No,' I forced myself to reply, though my voice shook. 'I'm looking forward to the noose. Nothing better than a good hanging.'

To my surprise, he smiled at that. 'You have courage. I admire that in a woman. But there comes a time when jests must be laid aside, and the sword taken up. And this is such a time.'

At these words, I glanced at his sword belt and saw that it was no longer there. 'Why do you wear a sword, anyway?' I demanded. 'I thought you were training to be a priest. Why carry a weapon? And all that armour you were wearing when you arrived . . .'

'I am a novice in the Holy Catholic Order of Santiago,' he said patiently, as though explaining something very simple to a three-year-old. 'We are a martial order of priests. That means we fight in battle for the honour of Jesus and all the Holy Saints, and are entitled to wear the armour and weapons of a soldier of Christ.'

'So where's your sword now?'

Alejandro looked momentarily taken aback. 'In my bedchamber. I do not wear it *everywhere*.'

'You surprise me.'

His brows rose once more. '*Mi querida*,' he said drily,

'I have not yet said what I came here to say, and my five minutes is almost up.'

'What does that mean . . . *mee . . . mee cereeda* . . . ?'

'It means . . .' His smile twisted. 'It means I don't want to see you hang. Now be quiet for a moment and listen. It will be dawn soon, and your witchfinder will be here to interrogate you—'

'You can leave Marcus Dent to me,' I exclaimed, then saw the black look on his face and realized I had interrupted him again. 'Sorry, you were saying?'

'I am going to need a diversion. Can you provide one?'

I searched his face. 'What for?'

'I intend to enter the Lady Elizabeth's bedchamber and tell her what has happened,' he explained, his tone so confident that I nodded, though I was finding it difficult to concentrate on his words, mesmerized instead by the velvety-dark lilt of his accent. 'I do not believe she has been told about this accusation of witchcraft, and I think it imperative that she is.'

'Elizabeth's door is always guarded.'

'Hence the need for a diversion,' he reminded me gently.

'It won't work. She's been sick for days. Blanche would never let you in.'

'The diversion,' he murmured again, picking straw out of my mattress.

I frowned, the strange intensity of his presence in my chamber suddenly catching up with me.

'I don't understand. Why are you helping me? I'm accused of being a witch, of worshipping the Devil. Don't you want to see me hang for it?'

His eyes lifted to survey me, serious again. 'I've seen enough Spanish women burned at the stake as witches and heretics to know that hanging is a merciful death. It would be a pity to stretch such a beautiful neck though.'

I swallowed, and with an effort pushed away that horrific, unwanted image of my last moments.

He hesitated. 'Besides, it is not too late to repent.'

'I have nothing to repent.'

'The charge is false? You are not a witch?'

Oddly, I couldn't lie to him. 'I didn't say that. But what I do is not evil.'

'Witchcraft is against God's law,' Alejandro pointed out. '*Thou shalt not suffer a witch to live*.'

'Yet Jesus performed magick in God's name. What else were his miracles but magick?'

'Blasphemy,' he muttered, clearly shocked.

'The truth,' I countered. 'If I were able to walk on water, would you call that a miracle? Or magick?'

'That's different.'

'Why?'

He sat back, staring at me. 'I see you have the makings of a theologian, Meg. Unfortunately, we have no time to debate the holy miracles of Christ. The witchfinder will be here soon. Once he removes you from Woodstock, I will no longer be able to help you. Which I very much wish to do.'

'Thanks,' I muttered. 'So you want me to create a diversion that will get Blanche Parry and the guards away from Elizabeth's chamber door long enough for you to go in and speak to her alone? It will have to be something amazing—'

This time, his eyes flashing, he interrupted *me*. 'Are you saying you cannot do it? That you do not have the necessary skill to—?'

'I can do it,' I said hurriedly, and sat up, tossing my unruly hair out of my eyes. 'Though I must admit, I do not understand why you would help me like this. You are to be a priest soon. I should be your enemy.'

A small frown tugged at his forehead. 'I have always been taught that witchcraft is the work of the Devil. Yet I would not see you die for it.'

My skin prickled at the sombre look in Alejandro's eyes. I did not press him further. 'When should I . . .?'

'Just as you are being taken to see this witchfinder, Marcus Dent. That is when I will need the Lady Elizabeth's door unguarded.'

'Consider it done.'

He smiled, seeming to relax. 'Good.'

'Good.'

We sat for a moment in silence, looking at each other. It was growing light outside. Then a brusque hand rapped on the door.

'Priest, your five minutes is up!' came a hoarse whisper from whichever guard he had bribed.

Alejandro stood up from the bed. Suddenly, I was terrified and did not want him to go. Alejandro de Castillo stood for everything that had made my life at Woodstock hard and bitter and false. Yet while he was in the room with me, it felt impossible that I might be going to die soon. And in such a horrible, agonizing way.

My hand went out to him. 'Don't . . .' I began to say, then I saw his gaze meet mine.

He was standing at the end of my bed, looking down at me intently, his eyes near black in the half-light. My hand dropped away, and I could not finish my plea for him not to leave.

Alejandro would not stay with me, nor touch my hand, because he knew his mission to be doomed. It was too late for me. Even if he managed to reach the Lady Elizabeth, she would never dare interfere with Marcus Dent's questioning. The same suspicion might easily fall on her too. Elizabeth was the daughter of a proven witch, and her own interest in astrology and divination was already being whispered about at court. Why would she help me when doing so might risk her neck too?

'I'm sorry, I must go,' Alejandro told me simply. 'To stay any longer would be to risk discovery.'

I nodded, and somehow managed to force my dry lips into a smile.

'*Adiós*,' he murmured from the doorway, and this time I did not need a translation.

I turned my face into the pillow as soon as the door had closed behind him, my heart gripped with a new and more terrible fear. Alejandro de Castillo had said his traditional farewell in Spanish, commending me to God. But I was a witch, and many believed that meant God was my enemy.

If that was true, all that awaited me after the hangman had done his work were the black, everlasting fires of Hell.

SIX

Witchfinder

They came for me late in the morning. Marcus Dent had been at Woodstock a good hour before I heard the tread of their feet approaching the room, and sat up, tidying the demure white cap I had chosen to wear over my yellow hair. By now he must have heard Joan's testimony, for I had caught the sound of the girl weeping again, and footsteps, back and forth between the various rooms of the old lodge.

I sat and tried to control my breathing. I was very nervous and my palms were clammy.

How would it feel to hang? I had seen men hanged in the marketplace before, and remembered how their legs jerked convulsively as the noose tightened about their necks, suffocating them.

My own breath seemed to stop at the thought. I did not want to die. Yet what chance was there that a man like Marcus Dent would accept my claim of innocence?

I guessed that Marcus had made me wait deliberately, that the witchfinder wanted me to be on the verge of breaking before he brought me in to be questioned. That way I would be more malleable, more open to whatever he might suggest to get me out of this tight corner. I had played the scene so many times in my head since being shut into this room last night, it was almost a letdown to see the door open and hear the guard's harsh command, 'On your feet, girl. Master Dent is ready to see you now.'

Do not betray Aunt Jane. That is all I need to remember. Not to betray Aunt Jane.

I twisted my hands before me, not meeting the eyes of the two guards who had come for me, and stepped out of my room.

I gave it five or six steps from the room, far enough for them to have relaxed, thinking me docile. Then I turned and said under my breath, in the silkiest voice I could muster, 'Fire! I smell fire!'

The boy nearest me was fresh-faced, barely old enough to be shaving. To my delight, he caught the suggestion straight away. His head went up like a stag's at the sound of the hunting horn, and he sniffed the air.

'Fire!' he exclaimed, and stopped dead, knocking into the older guard, who asked him irritably what he was doing. 'I smell smoke. Clear as day, I smell it.'

I looked at them both innocently. 'Fire?'

The older guard met my eyes. He stared about himself, his expression dazed, as though he had just woken up from a long sleep. 'I . . . I smell it too. Something must be burning in the kitchens.'

'I only hope the house is not alight,' I murmured sweetly.

'Something burning in the kitchens?' the younger one repeated. He shook his head, panic on his face. 'It's a heretic's bonfire. I tell you, the house is alight. Quick, call for the others! Tell them to bring water from the well before the whole place goes up.' The boy covered his mouth with the sleeve of his tunic as though he were choking. 'This smoke. Sweet Lord, I can hardly breathe.'

'We have to take the girl to Master Dent first. Those are our orders.' The older man was still struggling against the trick, frowning.

'Take her charred body, more like. Look, I'll go. You can stay here and brave the flames if you want. I'll fetch buckets, we can form a line from the well.' The boy ran for the stairs.

I looked at the remaining guard. There was sweat on his forehead and his lips were twitching. He did not know what to do.

'I wonder if it's reached the Lady Elizabeth's suite of rooms yet?' I murmured.

At this, the man finally broke, like a fishing line under the weight of a vast salmon, and began to shout, 'Fire! Fire!' up and down the narrow landing.

For the next few minutes, an age-old panic seemed to take over the household. Doors slammed, servants came running from all quarters, including a startled Blanche Parry with bulging eyes and an apron held up over her mouth. Up the stairs staggered guards with old buckets sloshing over with water. They rushed about in terror, throwing open doors and searching rooms, hunting in vain for a fire that had been conjured entirely from my imagination.

In all this, I stood quiet and still against the wall. I could only hope that this had been enough of a distraction for Alejandro de Castillo to enter the Lady Elizabeth's room and speak to her in private.

'Enough!'

As though a shutter had been thrown back, letting in the light, everyone stopped what they were doing and stared at each other in bewilderment.

It was Marcus Dent.

He was standing in the doorway to the long room. The thin-faced witchfinder looked past the crowd to where I was waiting in silence, and crooked his finger at me.

'Your turn to answer some questions, Meg Lytton. In here, if you please. The rest of you, get back to your duties. There is no fire.'

Prepared though I was to face his questions, I still shivered as I entered the room. Marcus seated himself in a deep chair by the window and looked up at me thoughtfully, one long thin leg crossed over the other. I curtseyed low, unpleasantly aware that the witchfinder held my life in his hands. He had not told me to sit, so I stood for my interrogation like a common criminal before a magistrate, my hands clasped behind my back so he would not see how they trembled.

'I am told you are a witch,' Marcus began, his tone pleasant enough, with none of the rhetoric or accusatory gestures I had anticipated. 'Is this true?'

'Of course not.'

'I see.' He smiled. 'So the maid Joan did not catch you casting a circle in the old palace yesterday evening?'

'She was confused. She must have seen a reflection of something . . . it was dark, we were playing a game.'

'Ah yes, hide and seek.'

I told him briefly what I had told Sir Henry Bedingfield the night before, though I knew that Marcus was a very different man to the Lady Elizabeth's gaoler. He would not be so easily satisfied by my flimsy explanation.

Marcus heard me out without interruption, then rose and looked out over the park. I studied him in silence, the tilt of his fair head, the straight back, the dirt on his boots from this morning's ride. It was hard to imagine that he could have ever proposed marriage to me.

It ought to have been a terrifying thought, reducing me to tears. Yet I was not terrified. Instead, I felt as though I were carved of ice, unable to feel anything as I stared at his back and wondered when he would call the guards to have me dragged away. Or what alternative he might lay before me instead of arrest and a public execution.

I did not have long to wait.

'What I have heard here today is enough to condemn you to the gallows,' he said lightly, and turned his head. His blue eyes held an odd expression. 'Meg, Meg . . .'

'Marcus, I swear that I am innocent.'

This time my voice had no effect; he was ready for

it and merely shook his head, dismissing my words.

'Witches always swear that they are innocent.'

'I am not a witch.'

Marcus came towards me and I shrank away at last, guessing instinctively that he meant to touch me. He halted a few feet away, and I could see that my reaction had angered him.

'Well,' he murmured, 'perhaps you are not a witch. Not yet. But perhaps you are apprenticed to one.'

My heart almost stopped.

'Who . . . what do you mean?'

'Come, Meg, the time for such pretence is long past. Your aunt never married, did she? I have met many such lone women in my time, growing old without a man to keep them on the straight and narrow path to salvation. Perhaps she practises the dark arts behind your father's back.' His smile was cold. 'Or perhaps he knows, and allows it out of fear.'

I stared at him, an icy terror gripping me. If they were to search my aunt's bedchamber at Lytton Park, what would they find? Magickal instruments enough to hang us both thrice over, and books that no respectable woman should possess.

In desperation, I strengthened my voice. 'My aunt is not a witch either. I thought you were a learned man, but you must know this is mere superstition. Every unmarried woman past twenty years of age must be a witch these days, it seems.'

My gaze fixed on his blue eyes, I let the silence between us grow long and heavy, the room suddenly clammy with it, like a mist thickening into fog.

I imagined Marcus Dent becoming confused in that oppressive silence and forgetting what he had come here to do. In my mind's eye, I heard the witchfinder declare me innocent. He would leave Woodstock and never come back. He would forget the accusations against my aunt. He would . . .

'Do not waste my time with these childish tricks.' Marcus clapped his hands, and the dark, clammy atmosphere I had conjured was gone from the room. So was the feeling of confusion. Only Marcus Dent remained. He stood in front of me, his gaze assessing. 'Truly, is that the life you wish for yourself, Meg? To become an old maid like your aunt, accused by your neighbours of worshipping the Devil and turning milk sour wherever your feet pass?'

He was only a man, so he could not understand. A woman did not choose the gift. The gift chose her, and even if she averted her face for years, there could be no ignoring the small, insistent voice in the dark watches of the night that told how she spent her power on sweepings and cradlings and nothings, how she poured the gift away in dirty water every day, while her true self lay hidden and unused, like gold at the back of a drawer.

'You are so beautiful,' he said more huskily, and raised a hand to trace a line down my cheekbone. 'Come to me. Let me protect you.'

'Come to you? In what way?'

He hesitated, then allowed himself to meet my gaze. There was a strange burning hunger in his blue eyes, and an uncertainty too.

Was Marcus Dent in love with me?

I had thought him merely in lust before, and desperate to make an heir for his estate. But if he was in love with me, that made him vulnerable to my power, whatever he might claim. Perhaps it was not beyond my skill, after all, to turn this man to my will.

I felt sick to think of lowering myself to such a thing. To encourage his love, and then escape him once I had the chance. Yet what choice did I have? This was not just my own neck I would be saving from the noose, I reminded myself, but my aunt's too.

'So?' I prompted him.

He came closer, and I felt the warmth of his breath. 'Accept my protection, and you will find out.'

I shivered and closed my eyes. His hand cupped my cheek. Suddenly, I was unsure that I could go through with this, even to save my life. The man was sadistic and cruel – how could I take him as my husband?

'Whatever you may think,' he continued, 'I am not a heartless man. I have watched you grow from a child into a beautiful creature, soft-skinned and alive. I don't wish to see you dangle at the rope's length, Meg, and watch your light put out so cruelly. But if you won't give me a good reason to discredit the kitchen maid's testimony, I must do my duty and send you to trial as a witch. And then you *will* hang.' Slowly, he leaned forward and touched his lips to mine. Even that brief contact seemed to burn my skin. It was all I could do not to push him away. 'Do we understand each other?'

I opened my eyes, staring at Marcus, and knew I had no chance against him physically. But I still had my skill as a witch. My hands bunched into fists at my side. Reaching out with my thoughts, I tried to repel him with the power of my mind alone.

Marcus Dent stood like a rock, his breath warm on my face, seemingly untouched by my magick.

My lips curled into a grimace and my eyes narrowed to slits as I redoubled my efforts. Still nothing. My belly hurt and sweat collected on my forehead. I pushed so hard against him with my mind that in the far corner of the room an elegant blue glass flagon teetered on the edge of a table and fell, shattering on the floor.

Marcus Dent merely laughed. He withdrew a small white stone from the pouch at his belt and held it up to my face. 'To ward off a witch's power, use her own instruments against her,' he quoted softly. 'This is your charm-stone, isn't it?'

Fury and helplessness snarled inside me. Marcus Dent seemed to have an answer for every trick I knew. How could I ever hope to win against such a man?

'Isn't it?' he repeated, waiting for my answer.

Before I could tell him to go to Hell, the door was flung open, and we both turned.

Startled, I stared at the Lady Elizabeth, who stood in the doorway with her guards behind her, wrapped in a rich red mantle that covered her right up to the neck, her face stern and more regal than I had ever seen it.

Marcus Dent appeared astonished by this unexpected interruption, and perhaps even a little fearful. He took a few steps back from me, no doubt realizing how intimate our closeness must seem, and thrust the white charm-stone back into his pouch. He remained defiant though, sure of his ground here. He was the witchfinder, after all, and not without power of his own.

Clasping his hands behind his back, he bowed with rather less respect than he ought to have shown the heir presumptive to the throne.

'My Lady Elizabeth,' he murmured, raising his head to meet her accusing gaze. His colour was heightened, his breathing a little fast, but he was back in control. 'I must apologize for my presence here. You were unwell, so I was called in to question your servant—'

'I have heard the servant girl's story, and it is clearly nonsense.' Elizabeth's tone was icy, though her eyes flashed across the room at me as though promising dire consequences later. 'I thank you for your diligence in this matter, Master Dent, but your presence is no longer required. Please leave us.'

He persisted. 'Madam, an accusation of witchcraft has been made—'

'There are no witches here, sir. Only two very foolish girls. I may be a prisoner of my sister the Queen's Grace, but I am still mistress of my own household here at Woodstock and shall punish my own servants as I see fit. Nor are your skills as a witchfinder needed. It was not witchcraft, as you will hear, but a jest gone wrong.'

She turned her head and spoke a command softly to Blanche Parry, who had stood silent and watchful at her shoulder the whole time.

Joan was produced, cringing and rubbing her eyes, from behind Blanche's voluminous skirts and pushed forward into the centre of the room. There she gave a shivering, tear-stained denial of her original tale and agreed with the Lady Elizabeth, after being prompted, that it had been 'nothing but a poor jest' and 'all made up'.

'A poor jest, indeed,' Marcus said tightly, but I could see that he knew he had lost.

Sir Henry Bedingfield came through the door, his florid face redder than ever, demanding to know what on earth had been going on while he was out with the guards in the old palace, searching for suspicious items that might have been left there. He had heard shouts of fire from the lodge, which had turned out to be false, and now the Lady Elizabeth was out of her sickbed and speaking without permission to the local witchfinder.

Elizabeth fixed her gaoler with a stern eye. 'Sir,' she said simply, 'your efforts here have made a mountain out of a molehill. Two silly girls played a game that went awry, and that is all there is to be said about it. Regardless of the country of my sister's prospective bridegroom, this is still England and we are not yet obliged to accept the Inquisition into our houses.'

Marcus Dent bowed, and reached for his cap and cloak. I could guess what he was thinking. To press his moral duty to examine me as a witch would have been to invite possible disaster in the future. If Queen Mary died without an heir – though that was in serious doubt, with her wedding to Philip of Spain about to take place – Elizabeth would be within her rights to claim the throne. And any fool knew that those who scorned the Lady Elizabeth during her exile from court would be repaid with equal scorn if she were to become Queen herself.

Once Marcus Dent had safely gone, accompanied by a tight-lipped Sir Henry Bedingfield, I waited in silence, with downcast eyes, for the Lady Elizabeth to chastise me.

In the tense silence that followed, I glanced discreetly at the princess and noticed for the first time how unwell she appeared. Her face was lily-white, her eyes swollen and red-rimmed, and she had seated herself in the same chair by the window that Dent had only recently occupied. For her to sit in company was rare, for Elizabeth was a restless person and preferred to stand or walk about whenever possible. I had not seen her so affected since her mysterious illness in June, from which she had taken so many weeks to recover.

'Now, Meg Lytton, I intend to discover the truth of this botched affair that forced me to rise from my sickbed and have Joan lie to that gentleman on your behalf,' Elizabeth told me, her white hands tightening on the arms of her chair.

Her shrewd gaze was hard to meet. 'What *precisely* were you doing in the old palace last night?'

SEVEN
Immortal Soul

We were alone together, the door was closed for once, and there was no one to hear us.

'Speak,' Elizabeth commanded me impatiently.

'I was casting a circle,' I admitted flatly, and saw her face tighten. 'I didn't know Joan had followed me out there. I'm sorry. It was careless of me.'

'I thought we had agreed it was no longer safe to work magick in the old palace. Besides, to go out there alone at dusk was madness. Simply being caught out at such an hour without good reason would be enough to draw suspicion on yourself.' She looked at me in silence for a moment. 'You could have been hanged for this, you understand that?'

I blenched and whispered, 'Yes, my lady.'

'Why in God's name do it, then?'

'I wanted to strengthen my skill. To see if I could work magick on my own, without my aunt to help me.'

'You were a fool to do so.' Her voice hardened. 'Did you never consider the danger you were putting me in? If the Queen heard that a member of my own household had been taken as a witch, do you think she would rest until I too had been summoned back to the Tower and questioned on the same charge?'

I was ashamed, realizing too late that she was right. 'I'm sorry, my lady.'

She must have read the contrition in my face. 'Well, if you are resolved never to be such a fool again, and to celebrate Mass with me every morning and evening for the next month like a good Catholic, then we may yet save you from the rope.'

'I am, my lady. Quite resolved.'

'Then we shall say nothing more about it.'

I curtseyed. 'Thank you, my lady.'

'Not that you must abandon your powers altogether, of course, for I may yet have need of them. But you must be more discreet from now on. I will not be able to lie for you a second time, not without drawing too much attention to myself.' Elizabeth thought for a moment, staring down at the fine red threads of her mantle. 'Do you know how to work astrology, Meg? To divine the future from the movements of the stars?'

'A little,' I agreed. 'And to tell the future from the bones, or the entrails of a dead animal, or even the patterns in a bird's flight.'

'Good,' she said. 'For I would have you teach me some of these skills. But not until we can be sure we are not overheard.'

We had been speaking in whispers, our voices so low that no one listening outside could have heard a word. But now Elizabeth straightened, raising her voice for the benefit of anyone with their ear to the door.

'I have accepted your innocence this time, but there must be no more doubt about your character. Nor will you disgrace my household again, is that clear? If you are so much as suspected of casting a tinker's spell or making up a love potion, I shall put you back in the hands of that despicable witchfinder myself. Yes, and come to see you hang, if you are found guilty.'

It was all pretence, yet still I shivered, not entirely sure that Elizabeth did not mean that threat.

'Let this be a lesson to you, girl,' she continued harshly, 'to keep to your daily work and your prayers, and not stray too far from the confines of the lodge.'

Elizabeth rose and looked out of the windows, as Marcus had done, across the sunlit lawns down to the river. Her long-fingered hands trembled on the windowsill. Elizabeth seemed very young suddenly. Yet she had already suffered so much in her short and troubled life. I wondered if she was thinking of her mother, the beautiful Queen Anne, executed as a witch and a heretic as well as an adulteress.

But she went on after a moment, in a lighter tone, 'You have that young Spaniard to thank for your life, by the way. He came to see me this morning. Had the impudence to break into my bedchamber unannounced and beg me to help you.'

I said nothing, but felt heat flood my cheeks.

'What is he to you?' she asked idly.

'Nothing, my lady.'

She made a noise under her breath, and I felt sure she did not believe me.

'You know why he was sent here, of course,' she bit out, still staring out of the window. 'He and his "holy" master.'

'To . . . to instruct you further in the ways of the Catholic faith?'

'To spy on me!' Her jewelled hands gripped the window-sill convulsively, then Elizabeth seemed to force herself to relax. She beckoned me closer and lowered her voice again. 'My sister does not trust me. Nor does Prince Philip, her Spanish husband-to-be. These two Catholic priests have been sent here to watch whatever I do and say. I am observed at every turn, and my movements reported to my sister. Who then tells me she keeps me prisoner here for my own safety and well-being!'

Father Vasco was a hostile and unpleasant man who seemed to hate Elizabeth and the Protestant faith she had professed under her brother's reign. I could well believe he was here to make mischief for the princess. But could Alejandro be spying on Elizabeth and sending secret reports back to London? Was such a thing possible?

I thought of those cool dark eyes, his swift and calculating intelligence, the way he had bribed that guard so he could speak to me last night . . .

Oh yes, it was possible.

'I have no proof,' Elizabeth continued under her breath, her voice bitter. 'Nor can I send them away without sinking myself deeper in trouble, for I promised to offer hospitality to any priests who should come to instruct me. But I would have you befriend Alejandro, since he finds you of interest. Watch him for me, both him and Father Vasco. Let me know if my suspicions are correct. Only be cautious. Do not grow too close to him. These priests are dangerous and not to be trusted, you understand?'

'Yes, my lady.'

She turned away from the view, seeming to shake off her anger. 'Now, I imagine the boy is still waiting outside to discover the outcome of this interview. Better call him in quickly, before Bedingfield returns.'

'Yes, my lady.'

I curtseyed and opened the door to find Alejandro de Castillo waiting there, two guards blocking his way with crossed pikestaffs. His dark eyes searched my face.

'The Lady Elizabeth wishes to speak with the priest,' I told the men coldly. They dropped their pikes aside and let him enter.

I closed the door in their faces, though I knew that as soon as Bedingfield returned he would demand the door be left open, so there could be no secret discussions between us. Elizabeth was, after all, still under suspicion of treason herself.

'Alejandro de Castillo,' she addressed him formally, and signalled him to rise from his respectful bow. 'You came here with your master to keep us all in the Catholic faith when we are far away from court. But will you pray for this girl too, priest?' He began to reply, but Elizabeth cut him short. 'Will you watch over one who has been accused of practising the dark arts?' She looked at me, her voice shaking slightly, and I did not know why I had always thought her cold and distant. 'I believe Meg to be innocent of those charges. But her immortal soul stands in some danger, I fear.'

We could hear Bedingfield returning. His familiar tread echoed up the wooden stairs, heavy in his outdoor boots. Blanche Parry's voice was raised as she followed him, perhaps as a covert warning to her mistress that she would soon be under observation again.

Alejandro bowed again, his face solemn. 'It is a great honour to serve you in this way, Your Highness. I shall indeed pray for Meg Lytton, and watch over her immortal soul while I am here at Woodstock.'

Elizabeth's mouth twisted in a smile. 'Sir, I thank you, but you must address me as "my lady". I am no longer a princess.'

'You are the daughter of a king, Your Highness. Until you are Queen yourself, you must always be . . . *una princesa*.'

'Hush, sir, are you trying to land me in trouble too?' But Elizabeth laughed, and already she looked better, her cheeks lightly flushed, her eyes sparkling at this flattery. She allowed Alejandro to kiss her hand and, as Bedingfield and Blanche Parry entered the room, even addressed him in fluent Spanish, which I had heard she had learned as a child.

Alejandro smiled at the princess with sudden, glowing warmth. He replied in the same language, only falling silent when Bedingfield interrupted, asking him irascibly to 'Speak English!' before adding to the princess, 'You are fortunate, my lady, in your gift for foreign tongues. But alas, I have been instructed to hear all your conversations and so must request you to stick to plain English when you speak in front of me.'

Alejandro bowed again to Elizabeth, and led me from the room, still doffing his cap with great courtesy.

Outside the door, I stared up into his bronzed face. I was suddenly breathless, aware of how lucky I was to have escaped with my life today.

'What did she say to you?'

Infuriatingly, Alejandro shook his head, still smiling. 'I will tell you one day. But not today. Come!' He seized me by the hand and began leading me down the stairs.

'Where are we going?' I demanded.

'I have been put in charge of your immortal soul,' he told me firmly, 'so we are going to take the Holy Sacrament. I shall wake Father Vasco from his siesta and he will hear your confession.'

'But I don't have anything to confess.'

'Nothing?'

'No,' I insisted stubbornly, hanging back against the tug of his hand. 'Nothing at all.'

'*De verdad?*' Alejandro stopped and looked back at me. 'I

find it hard to believe that, Meg Lytton. Especially when I was exploring the old palace early this morning and happened to find this.' He felt beneath his jacket, and drew out my aunt's black-handled dagger.

I stared, speechless.

'Your immortal soul . . . ?' he queried again.

'Is perhaps a little bit in danger,' I breathed, nodding. How had he found my aunt's athame? I thought I had hidden it safely. There were footsteps below us on the stairs. My eyes met his. 'Put that away. Would you see us both hanged?'

He handed me the dagger. I drew up my heavy skirts, not caring what he might see, and hid the dagger in the top of my woollen stocking. By the time the guard passed us, I was respectable again, if a little red in the face.

We went downstairs together to find Father Vasco. Considering what the princess had told me of his mission here, I was surprised that Alejandro had neither betrayed me nor used the dagger to blackmail me. After all, he could easily have threatened to take the dagger to Marcus Dent.

What Alejandro might have demanded in return for his silence, I dared not consider. Though I couldn't help but think that it would not have been a hardship to give in to *his* demands.

I caught myself staring furtively at my unlikely saviour during Mass, perplexed by Alejandro's unexpected help in avoiding the hangman's noose. I had never found it too hard to understand people, to see almost at a glance what they wanted and why. Yet Alejandro was a riddle I could not solve. It seemed as if I had been mistaken in thinking him my enemy, but yet I must remain cautious.

I was in the old palace herb garden a few days later, sent on an errand to gather fresh bay leaves for the cook, when Blanche Parry finally cornered me. She had been trying to get me alone all day and so far I had carefully avoided her. I did not know what she wanted, but I could see from her flushed cheeks and sparkling eyes that she was angry.

'Not so fast. It's time you and I had a talk,' Blanche insisted as I tried to slip past, a muttered excuse on my lips about the cook waiting for me.

I said nothing but waited, eyes downcast, herb basket cradled on my arm, to hear what I had done to offend her. There was never any point arguing with Blanche when she was in this mood.

'You may have fooled the others, but you can't fool me,' Blanche said fiercely. 'I know you for a witch.'

I raised my eyes to her face at that. Knew me for a witch, did she? I considered a few spells my aunt had taught me, methods of ensuring a person's silence. But they were all dangerous and could easily go wrong. I knew Elizabeth would never forgive me for working magick against her faithful lady-in-waiting.

Although I had stayed stubbornly silent, my expression must have betrayed my anger. Blanche made the sign of the cross, as though afraid I might turn her into a toad at any moment.

'Don't look at me like that, Devil's child.' She saw my involuntary movement, and her face twisted with malice. 'Oh yes, I remember the gossip about your mother. Cat Canley was a witch too, though she knew better than to flaunt it at court. But she was too friendly with poor Lady Elizabeth's mother, and look what happened there. Queen Anne suffered a terrible death, her head struck clean from her body!'

'That was not my mother's doing,' I said coldly, struggling to control myself.

'Perhaps not.' Blanche Parry levelled a shaking finger at me, her voice a vehement whisper. 'But the same will happen to you one day, Meg Lytton, if you keep encouraging my mistress in the dark arts.'

A tide of red moved across my vision, and I could no longer see Blanche Parry; she was just a dim figure against the sunlight. The herb basket tumbled to the floor, spilling bay leaves across the narrow sandy path. I raised my hand, pointing at Blanche with stiffly outstretched fingers, and vaguely heard her shriek.

But before I could speak the words, a familiar voice cut across my rage like a dash of cold water, shocking me back to myself.

'Meg?' It was Alejandro, suddenly at my elbow. 'What's this? You've dropped your basket. Here, let me help you.'

Blanche Parry had backed away into a privet hedge. She stood now, covering her face with her apron and blubbering. 'Witch! Witch!' She raised her head to Alejandro and gasped, 'You saw what happened, *señor*. She was going to put a spell on me.'

'I saw nothing,' Alejandro said sharply. He bowed to her formally. 'Give you good day, Mistress Parry. I must take Meg back to the house, for Father Vasco has urgent need of her.'

'Father Vasco?' Blanche echoed blankly, staring at him over the edge of her apron.

'Some robes that need mending before tonight's Mass. Bedingfield will spare none of his servants for the task, and I have no skill with a needle and thread. Forgive me, Mistress Parry. My master is waiting.'

Alejandro pushed the herb basket back into my arms and led me away from the garden, his hand firm on my shoulder.

I was still trembling with rage when we reached Father Vasco's dark little room at the top of the lodge. Alejandro gestured me inside and shut the door. There was nobody there. He threw back the shutters and the tiny room was flooded with daylight.

I stood blinking. 'Where is Father Vasco?'

'In the chapel,' Alejandro said calmly.

'But you said—'

Silently, he indicated a pile of old robes on the bed behind me. I sat down beside them and began to turn over the robes, hunting for rips and tears as though my life depended on it. At least it gave my hands something to do while I cooled my temper.

'What was all that about?' he demanded. 'What did you think you were doing, behaving like that in broad daylight where anyone might have seen you?'

'Mistress Parry insulted my mother,' I muttered.

Alejandro drew a sharp breath. 'Did she indeed?' I looked up to see him nodding, very sombre today in a plain shirt and hose, his dark jacket unfastened. He leaned back against the wall, watching me. 'Then I can see how you might have lost your temper with the foolish woman. But that is still no excuse for working your . . . your . . .'

He could not seem to bring himself to use the word. 'Magick?' I suggested.

'Yes,' he agreed. 'For working your magick against her. You cannot be too careful after last time.'

The room was silent for a moment. My skin prickled with apprehension. Why had he brought me here?

I glanced at the closed door. 'We should not be alone together,' I pointed out lightly. 'Father Vasco would not approve. Nor would Sir Henry Bedingfield.'

Alejandro did not move, leaning at his ease, his arms folded across his chest. 'True.'

So he was living dangerously now. I could not help some amusement at the thought and hurriedly bent my head to hide my smile, running my hands over the old priest's coarse robes. There was a tiny rip along the hem of one white robe, barely worth the mending. But I would play along.

'Where is this needle and thread, then?' I asked.

'Do you not have one?'

'In my chamber, yes. I don't carry them about with me,' I told him tartly.

Our eyes met. I could see Alejandro was remembering the last time he had been in my bedchamber, just as I was too. I had thought that would be my last night on earth.

'Promise me,' he said softly, 'you will not work magick again.'

'I cannot promise that.'

Alejandro frowned, and came to crouch before me. 'Do you not see how magick puts your life in danger?'

'What is my life to you?'

'I care what happens to you,' he said simply, and took my hands in his.

I looked down at him mockingly. 'What, will you pray with me now?'

'If not with you, then for you. Your immortal soul is under my protection,' Alejandro reminded me, 'by order of *la princesa*.'

'Magick is my power. You are asking me to lay aside my only power in the world.'

'There is power in being a woman.'

I raised my brows at that, and Alejandro laughed. His hands tightened on mine. 'Come, Meg. You are still young in the dark arts, not yet an accomplished witch. Lay magick aside before your soul is burned away for ever.'

'I am not as unaccomplished as you think,' I muttered.

He was smiling. 'Have I touched a nerve? I beg your pardon, Mistress Witch. Do not hurt me, of your kindness.'

'You want me to prove my skill?'

'No more tricks, I pray you.'

'Tricks?'

Anger stirred inside me, mingled with a certain pride in my skill. I narrowed my gaze on his. So he thought my power was that of a trickster, a street magician with his cups and cards, not a true witch?

'Meg,' he whispered.

'Hush.'

I focused my attention on the cross hanging from his neck. It was a heavy silver cross, ornate in the Spanish style, beautifully engraved along the cross-beam. I allowed its weight and substance to enter my mind, to become one with it. Then I imagined the metal growing hot again, almost as hot as it had been at its first making, the silver beginning to glow and soften against the plain linen of his shirt, too hot to touch now.

Alejandro frowned, and shifted uncomfortably at my feet. He seemed aware of the growing heat at his chest. 'Meg, what . . . what are you doing?'

'Touch your cross,' I instructed him. 'Go on, touch it.'

Alejandro stared up at me, then slowly released one of my

hands to touch the cross. He recoiled, his hand jerking away.

'It's hot!'

I relaxed my mind, and felt the heat leave the cross on my command, hardening to cool silver again.

'Try it now,' I prompted him.

When Alejandro's fingers gingerly touched the cross again, I saw his eyes widen and fix on my face.

'So tell me,' I demanded, 'was that a trick? Or a mark of true power?'

'*Madre de Dios*,' he muttered under his breath.

I smiled then, childishly pleased that I had impressed him. 'God gave me this gift, surely? I do not believe God would give me such a powerful gift, yet not allow me to use it. And if I hurt no one, what harm can there be?'

Alejandro said nothing for a moment but continued to stare at me, his eyes troubled. Then he raised my hand to his lips and brushed the lightest of kisses across it.

'Tread carefully, *mi querida*, and do not risk the sin of blasphemy,' he warned me, his voice quiet. 'Your gift may indeed be from God. But you are right, the Lord does not give such power lightly. Some gifts are a test, and others are a curse.' He met my eyes seriously. 'Which is yours?'

EIGHT

A Face Amongst the Leaves

Within a few weeks of my interrogation by Marcus Dent, Elizabeth received several more letters from friends at court. One of these letters she read out to us, her voice steady despite the momentous news. This was what the whole country had been waiting for all these months. The worst had finally happened: we were now a Catholic nation.

Her sister Queen Mary had married the Spanish prince in the great cathedral at Winchester before many hundreds of courtiers, lords, ladies and exalted guests from Spain, along with other foreign dignitaries and ambassadors, in a ceremony of great pomp and expense. And although many had grumbled privately about this Spanish marriage, thousands of the common people, we were told, had lined the streets on her journey back to London.

Elizabeth came to the end of the letter and laid it aside, staring into the distance.

It was early August and the three of us were sitting on our cloaks by the river in the afternoon sunshine: Elizabeth, with Blanche Parry and myself serving lunch from a cloth-covered basket. Thirty paces away, seated on a fallen tree trunk and munching stolidly on an apple, was the solitary guard who had come to watch over the Lady Elizabeth.

Blanche moved into the gentle shade of a birch tree after she had finished eating. She was mending one of the princess's gowns and seemed drowsy, with nothing much to say, besides tut-tutting from time to time as the names of various courtiers who had attended the wedding were read out.

I looked at Elizabeth and wondered how she must feel, knowing that any hopes of her becoming Queen would be destroyed by a child from this Spanish marriage – though she seemed less concerned by that possibility than by her exclusion from court. She could not have expected to be invited to Mary's wedding, for she was still under suspicion of treason against her sister. Yet it must have stung, the thought of these great events happening so far away, while she – an English princess of the blood royal, daughter of King Henry and half-sister to the Queen – was left to pace a few cramped rooms in the dilapidated gatehouse at Woodstock, alone and unvisited.

Somewhere off in the old palace grounds, one of the wild peacocks screamed, a last bedraggled remnant of the manor's ancient glory.

Elizabeth suddenly laughed. 'So it begins,' she murmured, then shrugged as though such fine doings meant nothing to us here at Woodstock, and asked me to pass her a dish of raspberries.

Squinting up at the afternoon sun, a fine perspiration on her forehead, Blanche Parry paused in her needlework.

'I can't remember a hotter summer. Come under the shade with me. You'll brown like a blackamoor in this heat, my lady.'

Elizabeth looked up with some quick retort on her lips, shielding her eyes, then exclaimed, 'Señor de Castillo!'

I sat up, rearranging my untidy gown and cap, suddenly flustered. When I looked round to see our visitor, Alejandro was rising from his bow.

'I trust that I do not intrude on your meal, my lady,' he addressed Elizabeth, replacing his feathered cap on his head. 'I was walking out in this fine summer weather, and saw you and your ladies unaccompanied' – he glanced sideways at the guard – 'by any gentleman.'

Elizabeth smiled at him invitingly. 'You are most welcome, sir,' she murmured, and signalled him to join us. 'Are you thirsty? We have wine and ale.'

'Thank you, my lady, I am not thirsty.'

'Perhaps we should both join Blanche Parry in the shade of that tree, then. If there is one thing I cannot abide it is freckles, and she claims I will freckle in this sun.'

Alejandro examined her face seriously. 'If there is any danger of that, allow me to help you to a shadier spot at once. Mistress Parry is right, your skin should not be exposed to this heat.'

I felt my skin prickle, and had to look away before my frown betrayed me. For some reason, the thought of Elizabeth lying under that tree with Alejandro made me . . .

not angry, but uncomfortable. And her smile seemed to be for him alone.

Was this jealousy?

I did not want to feel jealous. He was nothing to me, the young Spaniard. Besides, he would be a priest soon, he had told me himself. Only another year, and Alejandro would return to Spain to be examined for his readiness to enter the priesthood.

Still, when Elizabeth laughed and did not move, I knew a lightening of my mood that could only be relief.

Irritated by my own weakness, I jumped up, averting my face from Alejandro's. 'Shall I hunt for more honeysuckle for your skin lotion, my lady?' I suggested, fearing my desire to escape must be transparent to everyone there. 'It is so scarce near the lodge. And your last pot is nearly finished.'

The princess looked surprised by my sudden request, but readily agreed. My aunt had taught me how to make skin lotions when I was young, and Elizabeth had been delighted with the ones I had already made for her, with Blanche Parry's help, from easily found plants such as the yellow primrose, blue-flowering rosemary and the soft-scented ground-rambling honeysuckle. Ground into pulp and mixed with spring water and vinegar, they kept Elizabeth's face and throat soft and white in the dry heat of summer.

Much to my annoyance though, she did not want me to go alone, which had been my only motive in asking.

'You may go, but Alejandro de Castillo will accompany

you,' Elizabeth said pointedly, and her sharp look reminded me that I was supposed to be finding out whether or not the Spanish priests were here to spy on the princess. 'It is not fitting for you to be wandering about on your own.'

Alejandro rose at once, his movements fluid and graceful, and bowed to the princess. 'It will be my honour, madam.'

Elizabeth smiled, and made some remark in Spanish. He replied quietly in the same language, bowed again, then gestured me to lead the way. 'After you, mistress.'

'This way,' I said, a bite in my voice, though I made sure the others could not overhear me. 'But I hope you don't mind thorns. We may need to go deep into the thicket to find the best honeysuckle.'

'As long as the thorns are no sharper than your tongue, Meg Lytton, I shall survive the encounter.'

Narrow-eyed at this reply, my cheeks a little flushed from the day's heat, I walked into the little thicket, holding my skirts tight about my legs, in case any thorns should snag at the material.

Alejandro followed close behind me, silent.

The trees and bushes were so crowded together there that it was hard to get close to where the honeysuckle grew, twined fragrantly about the trunks. Spotting a strong, darkly green honeysuckle still in bloom ahead, I pushed back the thorny twigs to avoid them scratching me, then let them swing back so violently that he had to jump aside.

What was it Alejandro and the princess said to each other when they spoke in Spanish?

It was so frustrating, not being to understand their muttered comments and jokes. Small wonder that Sir Henry Bedingfield forbade the speaking of foreign languages in the lodge, for he thought it a breach of security to allow such conversations to go unmonitored. I loathed the man's strict rules, and his stern lectures on decorum for royal prisoners, but in this I shared his dislike. Elizabeth was an incorrigible flirt, and there was something unsettling about Alejandro's smile when the princess addressed him in his own tongue, her voice like warm honey.

I kneeled to gather a few of the thicker strands of yellow-flowered honeysuckle, tracing the long tendrils back to the main stem. But they were tough to pull free, and my hands were soon sore, with red lines scored across my palms. My hair fell into my eyes as I wrestled with them, and I brushed it back irritably, hot-faced.

'Permit me,' Alejandro murmured, and leaned past me with his knife. With a few neat cuts, he severed the strands of honeysuckle, twisted them into several thick green coils and handed them to me. He crouched a moment longer, wiping his blade on the underside of his tunic, then looked into my face.

We were so close, almost touching. I could smell his breath on my face, sweet as the honeysuckle I was clasping to my throat and chest. I felt dizzy, as though the sun had been too strong for me after all.

I had the oddest feeling that Alejandro was going to kiss me, and tilted my face towards his, watching his mouth through lowered eyelashes.

But it seemed that I was wrong.

Through the yellow tumble of hair over my face, I saw Alejandro's eyes, so warm and laughing before, grow distant, almost aloof.

It was as though the novice priest had thought to amuse himself with the princess's humble country servant, and then had suddenly remembered who I was – a suspected witch. Someone to be shunned, not kissed.

Then Alejandro was gone, straightening into the sunshine as he returned to the Lady Elizabeth's side.

Following on with my fragrant armful of honeysuckle, sweaty and a little angry at having suffered such a humiliation, I caught a rustle behind me in the thicket, the crack of a twig underfoot.

Turning swiftly, fearing it might be a boar or some other dangerous animal, I glimpsed a man's face amongst the leaves. My mind flashed to the Green Man, the wild pagan god who lurks unseen about the woodlands and to whom we sometimes dedicated our sabats. Then I saw the coarse edge of a cloak, a plain cap, and knew it was the face of a man there, not a god.

Someone had been watching us!

Yet even as I drew in my breath to call for help, the dark cloak whirled and the man was gone.

I stared a moment longer, blinking into slanted sunlight. The little thicket stood empty and silent except for the piping of birdsong. Bemused, I turned back to rejoin the others, and sat down by the princess without saying anything, and certainly without meeting Alejandro's searching gaze.

But I was flushed and worried. For I had recognized that face amongst the leaves. The man watching us through the undergrowth had been my cousin, Malcolm Lytton.

'Show me again!'

I sighed, using my sleeve to wipe fingermarks from the face of the scrying mirror. 'Divination does not work like that, my lady. The mirror will remain cloudy if asked to reveal the same vision again. Each glimpse of the future can only be seen at one fixed time, and no other.'

'And how is that time determined?'

'By the asking of a question,' I replied, as patiently as I could. We had already been through this twice, both of us sitting cross-legged on her bed, the door to her chamber securely locked and only a single candle lighting our work. I repeated what my aunt had told me many times. 'The scrying mirror must be consulted at the moment when the question is asked, not before or after.'

Elizabeth looked at me stubbornly. 'Very well. Then I ask the question again. When shall I be Queen?'

'Better to change the terms of the question, my lady, or

the outcome will be unclear. To ask the same question twice is like stirring the depths of a pond with a stick . . . all you do is muddy the waters.'

Elizabeth seemed to understand that comparison, though she was clearly dissatisfied by the way magick worked. No doubt the princess was too used to bending the rules to take kindly to being told these rules were utterly inflexible. 'Let me see . . .' Her eyes sparkled mischievously in the candlelight. 'When will my sister die?'

I stared at her, and the twinkle in Elizabeth's eyes faded.

'Oh, very well,' she said reluctantly. 'Maybe that is a dangerous question. And a cruel one too. I do not wish my sister dead. Though she wishes for my death, I suspect. We were never close as children, for Mary is much older than I am, even old enough to have been my mother. She was forced to look after me sometimes at court. I know she must have resented that, for my father divorced her mother to marry mine. Yet Mary was always so devout she would say it was her Christian duty to care for me. Never any word of sisterly love, but only duty.'

Hunched over the dark mirror, I waited for her question.

Elizabeth bit her lip, as though struggling with her own conscience. 'Ask then if I will ever return to London, or if I am doomed to die in this dreary prison. There can be no harm in such a question. I am so sick of captivity, Meg. With each day I spend hidden away here in the country, it becomes harder to imagine ever dancing at court again.'

I passed a hand across the dark mirror and spoke a few words in Latin that I had learned from one of my aunt's spell books. The surface began to move, coiling smokily. I gazed down through rippling coils to the black velvet heart of the mirror, and repeated her question: 'When will the Lady Elizabeth return to London?'

In the mirror I saw a broad road cutting through green fields towards distant towers, then a dreamlike procession of horses, carts, a swaying covered litter . . . and knew at once that this was Elizabeth returning to London. But when?

The wind blew strongly, flapping the litter curtains. There was a white scattering of blossom in the hedgerow and freshly unfurled leaves on the trees.

With a shock I saw a shadowy vision of myself, seated on a cart behind the princess's litter. It was only a glimpse, then my future self turned to stare across the fields. I did not look much older though. A year, perhaps?

Under the cap I was wearing in the mirror, my fair hair seemed painfully short. My eyes widened and I felt instinctively for the long thick tresses now lying unbound about my shoulders.

Then my eye was caught by an odd thing. In the mirror, something dark stirred in the air behind the jolting cart. I looked more closely, holding my breath. A massed shadow grew and flickered at my back in the vision, as though some hideous creature of darkness were half creeping, half flying after us on the road to London. Yct my future self did not seem to have noticed it, smiling and looking ahead at the glinting towers in the distance.

'What is it?' Elizabeth demanded, leaning forward eagerly to stare down into the dark mirror. Some of the shock I was feeling must have shown on my face, for the princess sounded urgent. 'What do you see?'

'I see myself,' I murmured, feeling a little sick and off balance.

'You?' Elizabeth appeared affronted by this. Her small mouth pursed tightly. 'But what of me? Tell me what you have seen, and leave nothing out. Am I in the mirror? When will I return to London? How long must I waste my life in this prison?'

The mirror began to cloud over again, like the sun on a windy day. The vision of our procession was lost. I passed a hand across its smoky surface again, but nothing happened. Her question had been answered, and could not be asked again.

'I can't be sure,' I admitted, sitting back. I saw her disappointment and hurriedly sketched out some details for the princess. 'Next year. In the springtime, perhaps. I saw a procession on its way to London, but nothing to tell me when or why you were returning to the city.'

I did not mention the terrifying shadow-creature I had seen creeping at our backs. It might have been nothing but a trick of the mirror, after all. Instruments of witchcraft were tricky, highly unreliable, and often exacted some kind of payment for their services from the user. My fear might be what the scrying mirror wanted in return for showing us the future.

'But was it a triumphal procession?' Her voice dropped to a hiss. 'Was I returning as Queen?'

I shook my head. 'I'm sorry, my lady. The mirror did not show me that.'

Her pale cheeks flushed with sudden anger. 'Then what use is this "dark mirror" of yours? You had your aunt send this magickal object to Woodstock, and promised it would tell my future, then you give me hints and whispers, half-truths and maybes instead.' Elizabeth slid off the bed, contempt plain on her face. 'You told me you had power, Meg. Yet you show me what I already know and call this divination.'

'I do have power,' I snapped, forgetting to sound deferential, my pride stung by her accusation.

'Then show me some!'

My aunt had wrapped up a few of her old magick books along with the dark mirror. I had been playing all that week with one of the trickier spells in her books, and thought of it now, knowing how it would impress Elizabeth and banish her doubts for ever.

Without thinking of the risks, I raised a hand and pointed stiffly at Elizabeth. '*Obscure!*'

The spell had not fully worked for me yet, but I knew it would make at least a part of the princess invisible. What I had not counted on was it working perfectly this time.

Perhaps the anger in my voice had been enough to push this most difficult of spells beyond my half-hearted efforts earlier. It was all in the power of the voice, I knew that much. But whatever the reason for it, the spell suddenly worked. Where Elizabeth had been standing was nothing but a thin shadow, shifting subtly in the candlelight.

'Well?' her voice repeated impatiently. Presumably she could see me staring at her, my mouth agape. 'What was that supposed to achieve?'

I swallowed, and pointed to the gilt hand mirror on the bedside table. 'Look . . .' I could hardly speak. 'Look at yourself.'

The hand mirror floated into the air, then I heard a gasp. 'I'm not there!' The mirror was replaced on the table, and a silence followed.

Then I saw the shadow of her presence change, turning more solid in the middle. Her hands were becoming visible again. It was always the hands that came back first, my aunt had told me. They seemed to hate being invisible.

There was a muffled shriek as Elizabeth examined her hands, turning them over. Just a pair of long, white-fingered hands and a hint of her nightdress sleeve floating about in thin air.

This spell was clearly not a strong one, or not the way I had cast it. I wondered if it would be possible to strengthen it enough to last a few hours. It could prove useful when creeping about the old palace after dusk. But if the spell was unreliable, it would be best not to chance it. Becoming suddenly visible at a dangerous moment would surely land me in the hands of the witchfinder again.

'My lady?' I whispered, worried that she might faint.

Her voice shook, but Elizabeth sounded surprisingly calm. 'I'm invisible. You did this?'

I nodded.

A sharp slap across my face shocked me and I fell sideways on the bed.

'Make me visible again at once,' the princess demanded coldly. Part of her face reappeared, scowling down at me. Then her hair also thickened into being, as ruddy as her flushed cheeks. 'How dare you tamper with me in this wicked, freakish way? I am Elizabeth Tudor, daughter of a king, not something from a cheap street spectacle.'

'I'm sorry.' I rubbed my cheek, forcing myself to swallow my temper, and pointed at her shadowy form. '*Reveni!*'

Once more the princess stood before me, plain to see. I almost wished she was still invisible, sensing her prickling anger. Her arms were folded, her lips pursed tight. 'You had better take your witching instruments and go to bed,' she told me curtly. 'And send Blanche to me.'

'Yes, my lady.'

I covered the dark mirror with a cloth, tucked it under my arm, and scrambled off the bed.

'Wait,' she said, her voice sharp. I saw a glimmer of respect in her face. 'It was a good spell, Meg. But never play such a trick on me again. Not without my permission, at any rate.'

'I don't know if I can work that spell again,' I admitted reluctantly. 'That was the first time I've managed it.'

'Well, it was very impressive. And a useful spell too, if I ever need to hide in a hurry. So perhaps you should keep practising it, just in case.'

I curtseyed and bowed my head in acquiescence, though the princess did not understand how magick worked. It was not merely a question of practising until the spell fell right. Sometimes these more complicated spells just refused to work as intended, or did not work at all, and that was down to the individual talent of the witch casting the spell.

It had to be my fault, there was no other explanation. The simple truth was, I did not possess as much witching power as my aunt, and never would.

Malcolm sent me a letter a few weeks after I had seen him spying on us by the river.

I read it quickly, then tore it up. Malcolm was returning to the Low Countries with my foolhardy brother in tow, whose studies had been abandoned while he pursued their hope of rebellion. Malcolm begged me to reconsider the favour they had asked of me at their last visit.

My cousin merely wanted to make mischief, and even if my brother Will had been unable to resist his arguments, I would have no part in it. Not when Elizabeth's life was at stake. One peep of sedition from the disgraced princess, and she would be marched straight back to London and the gloomy restraints of the Tower.

Nor would I escape punishment if we were discovered in such a dangerous course.

The penalty for treason was the most horrible death imaginable – to be hung until not quite dead, then drawn in agony, my guts spilled out onto the marketplace, my heart cut, still beating, from my butchered body, before finally being quartered with a knife. Only then would merciful death be allowed to close my eyes.

I threw the shredded remains of Malcolm's letter into the cesspit where they soon blackened into filth.

If my hot-headed cousin and brother wished to raise a rebellion together against Queen Mary and her new Spanish husband, they would have to do so without my help.

NINE

The Queen's Astrologer

We lived quietly at Woodstock for the rest of the summer, with no more letters from court. Distinguished visitors appeared in the village from time to time, however, much to Sir Henry Bedingfield's frustration and annoyance. They stayed at the Bull Inn, and although I could never see how these visitors were making contact with the princess, she often seemed to have a secret smile and would tell us news of court in a whisper when the guards were busy elsewhere. I wondered whether the same servant who had sometimes brought me letters from Malcolm and my brother was also carrying secret messages from the Bull to the imprisoned princess.

More and more frequently that summer, as Father Vasco concentrated his efforts on the princess's conversion to Catholicism, I found myself alone with Alejandro while his master and my mistress meditated together on the teachings of the scriptures. We spent these long hours in conversation, seated on the old wooden bench in the herb garden or strolling through the overgrown woodlands that bordered the palace. Sometimes we discussed philosophy, a subject that was relatively new to me, and sometimes darker matters, such as the origins of the universe and God's purpose for his creation. Alejandro was a fascinating conversationalist, his mind always sharp and alert, his knowledge of the world extensive. Apart from the unbearable Marcus Dent, I thought him the most intelligent and well-read man I had ever met.

Though not all our time alone was spent in conversation. Occasionally as we walked, our hands would brush, and for a few heated moments it would feel as though we were lovers, or destined to become so. But then Alejandro would seem to recall that he was a priest and thrust his hands safely behind his back, or I would grow suddenly shy and avert my gaze. At night in my bed though, I would secretly imagine the two of us lying together in the darkness, and could not help wondering if the very cool and controlled Alejandro ever did the same.

In late September, as the warmth of summer had begun to fade and the leaves to turn a reddish gold, Sir Henry Bedingfield came to see Elizabeth. It was early evening, not quite dusk, and the sunlight filtering through the cracked window panes was still just strong enough for us to sew by without the need for candles.

From his flushed countenance and breathless state it was clear as soon as Bedingfield strode into the room that he was in a temper.

'I can no longer allow these visitors of yours from court,' he blustered, barely bothering with his customary bow on entering the Lady Elizabeth's presence. 'I must insist that they no longer visit you, nor stay in the village inn where they cause a nuisance to the locals.'

'Sir?' Like the rest of us, Elizabeth had looked up from her embroidery at this intrusion, her tone astonished, her face the very picture of maidenly innocence.

'I am convinced you do not need this spelled out for you, my lady,' Bedingfield continued raggedly. 'These secret visits from your courtly followers must cease.'

'Indeed, I would readily agree to any commands that come direct from the Queen or her council. But I have had no visitors, sir, as you know very well. No one has come to me from court since early summer, not since I was first brought here at my good sister's will.' Elizabeth hesitated, then laid aside her embroidery, pretending confusion. 'Could you make yourself more clear on this subject, sir, for I cannot understand your meaning?'

Bedingfield withdrew a folded letter from inside his coat and waved it at her. 'Today, madam, I have received this letter from the council. In it, I am accused of failing in my duty towards the throne, and informed that messages of a dubious nature have passed between you and various named individuals who have come to visit you here at Woodstock. Yet I have not seen you leave the grounds, nor have I permitted any such contact between yourself and the outside world. So explain to me, if you will, madam, how it can be that you have met and spoken with these individuals without my permission and in breach of the Queen's express command?'

Elizabeth rose, clasping her pale hands before her. Her narrow face looked more pinched than ever, her tone a little more curt than usual. 'Sir, I am at a loss to understand these accusations. They mean nothing to me. You yourself have just confessed my innocence. For I have spoken with no one beyond these four walls, nor have I received nor sent any letters since my arrival here that were not sent directly through you.'

'Then how do you explain this information?'

She glanced at the letter he was holding aloft. 'May I be permitted to read the contents?'

'No, you may not.' His nostrils flared. 'I may not be as cunning a person as yourself, but I am not such a fool as to allow you to see which individuals have been named and what messages have passed between you.'

'In that case, sir,' Elizabeth pointed out coldly, 'if I am not permitted to know these things, how am I to defend myself against this accusation?'

'Have you,' Sir Henry Bedingfield thundered, 'or have you not, madam, received any visitors or news without my permission and knowledge during your time here at Woodstock?'

'No, sir, I have not.'

Her gaoler stood a moment, his jaw working furiously, then stormed out of the room, kicking one of the Lady Elizabeth's hounds out of the way as it tried to slink through the doorway.

Elizabeth waited a moment, listening to the noisy retreat of his boots down the stairway. Then she strode restlessly to the window and stared out across the palace grounds in the gathering dusk. Her back was very straight, her head thrown back in defiance. I heard her mutter something under her breath. The long white fingers of one hand tapped repeatedly at the cracked glass as though with some secret code.

When Elizabeth turned back to face us, I saw she had been crying.

'Blanche,' she said hoarsely, 'I am unwell, you must help me to my room at once.' She dried her damp cheek with the back of her hand, not quite meeting my eyes. 'Meg, where is Alejandro? I need . . . I need someone to read the scriptures with me. There is a passage in Paul's Epistles that I must have explained to me. Fetch young Alejandro to my chamber. Hurry!'

I curtseyed, dodged past the guard on the door and ran along the corridor to the small back room where the priests lodged. It had been Bedingfield's own room before Father Vasco and Alejandro had arrived, but now Elizabeth's gaoler had reluctantly set up a room for himself in the old gatehouse, allowing the two priests a more comfortable place in the lodge.

I knocked on the heavy wooden door and called out hurriedly, 'Alejandro!' I wondered what on earth Elizabeth could be planning.

She was not ill, that was for sure.

The door was thrown open within seconds and Alejandro himself looked out at me, rightly surprised to see me knocking there at dusk. His long white shirt was undone and worn loose, his dark robe discarded. I averted my eyes from his bare chest, feeling myself flush. Behind him, stretched out on his narrow bed, I could see Father Vasco already asleep.

'Meg?' Alejandro frowned. He glanced over his shoulder at the old priest and kept his voice low, presumably not wishing to wake his irascible master. 'What is it? What's the matter?'

Briefly, I informed him of Elizabeth's odd request but did not mention Bedingfield's accusations. Alejandro already disapproved of me, of that I felt certain, and I did not see why he should also disapprove of Elizabeth.

'It's lucky my master shows no signs of waking,' Alejandro whispered, and reached for his coat and his sword. 'I will come.'

I waited outside until he was respectably dressed, his shirt fastened and the sword buckled about his waist, then led him down the corridor to the Lady Elizabeth's chamber.

To my surprise, there was no guard on her door. Could Elizabeth have bribed the man to turn a blind eye that evening?

My heart was beating fast – though with excitement, not fear. We had led such a narrow, stifling existence at Woodstock over the hot summer months. Now it all seemed to be coming to a head. Suddenly I was filled with a terrible restlessness, an irresistible itch in the palms of my hands that I recognized as the desire to work magick.

I scratched softly at the unguarded door, and heard the princess herself call 'Come!' immediately.

I had expected to find Elizabeth in her nightclothes, collapsed in bed, with Blanche Parry hovering at her side with some refreshing herbal concoction. Instead, she was standing against the wall, a few feet away from the now shuttered windows, fully dressed and wearing an old patched and hooded cloak I recognized as one sometimes worn by Joan, the simple-minded kitchen maid who had accused me of witchcraft. Blanche was fussing about the princess, tucking Elizabeth's hair back under the hood.

Elizabeth met Alejandro's surprised gaze with a level stare I had not seen since the day she had asked if I was truly a witch.

'Will you help me, sir?' she asked him directly. 'I am in trouble and must go to the Bull Inn at once. There, I must meet with one who awaits me secretly and then return unseen. Blanche will guard the door here and tell anyone who asks that I am sick with the toothache and can speak to no one. But if this fails and Sir Henry discovers that I have left his custody, I shall be taken back to London, perhaps to my death.' Her dark narrow eyes seemed to search his face. 'All I ask is your help in seeing me safely there and back. Will you do it?'

I was astonished. If Alejandro and his master had been sent here by Queen Mary, the most likely explanation was not that she was concerned for Elizabeth's soul but that she wanted her watched and reported on. Now Elizabeth was planning to trust the spy in their midst with this most dangerous of secrets?

Alejandro glanced sideways at me, his eyes filled with a kind of subdued laughter, as though mocking my surprise. He looked assessingly at Blanche Parry's worried expression, the handkerchief she was fretting at nervously, then at the Lady Elizabeth, standing cautiously with her back against the wall.

'Madam, is this visit treasonous?'

Defensive, she shook her head. 'It is not, sir.'

He bowed. 'Then I am at your service,' he said simply. 'When do we leave?'

'Straight away.'

Blanche pulled at her lower lip in distress, her face beginning to quiver. 'I beg you not to go, my lady. It is too dangerous. My husband is staying at the Bull tonight, with others of your faithful followers who could not bear to be parted from you. Let me bear a message to him, pray do not go yourself.'

'I must go in person. This is not something that can be written down and given to another person to carry.' Elizabeth turned to me sharply, ignoring Blanche's little whimper of despair. 'Meg, you will accompany me to the village. We will take the back way, it will be safer. But if the guards see me in this cloak, with any luck they will believe I am Joan. You must tell them she is visiting her sick mother in the village, and that she is too upset to speak.'

I nodded.

'Sir, you must follow without being seen until we have left the palace grounds,' Elizabeth instructed Alejandro. 'I will be one hour at the Bull in a private room, and afterwards will return here. I trust we shall not be discovered on the way. But if we are, you may be required to use your sword in my defence.'

Alejandro said nothing, his face sombre, but he rested his hand lightly on the hilt of his sword.

I spoke up at last. 'Where is the guard on your door?'

Elizabeth hesitated. 'Blanche offered him a hot posset to keep out the chill. As soon as he had finished drinking it, he had a sudden urge to . . . to visit the privy. The poor man may be gone for quite a while.'

This confession broke the tense atmosphere. Blanche giggled into her handkerchief. Even Alejandro smiled, then went to the door and opened it a crack, his eyes alert for danger.

'Shall we go?'

The Bull Inn was livelier than I had seen it before. The arrival of chilly autumn weather must have drawn men from the village to the inn's roaring fires and cosy backrooms, to the blood-heating tang of its ales. As we approached quietly by a side alley, the battered front door was yanked open, throwing a stream of smoky light across the road. Two large, burly men spilled out of the inn, cursing each other for fools, their mangy dogs underfoot, barking and snarling as their owners argued.

Over their heads, the sign of the Bull swung in a sharp breeze, creaking.

I shivered, and saw Alejandro's eyes on me. My chin rose another inch and I looked away, trying to appear unconcerned.

Yes, I was afraid of being captured along with the disgraced princess. The memory of Marcus Dent's interrogation still prickled under my skin, the knowledge of how close I had come to death.

But I would not admit that to him.

Cautiously, we moved out of the shadows at a signal from Alejandro, who had rejoined us after we had successfully forded the stream without being seen. It would have aroused too much suspicion for us to be seen leaving the grounds with the young Spaniard. But if we had been stopped and questioned alone, no one would have questioned our story: two girls hurrying to the bedside of a sick relative.

Alejandro led us to a side door and guarded it while we hurried through, both of us hooded and cloaked, only a few strands of Elizabeth's reddish-gold hair peeping out to suggest her true identity.

He went through into the noisy taproom to speak to the harassed landlord, and returned a few moments later with a stinking tallow candle, gesturing us towards the unlit stairs.

'The first room on the left upstairs,' was all Alejandro said, but I caught a flicker of disapproval in his eyes.

I turned to the stairs, but there was a man descending, swaying slightly as he came. I glanced up and froze in shock at the sight of that familiar face.

My father!

My first impulse was to throw my arms about him, for I had not seen my father since he had taken me to Woodstock that spring to serve the princess. But then I remembered our secret mission, and the disguised princess at my side. I could not endanger Elizabeth's life by announcing myself to my father, knowing our meeting might be observed by her enemies.

My heart beating hard, I drew back hurriedly into the shadows and threw my hood further forward to hide my face. Elizabeth too shrank back, burying her face in my shoulder.

When he had gone into the taproom, I straightened again and saw Alejandro's questioning gaze on my face.

'That was my father,' I breathed. 'Do you think he recognized me?'

Alejandro shook his head. 'He was drunk.' He touched my arm, frowning. 'Let us hurry though, in case he comes back.'

Upstairs, there was a strong smell of urine, and behind

that, the sweeter smell of something rotting. Elizabeth grimaced and cupped a hand over her nose and mouth. I too held my breath, feeling sick, and trying not to fret that my father was in the Bull Inn tonight. He had not recognized either of us, and he did not know Alejandro, so there could be no harm done. Yet I could not remember ever seeing my father drunk before. It left me uneasy, wondering if there was something wrong at home.

Alejandro knocked at the door. It was opened by a man in his late twenties.

Even in the dim flickering of the candle, I could see that this man was quite beautiful, with flowing hair past his shoulders and intelligent, light-coloured eyes. He looked other-worldly, yet wore a neat white ruff and dark, floor-length robes like a religious cleric.

'Your Highness,' the man said at once, turning his eyes to Elizabeth. He dropped to one knee before her.

'For God's sake, get up quickly, before someone sees,' Elizabeth instructed him, and whirled into the candlelit chamber, throwing back her hood.

I followed her in silence, nervous but excited. My gaze moved at once to the broad desk under the window on which were arranged curious instruments of metal and glass, an untidy stack of documents and a small cask of wine with several glasses set out.

'One hour,' she told Alejandro firmly, who had stepped inside after us. 'Hold the door for us, sir.'

Alejandro bowed, withdrew and closed the door behind him. I wondered if he would see my father again, and frowned.

Could there be some other reason why my father had ridden over here tonight, other than to drink in company? I knew he liked to visit the Bull sometimes, and often did so when my brother was at home to accompany him, for it was widely acknowledged to be one of the best inns for miles around. Yet it seemed the height of bad luck that we should have met him on the way up here. Of all the nights to have chosen . . .

Then I forgot my father's presence as the man turned to me, his long-fingered hand taking mine and opening my palm to examine it.

'But who is this?' he murmured, staring into my eyes as he stroked my skin, tracing the lines on my palm, back and forth. I felt mesmerized, a cold chill running down my spine. 'There is power here. Fear too, but power.'

'She is no one. A country witch, that is all,' Elizabeth said impatiently, and did not meet my surprised glance.

Why did she not want this man to know the extent of my powers? Though perhaps Elizabeth really did see me as a simple country witch, nothing more. That idea rattled me, but I said nothing.

'Pardon, Your Highness,' he said, 'but will you introduce us?'

Elizabeth was clearly annoyed by his insistence. Yet she obeyed nonetheless. Again, I was surprised. I sensed that she was a little afraid of this man.

'This is Meg Lytton, a maid of mine whose mother served at court when I was young.' She hesitated. 'Meg, this gentleman is Master John Dee, a great astrologer.'

'Oh, not great yet,' Master Dee said lightly, but he was smiling. I stared at him, for even I had heard of the famous astrologer John Dee. His fingers were still stroking my upturned palm, my hand held captive in his. 'Meg Lytton, you say? Hmm, this one would make an excellent subject for my studies. Tell me, child, have you ever conjured the spirits of the dead and spoken with them?'

'Sir . . . ?' I stammered.

'Leave the girl alone,' Elizabeth commanded him coldly, and he dropped my hand with obvious reluctance. 'We do not have much time, Dee, so let us get to the matter in hand. In your note, you indicated that you had cast my sister's horoscope, and had many secret and terrible things to tell me.'

'Indeed.' The astrologer nodded. His eyes narrowed to bright slits. 'Your sister the Queen has not been as generous as I had hoped. I fear she listens to her priests too much, who find my work challenging. And so I have come to you with my findings instead.'

'You need money?' Elizabeth asked astutely.

'To expand my library,' he agreed smoothly. 'And for my travels abroad. The most important books are rarely to be found in England, alas. But such endeavours cost me dear, and my family's coffers are nearly empty.'

Elizabeth raised her eyebrows. 'I am a prisoner of my sister here, Master Dee. I have no money to help you build up your library.'

'Indeed, my lady. But you may not always be a prisoner. Nor poor.'

Elizabeth's eyes widened at the astrologer's bold assertions. Yet still she hesitated, a habitual caution in her face. 'You have proof of this?'

'Astrology is a slippery art,' he admitted, and smiled at us wanly. 'The charts are not always easy to decipher. But follow me, my lady, and I shall be glad to show you what I have discovered.'

John Dee went to the desk and unrolled a sheet of parchment covered in dense marks and symbols. A quartered square had been drawn across it in a spidery hand. Carefully, with great delicacy, the astrologer placed paperweights at its four corners to prevent the parchment from curling up, and set out two chairs beside the table.

He held his hand out to Elizabeth in courteous invitation. 'Shall we sit, my lady?'

The two sat together at the desk, heads bent over the parchment, and I stood awkwardly behind the princess, unsure of my place in this secret meeting. Was I here as chaperone to the princess or as apprentice to the astrologer? A little of both, perhaps.

Over the princess's shoulder, I examined the diagram spread out on the desk. So this was a horoscope. My heart leaped with excitement, for I had never seen one before. I had told Elizabeth I knew how to read the future from the movements of the stars, but my knowledge was scanty and only extended to what my aunt had told me of the night sky. These tiny markings and endless rows of mathematical calculations meant little to me. It was a skill of which I had no understanding.

Quietly, John Dee began to describe what he had seen in Mary's horoscope, pointing to each crowded sector of the square as he spoke.

I listened with fascination to the ancient names of the planets and their rulers, where they stood in Exaltation or were at their Fall. I quickly grasped Dee's explanations, and felt almost disappointed when he drew his comments to an end. I knew there was much to learn about this ancient art. Yet I dared not ask any questions, for I had seen Dee's gaze rise to my face several times as he spoke and feared drawing any further attention to myself.

'So you see,' he concluded, 'this chart for the Queen's wedding contradicts itself. It tells me your sister is to have a child, who would be heir to the throne of England, and yet that child's fate is crossed by these malevolent stars. I cannot be sure if that means an early death for the babe, or whether the birth itself will be hard and the child ultimately healthy. In which case, of course, you would lose your claim to the throne.'

Elizabeth stared down at the horoscope for a long while, her face very pale. 'No, Master Dee,' she said in the end, and shook her head vehemently. 'I feel it deep down here,' she whispered, laying a hand on her belly, 'in my gut. I shall be Queen of England one day.'

John Dee sighed but did not contradict the princess. Instead, his gaze moved curiously to my face. 'What say you, Mistress Goldenlocks?' he asked me. 'Where does your skill lie? Can you read this horoscope?'

'No, sir.'

I shook my head but already I was looking at the chart again, trying to decipher its strange symbols.

'Here,' John Dee murmured, standing so I could take his seat. 'Sit at the table, girl. Take a closer look at the chart and tell me what you see. What draws your eye?'

I sat down at his urging and looked at the chart. Slowly, I traced a finger across the figures. To the right of the lower quadrant, I paused on an odd symbol. 'What is this, sir?'

'The planet Saturn.'

'And these?' I ran my finger halfway up the chart and paused on two other symbols which had been drawn very close together, almost on top of each other. There was a key to the side of the chart, but it was all in Latin, and I did not feel confident enough to tease out the crabbed black lettering.

'That is Jupiter conjunct the Moon,' he told me.

My fingers began to tingle and I felt a sudden headache nagging behind my temples. 'And are they not clashing? Saturn, I mean, with these other two?'

John Dee smiled. 'You are right, Meg Lytton. They are ninety degrees apart, and form a square to each other.'

'A square?' Elizabeth sounded impatient. 'Don't speak in riddles, Master Dee. Tell me plain what this means.'

'Saturn is ninety degrees from Jupiter, which on this chart conjoins the Moon,' John Dee explained, showing her the symbols on the chart. 'Jupiter paired with the Moon suggests a child, for the Moon is the planet of motherhood and Jupiter the planet of fertility and increase. As I told you, this pairing led me to believe that your sister must be with child. But with the maleficent Saturn forming a square to their conjunction, I cannot be sure of that child's fate.'

Elizabeth's eyes flashed. 'Sir, is my sister to have a child or not?'

'If she is,' John Dee said hesitantly, staring at the chart, 'the child may be stillborn. Or else the Queen herself may die during the birth.'

The princess stared at John Dee, her mouth slightly open, clearly taken aback by such a shocking suggestion. I suspected we were all thinking the same thing – that if the Queen were to die in childbirth, there would be no one to stand between Elizabeth and the throne.

She shuddered, then glanced at me as though for confirmation of what the astrologer had said.

'What do you say, Meg?'

I laid my palm flat on the horoscope with its spidery symbols and numbers. It seemed to throb and pulse under my fingers as though alive. I closed my eyes and let my mind wander through what I had seen: the planets calling to each other across the chart, the tiny rows of numbers and Latin names, John Dee's delicate handwriting.

I gasped as the answer burned itself into my brain, too incredible to speak aloud.

'Well?' Elizabeth prompted me impatiently.

'The Queen will not die. The Queen is not even with child,' I whispered, barely able to believe my own words.

'But all the rumours at court—' John Dee began.

'It is a false pregnancy,' I hissed, cutting off his voice. 'Yes, the Queen will begin to bloat. Her monthly courses will stop and her breasts will swell. Then her doctors will tell the world Queen Mary is to be a mother and all the church bells will ring in celebration. But there is nothing in her womb, and there will be no birth when the time comes for her lying-in.'

Elizabeth's hand gripped my shoulder painfully. 'You are sure?'

John Dee shook his head, staring at me. 'There is no way for her to be sure. Not from this chart alone.'

'Let the girl speak for herself.'

Shakily, I lifted my hand from the horoscope and the room seemed suddenly darker. The candles flickered in the draught, casting long thin-fingered shadows across the chart.

My hand had stopped tingling. The power was gone. Yet Elizabeth was still waiting for my reply.

I hesitated, frowning at the incomprehensible tangle of symbols, no longer certain what I had seen. Yes, the future of England had revealed itself to me in a sudden dazzling flash of insight. But now the vision had faded, I was left blinded and unsure of myself, unwilling to pretend a knowledge I did not possess.

'I . . . I am not sure,' I admitted, avoiding John Dee's sharp gaze. 'Master Dee is right. He is more skilled in these matters, perhaps we should listen to him. I am sorry, my lady.'

Elizabeth made an angry noise under her breath, then snapped her fingers at me to rise. 'Come, we must get back to the lodge before I am missed. This meeting has been a waste of my time.' She looked coldly at the astrologer. 'I shall not require your services again, Master Dee. You might as well return to London. I only pray the Queen does not learn that you have visited me.'

'She will not even suspect, my lady. The stars are most propitious tonight for matters of great secrecy.'

John Dee bowed very low, and opened the door for the princess to leave. As I trailed out in her wake, his gaze did not leave my face. The great court astrologer ought to have been annoyed by my interference in his fortune-telling, yet he seemed more fascinated than angry.

'Another time,' Dee murmured, and I suspected he was addressing me, not the Lady Elizabeth.

TEN

A New Year Kiss

I was dreaming.

I knew that in my heart. Yet somehow the dream felt so real, I was still afraid. I could not quite shake off the illusion that the astrologer John Dee was in the room, that he was standing at the foot of my bed, watching me through the darkness.

Tell me, child, have you ever conjured the spirits of the dead and spoken with them?

I wanted to cry out 'No!' but my face had been stopped. With sand, or perhaps earth.

That was it: I was lying deep in a pit under the earth, my arms folded across my chest, a thin, coarse shroud barely covering my white body. I had been buried alive and John Dee was standing above me, staring down at my freshly dug, unmarked grave.

My hands scrabbled desperately at the soft, crumbling darkness around me. But it was no use. Dirt covered my face with its black whispering death. It choked my eyes, my ears, my mouth. I had not been buried alive. Dee had killed me, had come in the night and strangled me, and now he was trying to conjure my spirit, to speak with me and learn the secrets of the other world that lay beyond the gates of life.

A hand was shaking my shoulder. Dee had brought a spade. He had dug down to my poor strangled body and was attempting to resurrect me.

'Meg!' he was saying insistently. 'Meg!'

My eyes flew open.

It was daylight and I was lying on my back, tangled up in my bedclothes, one arm flung out of the narrow cot as though reaching for something. I must have been lying on it, for as I moved, my whole arm tingled with pins and needles.

'Ouch!' I sat up, rubbing my numb arm as it came painfully back to life.

Blanche straightened above me with a sigh, shaking her head. 'Time to get up, slack-a-bed. It's Christmas Eve, and there's much to be done.'

I stared at her stupidly. How had I overslept?

Blanche watched me struggle out of the tangled covers and begin hunting for my white cap. She shook her head, a tight little smile on her lips, clearly enjoying this heaven-sent opportunity to reprimand me for laziness.

'You've missed Mass,' she pointed out. 'Our mistress has been up this past hour, and done her prayers. Though I can tell you, having to pray for the Queen and her unborn child stuck in both our throats today. By next Christmas that babe will be the new heir to the throne, and my dear mistress will be all but forgotten at court.'

The Queen's pregnancy seemed to be all we ever talked about these days. I licked my fingers and tried to straighten my wayward hair. 'I do not believe there will be a babe. The Queen is too old to bear a child.'

'Well, we shall see what we shall see,' Blanche muttered dismissively. 'Now hurry. Just comb your hair, put on your oldest gown and come down to the kitchen. There's a goose to be plucked, and dried herbs for the sauces to be cut and prepared. You cannot expect young Joan to help the cook on her own.'

When she had gone, I wearily splashed my face from the bowl, then dampened my unruly hair and combed it into some kind of submission.

Why had I dreamed of John Dee again?

For months now, ever since meeting him that night at the Bull Inn, the young astrologer had been creeping into my dreams. Sometimes I dreamed of conjuring the dead with him by the light of a single, tall candle. Other times the crabbed black symbols of his star charts would float weirdly before my eyes as I drifted into sleep.

There is power here. Fear too, but power.

I was afraid of Dee, certainly. But not of the knowledge he possessed of astrology and the secret world beyond death. Of such hidden things I would be willing to learn more, if the opportunity was ever granted me. I still did not know how I had been able to read the meanings in the Queen's horoscope, but if no baby came of this pregnancy, I would know for sure then that my power was true.

Alejandro knew of my yearning to learn more about astrology and he clearly disapproved of it. I had caught anger in his face that night at the Bull Inn, and a strong dislike for what we were doing there.

But Alejandro was a creature of the midday sun, of broad Spanish plains under the scorching heat of summer. He was a follower of the sword of Christ, the lightbearer. Such a man would have no time for the secrets of the night, for astrology and witchcraft and the spirits of the dead, or my childish nightmares of being buried alive.

I ran down to the kitchen. The oven was already smoking strongly, the rushes on the floor filthy with a good week's grease and spilled food. Everywhere was a stench of burned oil and herbs, and all the doors and windows were standing open in the chill wintry air. Joan did not look up as I entered; she was hard at work scrubbing the burners clean. Besides, the simple-minded girl had barely a word to say to me these days, still suspicious of my witchery.

The cook was not much friendlier. With just a few terse words, he laid a limp, heavy goose across my arms and told me to pluck it.

I took it outside, sitting on a three-legged stool in the feeble winter sunshine, and wedged the dead bird between my skirted thighs, a bowl on the floor beside me to receive its feathers. One dull eye stared up at me accusingly as I dragged on its glossy white feathers, their quills fixed so firmly in the pale, pimpled skin beneath that my fingers were soon sore and aching.

'Good morning.'

I shivered and glanced up as a shadow fell across me. It was Alejandro, still in his robes from this morning's Mass, his silver cross hanging about his neck.

He looked down quizzically at the dead goose between my thighs. 'Is this what you missed Mass for?'

'I overslept,' I told him, and threw another fistful of sharp-tipped white feathers into the bowl, not bothering to look up at him again.

Let him think me rude, I told myself crossly. I knew Alejandro disapproved of my magick, and it irked me. I was also aware of a secret frustration eating away at me, for we had spent many hours together without Alejandro ever once declaring his interest in me. Yet I knew he felt something, that there was an intimacy of a kind between us. Part of me almost hated the young Spaniard for his iron self-control, yet part of me wanted to discover what it would feel like to have him lose that control and kiss me. Not that Alejandro de Castillo would ever dare to kiss a girl, whatever provocation was offered. No, he was too fixed on becoming a priest and dedicating himself to the Catholic Church.

'This goose is for our Christmas dinner. Forgive me for not stopping to speak, but it will not pluck itself.'

He stood a while, watching me without comment. 'Are you not cold?' he asked eventually.

'A little,' I admitted. 'But this must be done outdoors. Besides, I would be warmer if you did not stand in the way of the sun.'

'I beg your pardon,' Alejandro muttered, and shifted at once, so that I was once more sitting in sunshine.

I gave him no thanks for it, but tore savagely at the shining goose feathers. For some reason, his politeness annoyed me more than any show of open dislike would have done. Why did he not go away? Why must he stand and watch me like this? Could he not see how his presence disturbed me?

'Doesn't Father Vasco need your assistance?'

His brows rose, though he answered levelly enough, 'My master is unwell again. He retired to his room straight after Mass and is sleeping now. This chill weather affects him badly.'

'My grandfather was the same at his age. You should ask Blanche to make up a hot posset for him.'

To my surprise, Alejandro laughed at that. I looked up and saw an oddly cynical gleam in his eyes, a smile curving his lips.

'What, after the last hot posset prepared by the skilled hand of Mistress Parry? That unfortunate man was sick for days.'

Reluctantly I laughed too, recalling how Blanche had managed to remove the guard from Elizabeth's door by drugging him.

'I'd forgotten about that. Well, I am sure it would not have the same effect.'

'Let's hope not.' Alejandro smiled, but it was a tense smile, not quite reaching his eyes. I noticed that he no longer seemed comfortable in my presence, that the tentative friendship between us over the summer had faded with the heat. 'Thank you for the suggestion. I will ask Mistress Parry this afternoon, before my master has to rise for evening prayer.'

'Will he join us for dinner afterwards? We eat late on Christmas Eve, but we should have games as well as goose to take us up to Mass at midnight.'

He frowned. 'Games?'

'I suppose it may be hard to celebrate Christmas here, with Elizabeth being a prisoner and in disgrace,' I murmured, and glanced cautiously over my shoulder. But the cook and Joan were too busy at their work to overhear us, and the windows above us seemed to be closed. 'At Lytton Park, where I used to live with my father, we would gather after dinner to sing Yuletide carols, then play some games. Sometimes we would exchange a few gifts at New Year too. It is an old English custom.'

'I have no gifts to give.'

I laughed at his concerned expression. 'Well, you have your lips. You could sing a Spanish song for us on New Year's Day. You must know a song or two.' I paused, left suddenly breathless by my own bravado. 'Or you could give a kiss.'

His eyes darkened at that, his voice deep and very Spanish. 'A kiss?'

Was that reproof I heard in his tone? For a moment there, I had forgotten that Alejandro de Castillo was only one step away from being a Catholic priest. I looked up at him and could almost smell his disapproval, taste it in my mouth like ashes. No doubt such playfulness as games and an exchange of kisses, even at Yuletide or the New Year, would be looked on as the work of the Devil.

My temper flared. 'Yes,' I continued, half angrily, my fingers buried deep in the soft feathery down of the goose's chest. 'The exchange of a kiss is traditional.'

I did not know why I was so angry. Or perhaps I did know but did not wish to admit it, even to myself.

Then I saw Alejandro draw back from me, and realized it was not disapproval I had seen in his face, but fear. Fear and caution, strong as my own. And beyond them, desire.

It was like that moment when the circle is cast, the four directions are called, and you feel the spirits rush in on you as sharp air through a winter's doorway.

Alejandro wanted me. Just as I wanted him. And there was nothing either of us could do about it.

I could not speak, and was grateful when Alejandro bent to move the plucking bowl a little closer to my stool, breaking the spell between us. As he straightened, I saw heat running under the olive skin, an odd haunted look to his eyes. His hand came up to steady the swaying cross about his neck, and lingered there a moment, as though seeking comfort from the silver.

'I should go and—'

He did not finish his sentence, but gave a curt bow and trod swiftly back inside the house.

I sat a while in silence after he had gone, my hands stilled on the shining white feathers. Then I began to pluck them again, humming over the limp body of the goose as though it was a silver gown I was sewing.

That night, after we had stuffed ourselves silly with goose in a piquant sauce, and pigs' trotters roasted with the last of the autumn's sweet, wrinkling apples, and our rough cook's brave attempt at a courtly delicacy – a syllabub – we played traditional Yuletide games such as Blind Man's Buff and Hunt the Thimble. For a while, breathless and giggling as we played our Christmas games, we could almost forget that Elizabeth was a prisoner under the constant threat of execution for treason. But every now and then she would stop by the window, staring longingly out at the darkness, and I would realize that Elizabeth must have spent some very different Christmases when her young brother Edward was King, showered with costly gifts and treated like a princess in the great courtly palaces of London. Cooped up here in the grim dampness of Woodstock's ruins, she herself could never forget the injustice and tedium of her imprisonment, not even for a moment.

Father Vasco came to pay his respects to the princess after dinner but was quickly fatigued by our noisy antics, seeming to disapprove of people enjoying themselves on a holy festival. The old priest excused himself soon after the midnight Mass, and was helped to bed by Alejandro.

We celebrated the coming of the New Year in traditional English style too. The weather had turned bitter by the last few days of December, with a thin scattering of snow on the ground, so we huddled together by the fireside in the narrow smoky room overlooking the park and took turns to exchange gifts. Elizabeth gave me one of her oldest gowns, with only a plain silk edging on the sleeves, for I was not noble and by law could not wear too much by way of finery. In return, I gave her a handkerchief which I had embroidered with her initials entwined with a spray of her favourite flowers, the white eglantine. To my surprise, the princess seemed delighted with this and took it at once to show Blanche Parry, whose gift from Elizabeth had been a leather-bound book of psalms.

I had also made a small gift for Alejandro, a neatly stitched purse for his coins. This I gave to him unspeaking, a little embarrassed, remembering our conversation outside the kitchen on Christmas Eve.

'Happy New Year,' he whispered, and leaned across to kiss me. 'Here is my gift to you.'

I think he had truly meant to kiss me on the cheek, in a brotherly Christian way. But I shifted at the last moment, startled and surprised that he had taken me at my word, and his kiss landed on my lips. That fleeting contact burned with a sudden ferocious heat that made me lose my head for a moment.

I gasped, as did he, both of us springing back from each other with hot faces.

Alejandro muttered something in Spanish, then seemed to groan. 'I'm sorry. I didn't mean . . .'

One of the window catches was broken and a chill air blew in constantly from the river below, barely warmed by the heat of the roaring log fire. I hurried to the window and pretended to fiddle with the broken catch, though in truth I was letting the night air cool my cheeks.

If we had been alone . . .

But we were not alone, and already the Lady Elizabeth was staring across at us through the firelight, surprised, and Blanche was reading one of the psalms aloud to herself in a low-pitched voice, unaware of any atmosphere in the small room.

We celebrated a quiet midnight Mass for the New Year with the princess, Blanche Parry, and even Sir Henry, who had risen specially from his bed to share the body and blood of Christ with us. Father Vasco's authoritative voice echoed about the chapel as he intoned the Latin prayers, his young assistant following behind with the wine chalice. This time I did not catch Alejandro's eye, but bent my head in prayer after receiving the Host.

After Mass, I made my way to my chamber, which I now shared again with Joan. The dark-haired kitchen maid was already asleep and snoring as I pulled the covers over my chin and tried not to think of Alejandro.

It had been an amusing game at first, the young witch teasing the would-be Catholic priest with mysterious smiles and stares. But now the game had grown serious and tasted of danger. I had too many secrets to hide and I could not rely on the young Spaniard to keep them all for me. There was risk all around us at Woodstock. The closer the sharp-eyed Alejandro came to me, the nearer I moved to the hangman.

Early one morning, three days after New Year, my father came unexpectedly to Woodstock Lodge. My aunt had fallen seriously ill over the holy season and my father begged Elizabeth to spare me to nurse her back to health.

Elizabeth was annoyed to lose me, as I had become a help about the house as well as in her chamber. But she could see the fear in my face, and relented at last, giving me her blessing to return to Lytton Park.

'Come back to us as soon as you are able,' she insisted, and told me to take food and drink for the journey, for she knew I had not yet breakfasted.

Alejandro met me in the shadowy hallway and frowned down at the bag I was carrying, hurriedly packed with all my belongings.

'How long will you be gone?' he demanded.

'My aunt is unwell,' I explained tensely, not looking at him. 'Please let me pass. I shall not return until she is better.'

Alejandro had thrown out an arm as though to bar my way. His voice seemed to deepen, echoing in the hallway. 'Meg.'

I raised my eyes to his, then. 'Yes?'

'I . . .' He stared at me for a moment, his gaze very dark. 'You cannot go. The Lady Elizabeth needs you here.'

'Her ladyship has given me consent to go.' Stubbornly, I looked past Alejandro to my father, who was waiting in the narrow doorway to the lodge. My stomach hurt. I felt sick with fear that my aunt would die and leave me alone in this world. But I would show him none of that. 'Please, I have to leave. My father is waiting for me.'

Reluctantly, Alejandro stood aside and I moved past him through the shadows.

'I shall pray for your aunt,' Alejandro said softly. 'As I shall pray for you too, Meg.'

I clutched my ramshackle bag to my chest, its handles cracked and broken, and tried not to cry. I felt his gaze on my back like a brand, and knew Alejandro must be examining my father too. But he said nothing and did not follow us out to say farewell.

I should have been ecstatic. I was being released from my long servitude at Woodstock; I was going home to see my beloved aunt and nurse her back to health. Instead, it felt as though my heart were breaking.

As I shall pray for you too.

I turned my face to the darkening skies as the cart lurched forward over the snowy ground. There had been no answer to that.

ELEVEN

Flesh and Blood

I found my aunt more seriously ill than I had imagined, and gave up all hope of returning to Woodstock before the spring. I immediately set about gathering the wild plants I would need to restore her to health, and preparing the solution according to her own spell books. With the ground still icy in places, I was not able to gather all the plants on the list, but found some dried amongst her stores, and substituted others with those that grew abundantly in the winter months. Soon Aunt Jane was able to sit up and sip the bitter-tasting draught from a bowl. But she did not recover her full strength, nor did I think she ever would. There was a sickness at work in her body that no potion could cure, however skilfully mixed, and we both knew it.

In February, she began to speak again, and I told her in whispered snatches of how I had been discovered by Joan, casting the circle, and how Marcus Dent had come to interrogate me at Woodstock Lodge.

She seemed frightened by this news of Marcus Dent's continuing obsession with me, yet her blue eyes sparked with some of their old power in her ravaged face, and she managed a fierce smile occasionally.

I did not wish to believe there was nothing I could do to

cure her wasting sickness, even with the evidence in front of my eyes. My aunt had become horribly thin since the last time we had met. Her ribs poked through skin as fragile as paper, a delicate blue tracery of veins spread across her throat and arms, and her persistent cough grew harsher and more ragged each day.

One afternoon, while my aunt was sleeping, I cast a circle about her bed, lit the four sacred candles and softly began a Latin incantation against sickness which she had taught me the year before.

'Meg, stop.'

I faltered in my spell, looking up to see that her eyes had opened and she was watching me across the candle flame.

'Hush,' I told her. 'Go back to sleep and let me finish. You know this spell will counteract your ills.'

Aunt Jane shook her head. 'It is no use, Meg.' She smiled weakly. 'Did I teach you nothing? You can mend the sick if your power is strong, but you cannot work magick against the deepest law of nature, which is death. To attempt such a spell would mean the destruction of your own soul, for nature would take your life in place of mine. It is the law of our kind, and we break it at our peril. There must be balance in all things.'

'No, I can do this. Listen—'

'I am dying, child. It is my time. Snuff out the candles and I will tell you something important.'

I did not want to believe her. But I could not continue the spell in the face of her refusal, so I did what she had asked me, blowing out the candles and reluctantly lifting the magick circle I had cast about us.

'Good,' she breathed. 'Now, is there anyone outside the door? Go and look.'

I peered out into the hallway. The upstairs rooms were quiet, the stairs deserted. My father had ridden to the village that morning to speak to the priest there, and I guessed that the servants would be about their duties downstairs.

'No, we are alone.'

'Then let us not waste any more time. I may not have many days left on this earth. There is a false bottom in the chest at the foot of the bed. Under it, I have hidden some of my old spell books and papers, and a few small instruments of the craft. They will tempt you, but you must not try to keep them safe, for they will bring nothing but death in these dangerous times.' She took a shuddering breath. 'Swear to me that you will burn them when I die, so they cannot lead you to the gallows.'

'You are not going to die,' I insisted.

'Promise! You must promise me this!'

My aunt's face was so wild, I was almost frightened. I clasped her hand and nodded to calm her. 'Hush, Aunt Jane. You will make yourself sick. I promise that I will burn them.'

Aunt Jane lapsed into a terrible coughing fit. When it was

over, she gestured weakly to the healing draught I had wished her to take. 'Give me a good spoonful of that brew, Meg. And mix it with honey, to take away the bitterness.'

My hand shook as I measured out the strong-smelling draught and mixed it with honey.

'Now,' my aunt said afterwards, licking the sweetness from her dry lips, 'you know what to do when I am gone, and I can die content.'

'No!' I exclaimed in horror, and cast about for some reason that might persuade her to fight this wasting sickness. 'You cannot die, Aunt Jane. Who will teach me the craft if you are not here?'

Aunt Jane smiled, and fell back against her pillows. 'I have already taught you everything a young witch should know, Meg. The rest you must teach yourself.'

Near the end of February, my brother and cousin returned from the Low Countries, where they had been studying together – or so they told my father, glancing hard at me as though daring me to contradict their story. I had no interest in betraying them as rebels against the Catholic regime, so said nothing. But I was worried to see them back in England again, for I knew they would soon attempt to draw me into their scheming.

Sure enough, they had not been back at home three days before I caught Malcolm in my room, searching through my possessions.

'What do you think you're doing?' I demanded, and my cousin had the grace to look sheepish. 'Please leave my room before I call my father.'

'I'm going,' he muttered, but suddenly caught at my arm as he passed and swung me to face him. 'Tell me true, and then I'll go – do you have anything here from Elizabeth that we could use to further our cause abroad? Some kind of token, a gift or letter . . . anything with the princess's name or initials on it?'

'Let me go, Malcolm.'

My cousin looked angry and frustrated, but released me nonetheless, perhaps responding to the strength in my voice.

'You do not understand, Meg. These men will not move against Mary without some reassurance of Elizabeth's support. And they get more restless the longer we delay. We have heard such terrible things about Elizabeth in the Low Countries. That she has abandoned her father's beliefs, that she feeds priests like friends at her own table, and hears Mass three times a day. That she is as devout a Catholic as her sister and will burn every one of us who does not turn to Rome when she comes to the throne.' He stared at me. 'You have lived with the princess most of the past year. Are these stories true?'

'The Lady Elizabeth is no fool,' I told him coldly. 'She has no wish to burn as a heretic. She kneels and takes Mass, and yes, she keeps the priests Queen Mary sent to watch her. But she is no more a Catholic than you are.'

Malcolm nodded slowly, as though the truth of this had penetrated his barriers of distrust and hatred. 'So the stories are false. I am glad of it. It helps to know that we can still count on Elizabeth to rid our country of Catholics if this Papist Queen and her husband are removed from the throne.'

'I did not say that.' I opened the door wide in a silent invitation for him to leave my room. 'Now I have answered your questions, Malcolm, so please go. There are no tokens or letters here that you can use to gain support in the Low Countries, and nothing more that we can say to each other.'

My cousin turned to go, yet hung back in the doorway, looking hard at me. 'Those priests at Woodstock . . . I saw you with one of them in the summer.'

I stared at him, my breathing suddenly constricted as I remembered seeing his face amongst the leaves. I wondered again what game he was playing. 'I know, I saw you watching us down by the river. What were you doing there? Spying on me? Or on Elizabeth? Is there no end to your plotting and intriguing, Malcolm? Did you see whatever you went there to see?'

'I saw you and that young Catholic priest kissing,' he said, on a note of accusation.

'Kissing?' My face was scarlet now. I found myself stuttering, falling over the words, barely able to speak coherently. 'You saw me . . . *kissing* . . . Alejandro? No, no, a thousand times no!'

'That's what it looked like to me.'

'Then you must be blind. *Alejandro?* No, I would never kiss . . . I would rather . . . Anyway, he's not even a priest yet,' I spluttered, giving up on the whole ludicrous discussion. I slammed the door shut in my cousin's astonished face. 'He's still in training.'

Marcus Dent came to our house one afternoon the following week. I hung over the stairs and watched my father welcome him into his study, then the door closed and I could not hear their conversation.

I was surprised to see Marcus at Lytton Park. Surely the witchfinder could not still wish to marry me? My father had asked about my time at Woodstock when I arrived home, but had not mentioned Joan's accusation of witchcraft, so I assumed that Marcus Dent had not yet informed him. No doubt Marcus would be telling him now, and relishing every unpleasant detail.

I sat upstairs with my aunt, who was sleeping. Her colour was a little better than it had been. But all the time I was waiting for the summons which I knew must come.

It was nearly two hours before I heard a servant come up the stairs and scratch at my aunt's door. I opened it and knew instantly from the woman's nervous face that Marcus Dent had asked for me.

'Your father wants to see you in his study,' she told me with a quick curtsey, then went in to sit with my aunt in my absence. I did not like Aunt Jane to be left alone for any length of time, her strength having so nearly left her.

In my father's study, I found Marcus Dent standing at the hearth, his arm laid along the mantel, one boot outstretched to the heat. It was a damp and chilly day in early March, and the logs had been piled high for my father's guest; they must have been fresh-cut in his honour too, for they were spitting and smoking busily, the room a little foggy.

Marcus turned as I came in, and took a full moment to look me up and down before bowing, his narrowed blue eyes a little sharper than I remembered.

'Meg,' he said as I curtseyed in return, using my name with easy familiarity. 'Living with royalty must suit you. You seemed but a girl when I saw you at Woodstock. You have grown into a fine young woman.' He hesitated when I did not reply. 'Do you not recall our last meeting there? Some foolish girl had accused you of . . .' His brittle smile grew even colder. 'Ah, but I see from your face that you remember the occasion perfectly. I shall say nothing further to upset you. How are you, Meg?'

'I am well, sir, I thank you.'

'That is good to hear. But I believe your father wishes us to speak alone for a moment.'

I looked at my father, who coughed and left the room without a word. I stared after him in disbelief. What had

Marcus said to make my father leave me alone with this unpleasant man? I remembered our conversation at Woodstock and grew horribly uneasy. Had Marcus threatened to expose me as a witch if my father did not press me to marry him?

Once we were alone together, Marcus came towards me and put a finger under my chin, lifting my face towards his. He had never done such a thing before, so openly and deliberately touching me, and suddenly I was afraid. My first instinct was to call out for my father, though I knew it must be useless to do so. He would never have left us alone together if he had felt there was any choice in the matter.

The struggle must have shown in my face, for Marcus laughed, rather brutally, and shook his head. 'No, you are right not to call for your father. Even if he came, he would do nothing. You are on your own in this, my dear. On your own . . . with me.'

Marcus bent and kissed me firmly on the lips, holding me by the shoulders so that I could not escape without losing my dignity by fighting him. It was not an unpleasant sensation, but it left me cold. Marcus's kiss could not touch what I had experienced when Alejandro had merely brushed his lips against mine.

'I still intend to marry you,' Marcus said, and laughed again at my shocked expression. 'Did you ever doubt it? Why, because I stayed away from Woodstock while you were there?' He shook his head. 'Our separation was unimportant.

I knew I would eventually gain your father's blessing of our marriage, so there was no hurry for us to wed. Indeed, it will be useful for my future wife to have experienced some degree of life at a noble level, for I shall take you to court once we are married. But do not worry. I will bring you home once you are safely with child, for my son must be born here in Oxfordshire.'

I opened my mouth to refuse, but could not seem to speak. My lips moved but nothing came out. I had been left speechless, like someone under a spell. Marcus was still smiling as he fetched a chair for me.

'Here,' he murmured, helping me to sit down. 'Sit quiet and breathe slow. I cannot allow my bride-to-be to hurt herself. Your father has agreed that I can fix a date for our wedding. Easter will be an excellent time. Do you not agree?'

Gently, his hand brushed my cheek, and I stared up at him, his words slowly trickling into my head. *Your father has agreed that I can fix a date for our wedding*. I tried to comprehend them but could not. My father could not have made such a deal with Marcus Dent. He knew what kind of man Marcus was, how his previous young wives had suffered and died in childbirth. My father loved me. He would never force me into such a marriage, whatever threats Marcus made against our family. It must be a mistake.

'Marcus, I cannot marry you.'

His fierce slap took me by surprise, knocking me from

the chair. I lay face down on the rushes, holding my burning cheek, barely able to breathe.

Dent kneeled beside me. His voice hardened. 'Don't be stupid, Meg. Your father has given his consent for us to wed next month, and that is an end to the matter. You do not have a choice. You only make a fool of yourself by persisting in denying my suit. And see what else happens when you do that?' He pushed the fallen hair back from my cheek and turned me over onto my back so he could examine me, ignoring my whimper of protest. 'Your beautiful face is bruised and ugly now.' He made a furious sound under his breath. 'That makes me angry, Meg. I want you to look your best for our wedding. But I shall not hesitate to strike you again if you do not agree to be my wife.'

It occurred to me for the first time that Marcus Dent was mad. Either mad or utterly evil.

Gathering all my courage, I managed to shake my head, whispering, 'I shall never be your wife, Marcus.'

His angry blue eyes narrowed on my face. 'Is that so?'

For the first time I felt real fear. Was he about to hit me again as he had promised? Or worse?

I sucked in a breath to call for my father, but Marcus was too quick, grinding his lips against mine before I could make a sound.

I pushed at his shoulders and tried to drag my mouth away from his. But it was no use. He held me still with one hand at my throat, his body pinioning me to the floor. He was far stronger than I had realized, and without my voice I could do nothing to influence him.

'Meg,' he muttered against my mouth.

He yanked at the bodice of my gown, revealing more of my breasts than was respectable. I felt him hesitate there, perhaps seeing the unsightly birthmark on my left breast. Then he groped for my skirts, touching me in a vile way that left me shaking and miserable. That was when I guessed what he intended. I was frozen in shock and horror, lying like a wooden doll beneath him.

My father's wolfhound, which had been dozing by the hearth all this time, leaped up and began to bark hysterically, seeing me with Dent on the floor.

As though he had been waiting in the hall for some signal, the door was flung open and my father came in. He stopped dead at the sight of Dent on top of me.

'Master Dent!' he choked.

Dent rolled away from me, straightened his rumpled coat and got back to his feet. He was breathing hard, his face a dark red.

'This little witch refuses to marry me,' he said violently, as though this was an excuse for what he had done. 'She refuses the protection of my name and wealth. I warned you, Lytton, what would happen if she refused me.'

My father shook his head, and there was open panic in his face. 'No, Dent. For pity's sake, let me speak to her first.'

'It is too late for that.' Marcus Dent left the room, the

wolfhound still barking at his heels. 'Get down!'

I half expected my father to comfort me once my attacker had left, to help me back to my feet and tidy my clothing. But he did neither of those things. Instead, my father stood in the doorway in silence, perhaps still hoping that Marcus Dent would return and claim me as his bride. Then he turned to stare at me, his hands clenched into fists.

'You wretched little fool!' my father managed, his voice strangled. 'You have no idea what you've done. That man could ruin us with his tales of witchcraft.'

I pushed myself to my knees, but could not speak. My throat was still aching from Marcus Dent's vicious grip.

My father called his wolfhound to heel. 'I never thought I would say this of my own flesh and blood, but I hope Dent catches you playing witch next time and you hang for it!'

Then he flung himself out of the house, his parting words burning themselves into my memory like a brand.

TWELVE

Devil Worship

The next morning, we were woken just before dawn by a hammering at the front door of Lytton Park. I ran out of my room, and saw Malcolm and Will, sleepy-eyed and still in their nightgowns, emerging from their own room at the end of the corridor. My father came out looking shocked and haggard. Dragging off his woollen nightcap, he stared down into the shadowy hall, then turned to Will and Malcolm. The three men spoke in urgent whispers at the top of the stairs, as though trying to decide what to do. Then one of the servants stumbled down with a candle to open the door, and was knocked aside by Dent and a mob of angry, torch-carrying men.

'Where is she?' one of the older men demanded hoarsely as they all poured into the hall. 'Where is the witch?'

Ashen-faced, my father hurried downstairs to face the intruders. He stood his ground at the bottom of the stairs, dragging a long black coat about his crumpled night-clothes. 'What are you doing in my home? Who gave you the right to come bursting in here at this hour? Master Dent, I demand an explanation!'

But his exclamations fell thin as the men held their

flickering torches aloft and Dent came forward without answering.

The expression on his lean face was menacing, a thick pikestaff in his hand. His blue gaze glittering with malice, the witchfinder looked first at my brother's dumbfounded expression, then at my cousin. At last he saw me standing behind my father and pointed a long accusing finger in my direction.

'You!'

I felt my knees almost go from under me, remembering how Dent had seized me yesterday and how powerless I had been to stop him. This must be what my father warned me of when he said I had ruined the family. Was Dent's revenge to have me strung up as a witch?

'Speak!' he insisted. 'Where is your aunt?'

This I had not expected. His demand left me speechless and stricken with horror. My aunt? I had thought him here to arrest me as a witch, to have me dragged away for humiliating him.

'Aunt Jane is sick. You cannot believe she is a witch. She has not even left her bed since before Christmas!'

'Since Christmas, you say?' Dent turned to the older man beside him, nodding significantly. 'You see, Lawson? Did I not say she had a hand in your youngest grandchild's drowning, back in December? And now this new tragedy in the village.'

My father was staring. 'What are you talking about? What new tragedy?'

'Little Alice Butterworth died yesterday morning. Not a mark on her when they found her poor little body. No, nor a fever when she was put to bed.' Dent looked up at me, a malicious light in his blue eyes. 'What is that, I ask you, but the work of a witch? A devil-worshipper!'

'Aye,' several of the men agreed, beginning to seethe and mutter amongst themselves. One of them stared so hard at me that I suddenly feared for my own neck too. These men were angry and frightened, and they would take my aunt and hang her from the nearest tree if I could not settle them.

I held out a hand. 'Please, good sirs,' I began, using my strongest voice, 'this is a mistake. My aunt is no witch but a sick woman who has not left her bed nor even looked outside her window for nigh on three months now. I beg of you to leave this house and not come back, for there are no witches here.'

For a moment, there was silence in the hall, broken only by the spitting and guttering of the torches. To my intense relief I knew my power had worked on them. Their madness had been contained and they would now listen to reason again.

Marcus Dent seemed untouched by my voice though. Perhaps he had been waiting for it, expecting it. Whatever the truth, he was able to resist, and that proved my undoing. He breathed deep and shook off my influence like a man shrugging off a heavy coat, then pointed once again up the stairs.

'Friends, do not listen to the Lytton girl!' he called out and turned to gaze steadily at each man in turn. His eyes seemed to burn into their souls. 'This girl is but a child, she says whatever she must to protect her aunt. Jane Canley is a witch who has murdered these poor babes for her master the Devil's delight, and she shall hang for her crimes in the sight of God.' His voice strengthened, just as mine had done before, as though seeking to influence the crowd. 'Now, let us fetch this filthy witch down and take her back with us to face her trial. Who's with me?'

The rabble of men, encouraged by Marcus Dent's voice, surged past my father and his protesting servants. For a few moments there was chaos, everyone jostling together on the stairs, my father shouting dire warnings of reprisals to come, a serving maid screaming hysterically somewhere below us.

One of Dent's men must have knocked my head against the wooden banister in his furious rush, for I collapsed onto the stairs, losing my senses briefly. I was lucky not to be trampled underfoot. When I opened my eyes again, it was to see them half dragging, half carrying my terrified, white-faced aunt down the stairs, her pale feet and legs showing under her bedgown.

'Meg . . . !' she cried.

Then my aunt was gone, and the shouting men with her, one of them spitting deliberately on the floor as he passed the threshold.

My father stood looking down at me when the door had closed behind them. He said bitterly, 'This is your fault, Meg. You should not have refused Master Dent's offer of marriage. Now do you see what comes of playing the witch? Your aunt has been dragged away to her death and our family is disgraced.'

He trod heavily back to his bedchamber and slammed the door. My brother and cousin had already disappeared back into their shared bedchamber, perhaps fearing to be taken by Dent's men too, or to hide any seditious literature they might be harbouring.

Shocked and silent, the servants melted away one by one into the kitchen and the downstairs rooms to begin their day, as if nothing had happened. Though one girl made a sign against the evil eye as she slipped past, no doubt suspecting, like the other servants, that my aunt was not the only witch in the house.

I sank down on the stairs in the dawn light and stared at the blood on my fingers. It must have come from a wound on my head, though I could feel no pain.

What was the use of my gift if I could not use it to save the one person in the world whom I truly loved?

I wanted to weep for Aunt Jane but the tears would not come. Instead, my teeth ground together, my fists clenched so tight that my nails bit into my skin. My heart beat with a cold, smouldering fury. I was hurt by my father's anger, but I knew he was right. If I had not refused to marry

Marcus Dent, my aunt would still be safe in bed and our family would not be the talk of the county.

Now Aunt Jane would be hanged as a witch, and it was all my fault.

The first thing to be done was to hunt out my aunt's hidden books of the magick arts and burn them. When the fire had been kindled downstairs, I levered up the false bottom of her clothes chest and brought out the last few trophies of her art. Bundling them into a cloth, I carried the books and instruments down to the fire. I was taking a chance, knowing I might be seen. But the deed had to be done, and swiftly too, before Marcus Dent came back for me.

To my relief, there was no one about. Perhaps everyone was lying low after the misery of this morning's cruel visit. The fire was soon crackling merrily as I fed it slim volumes filled with strange symbols and Latin writing, a faceless wooden doll, some kind of stick with feathers bound to it, and a pack of hand-painted cards whose significance I did not understand.

I disliked disposing of magickal items in this hurried, unceremonious way. The books in particular I would have liked to study before burning them. But at any moment, Marcus Dent might return with his gang, having wrung some terrible confession from my poor aunt about the whereabouts of her books. So into the fire they went. The smoke turned a dirty grey from the paper, then a bright green as it consumed the painted cards, and finally my hands were empty.

I turned at a creaking sound, my heart nearly leaping out of my chest. It was my father. He had come into the hall without a sound and was standing only a few feet away, watching in silence.

I forced myself to remain calm. Here I was, kneeling on the hearth, the smouldering remnants of my aunt's books and belongings still clearly visible amongst the flame-engulfed logs. My father had seen what I was doing, that I was burning the evidence of her witchcraft. But even as I tried to reassure myself that my own father would not betray me, I remembered what he had shouted the night before.

I hope Dent catches you playing witch next time, Meg, and you hang for it!

My father must know what my aunt had been at such pains to hide, I thought – not only that Aunt Jane was a witch, but that she had been teaching me her craft. Though that last could hardly have come as a shock, given that Marcus had already told him of my questioning at Woodstock.

My father moved closer to the smoking fire, his face twisted in a kind of grimace. I wondered if he was about to condemn me for having followed my aunt into witchcraft. But he surprised me when he spoke, his voice heavy with pain. 'Your aunt will not survive this accusation. Dent will see to that. He is determined to punish us for your refusal.

But you have some small protection against him now.'

I got to my feet, looking at him uncertainly.

'The Lady Elizabeth favours you,' my father explained. 'You must use that influence to shelter yourself from Dent's anger. He will not dare to touch you while she keeps you with her at Woodstock. Dent likes to visit the court occasionally, and I believe he is considered by some there to be a philosopher as well as a witchfinder. But if Queen Mary were to die . . .'

He hesitated, and I realized that my brother Will had come into the room and was watching us.

'Go on,' Will said roughly.

'If the Lady Elizabeth came to the throne,' my father continued more carefully, 'Marcus Dent would not wish to be out of favour with the new Queen.'

'Elizabeth would not protect me,' I protested.

'Yet she keeps you close at Woodstock,' my father pointed out sharply, then straightened, his features guarded once more. 'That shows some favour. You must return there at once and beg for her protection. Do not stay at Lytton Park even another day. Dent will be too busy to follow you.'

'But what of my aunt?' I felt hot tears prick my eyes and was angry at myself for that weakness. I looked at Will for help, thinking my brother would surely understand my pain, for Aunt Jane had been like a mother to him too. 'I cannot abandon her. I must do something.'

'There is nothing anyone can do for Aunt Jane now,' Will said huskily. 'Except pray for her soul.'

His words reminded me of Alejandro. Suddenly, I wished the young Spaniard were there in the room, holding my hand. Someone I could trust and confide in. My heart felt as though it had swollen in my chest to twice or three times its normal size and was pushing now against my ribs with a deep, aching hurt that almost stopped me breathing.

Dent had taken my aunt away from me, and I would never see her again. She would never survive the cruel torture of his inquisition. She would never come back to us.

'Perhaps if the Lady Elizabeth were to write a letter asking for our aunt to be pardoned . . .' My brother hesitated, then shook his head at his own bold suggestion. 'No, it would do no good. The princess has no power at Woodstock. She stands accused of treason and is a mere prisoner herself. She will have no power until she comes to the throne. Besides, Dent will allow no one to get in his way.'

I stared at Will. 'It's worth the attempt though, isn't it?'

Will looked back at me consideringly, his head on one side. 'I'm not sure. In truth, only you can answer that question, for you know the princess better than us.'

I thought about it, remembering how deferential Marcus had been with the princess. 'It's true that Marcus seemed in awe of the Lady Elizabeth when he came to Woodstock,' I mused, and felt a prickling along my scalp as though of excitement or possibly fear. 'Perhaps you are right, Will. Perhaps Dent would listen if the princess wrote and asked him to spare Aunt Jane.'

My father raised his eyebrows at the two of us. 'You understand nothing about Marcus Dent if you truly believe that.'

Anger flared through me. 'I understand he is an evil man and ought to be stopped.'

'Go and ask the Lady Elizabeth then,' my father told me coldly, and turned away. 'Try and save your aunt if you must. But do not waste your time coming home again when you fail, for the house will be empty. I do not intend to be attacked by my neighbours for harbouring a witch under my roof, and nor does your brother. We plan to make a trip abroad together and stay there until . . . until it is safe to return.'

'You're leaving Lytton Park?' I demanded, astonished, looking from him to Will.

Suddenly I was afraid, not only for my aunt, but for my father and brother, and even for myself. This was the first time I had ever known my father leave his ancestral home at Lytton Park for more than a few days. He would certainly not have made that decision unless he felt all our lives were in danger. But if he and Will were no longer in Oxfordshire, who would try to spare my aunt? I knew the answer, but dreaded the truth of it. Unless I asked the princess for help, as Will had suggested, my aunt would surely die.

'Do you have a better way for me to avoid the shame and dishonour that have befallen us?' My father glanced at Will, and it seemed to me that a message passed silently between them. 'Tell the housekeeper we will be leaving in a day or two, Will. Your cousin can travel with us to the Low Countries if he wishes. I know he has no love for this country any more.'

'And what of my aunt?' I asked helplessly.

My father shrugged. 'You must do what you can to save her, just as I must try to salvage the honour of our family.'

Outside in the hall, my brother embraced me and whispered in my ear, 'God speed to Woodstock, Meg. If anyone can save Aunt Jane, it will be you.'

I ran upstairs to my chamber and dragged my battered travelling bag out from the window alcove. Into this I thrust my aunt's precious athame, which I still kept under my pillow, then my spare gown and shoes, without much regard for how these would look when they emerged at the other end. I was more careful with the gown Elizabeth had given me for a New Year's gift, folding it into the top of the bag and covering it with a cloth to protect the silk edging to the sleeves and bodice.

If only Alejandro were here, I thought feverishly. I could hardly wait to get back to Woodstock to see him, to ask his advice. Though he too might think it was a hopeless case and I should leave my aunt to her fate.

I barely even questioned my belief that I could trust Alejandro de Castillo, that the young Spaniard was someone I could confide in.

He should have been my enemy. But yet he had proved to be my friend too.

I shook my head at this notion and came away dizzy, struggling to hold the weight of such doubleness in one heart. Alejandro had risked his position as a novice to help me evade Marcus Dent's interrogation.

But what would he say when he learned that my aunt stood accused as a witch and a devil-worshipper?

I had forgotten how beautiful the soft, sloping walls of Woodstock Palace were – particularly now, their ivy-covered stones bathed in the gentle reddish light of a spring sunset. Flakes of white cloud scudded across the sky behind the ancient towers, and below my feet the river rushed and gurgled on its way further into Oxfordshire. The small cart jerked and rumbled its wheels across the uneven stones of the bridge, and I sat down again, impatient to be home.

Home.

That word surprised me. I had not realized Woodstock felt so much like home that I would prefer it even to Lytton Park, the house where I was born and grew up – albeit without a mother.

Aunt Jane had always been like a mother to me. And now she would die because of me. Unless I could stop Marcus Dent.

As we approached the first buildings, I saw Alejandro leaning against the gates to Woodstock Lodge, a tall figure in the fading sunlight. He straightened and raised a hand. He must have seen the cart from one of the upstairs windows and come down to meet me. His dark hair was uncovered, his olive skin visible from a distance against his white shirt and soft leather jerkin.

I jumped down impatiently from the cart a few yards from the gate and ran towards him, eager to see a friendly face. But I slowed my pace as I reached him, suddenly unsure of how he would receive such an enthusiastic greeting.

'Sir,' I managed, curtseying as he bowed his head. 'Tell me, how does the Lady Elizabeth?'

His brows rose, and I knew he was surprised at my cool greeting after the manner of my departure, which had been far from cool.

'You must come in and speak to her yourself – the Lady Elizabeth will be pleased at your return. Is that all you carry?' He held out his hand. 'Here, let me take it for you.'

Clumsy with fear, I tripped over my own feet as I passed through the guarded gate. Alejandro caught me before I fell.

'Have a care you do not hurt yourself,' he said softly in my ear, low enough that none of the guards could overhear. 'How did you come by that gash on your forehead, Meg?'

'It's nothing,' I lied instinctively.

My head was throbbing from where I had hit it against the banisters at Lytton Park. I rubbed at my aching temples but each touch only seemed to intensify the pain.

'Come inside, you need to be examined.'

What did he mean by that? The remark seemed innocent enough, but perhaps there was a more sinister meaning underneath.

He spoke again, leading me forward, and I felt an agonizing pain shoot through my head. I saw traps in every word the Spaniard spoke, ambushes in every look he gave me. Even his smile held secrets. His gaze searched my face for the lies I was furiously trying to conceal.

Had Marcus Dent managed to reach Woodstock Lodge before me, and warn the princess and her household of my guilt?

It was cool and damp inside the lodge. I had forgotten what a shabby place it was. The passageway smelled of woodsmoke and wet dog. I leaned my forehead against the familiar crumbling brickwork and fought to control my breathing. Alejandro de Castillo was standing just a few steps ahead of me in the shadowy passageway, carrying my bag effortlessly under one arm, his brow knitted together in a dark frown.

He said something, but I could no longer hear his voice through the pain in my head. Then Alejandro gestured me to go upstairs, still frowning.

I stared at the swinging cross about his neck. He was

angry. He knew the truth. They all knew, and soon I would be condemned along with my aunt, and led to the gallows for my punishment.

I took a step towards the stairs, and my knees failed. I cried out and pitched face-first into a well of darkness.

THIRTEEN
The Letter

I woke to an unlit, curtained chamber and stared upwards in silence. Slowly, I recognized the crescent-shaped damp patch on the ceiling, then the yawning, uneven crack that ran from window to door. It was my old room at Woodstock Lodge, the one I had shared with Joan.

There was someone nearby, breathing quietly in the shadows.

I sat up gingerly, frowning in anticipation, expecting to feel more pain in my head. Miraculously the pain had gone. I put a hand to my forehead, and found to my surprise that the cut had been bandaged.

'Don't mess with the bindings,' Alejandro reprimanded me sternly from a chair near my bedside. 'Mistress Parry applied salve to your hurt, then spent some time bandaging it to stop the bleeding.'

'My head was bleeding?'

'After you fell, yes.' He stared at me, a tense frown in his eyes. 'How did you hurt yourself? The servant who brought you here would say nothing.'

Briefly, I remembered Dent's face, and his men rushing past me on the stairs, the jostling and crushing. Then my head knocking violently against the wooden rail of the banisters.

How could I tell him? Yet how could I not?

'My aunt . . .'

He prompted me encouragingly when I stopped, unable to find the right words. 'Your aunt?'

'You remember Marcus Dent, the witchfinder?' I closed my eyes against the look on his face. 'He came to our house and took my aunt away, accusing her of witchery. He had brought an angry mob of villagers with him. There was a struggle, and I banged my head.'

He spoke angrily under his breath in Spanish, and I had the impression that he was swearing.

'When was this?'

'Yesterday. No, today.' I shook my head in confusion. 'I don't know how long I've been asleep.'

'It is near dawn now. So, yesterday.'

Remorse pricked at me fiercely. How could I have slept so long when my aunt was all alone, lying sick in some dreadful cell?

'I must save Aunt Jane from that monster,' I whispered.

Alejandro shook his head, reminding me of my father. 'She's beyond saving. Once your aunt has been accused of witchcraft, there is nothing to be done. The law must run its course.'

'The law is corrupt!'

He did not deny this but sat looking at me steadily, his hands on the arms of his chair. 'Tell me, what exactly do you plan to do? Burst into the courtroom and deny that your aunt is a witch? I doubt they would consider that an effective argument. Or pin them to their seats, perhaps, while you whisk your aunt away on a broomstick?'

My eyes narrowed to furious slits, my face suddenly flushed with heat. 'So, you think I should do nothing?'

'I think you too will be accused of witchcraft if you are foolish enough to attempt a rescue.'

'You are as bad as my father,' I told him angrily. 'He wouldn't lift a finger to help her either. He just let Marcus Dent take her. I don't know why. My father has been nothing but an enemy to me recently.'

'I am not your enemy, Meg.'

Alejandro rose from the chair near my bed and threw back the rattling curtain, once a handsome green fabric, that hung dusty and threadbare across the window.

A pale misty light flooded the room, and I could see more clearly now that Alejandro was back in his priestly robes. The dark hem brushed his sandalled feet, the corded belt with its leather pouch hung loose about his hips. He must have helped Father Vasco at evening prayers after I had been brought up here, then come straight back to my room to sit with me. A true Christian act, tending to the sick.

Surely now, with my aunt accused of devil-worship, and my own head as good as in the noose, Alejandro should begin to distance himself from me. Not find ways of disgracing himself too.

It was suddenly very important to me that Alejandro did

not ruin his chances of becoming a priest by associating himself with me, already a suspected witch.

'Why are you here, anyway?' I demanded, forcing a note of contempt into my voice. 'I am well enough now and do not need to be minded like a child. Should you not be on your knees somewhere, praying?'

He turned to stare at me, and I saw a hard colour come into his face. My temper flared, edged with fear. I wanted Alejandro out of my room. Without delay. The longer he stayed, the more dangerous it would be for him. But I knew only one thing would drive him from my side: my contempt for his calling, for the Order of Santiago.

'Please leave,' I insisted coldly, and looked pointedly at the door, more to avoid his gaze than for any other reason. 'When I want a priest, I will send for Father Vasco. Though don't hold your breath for that. I shall not want a priest even when they drag me out to the gallows. The only good priest is a dead one.'

After Alejandro had gone, closing the door quietly behind him, I thrust the dagger hurriedly inside the loose straw of my mattress. Then I swung my legs out of bed and attempted to stand.

The four walls of my room spun like dancers around a ribboned maypole and I had to sit for a while, perched on the edge of my narrow cot. Eventually, my vision cleared and the sickness in my throat abated. I groped across to the water bowl, grateful that someone had refreshed it for me.

Splashing my face, I was surprised to find that I had been crying. Had Alejandro noticed in the darkness? I fervently hoped not.

Straightening my crumpled gown, I rummaged in my travelling bag for a clean cap, then went to the door. I would not think about Alejandro, nor remember the look in his eyes as he left the room. I knew he must hate me for what I had said.

None of that mattered any more. My aunt was facing the most terrible of charges. She was too weakened by her sickness to use her arts to save herself from execution, and I had failed to stop them dragging her away. I might not admire my brother for his seditious beliefs, but he was right about one thing: the only person who might possibly be able to save my aunt now was Elizabeth.

I felt my way along the unlit corridor to the princess's room, blocking out what I had said to Alejandro. If he hated me now, it was for the best. This thing between us would only confuse me at a time when I needed to be cold and clear and ready to fight.

Elizabeth was waiting for me in her chamber. While Blanche dressed her by candlelight, the shutters kept closed against prying eyes, she stood in the middle of the cramped room and heard me out. Elizabeth seemed more angry that I had been hurt during the arrest than that my poor aunt had been taken sick from her bed and now faced death by hanging. She asked if I had spoken to Alejandro since returning, and when I admitted as much, she brightened.

'He has been distracted since you left. Father Vasco had to reprimand him more than once for failing to cover the holy wine after consecration, so that it had to be drunk before the next service.' Elizabeth smiled indulgently at Blanche's giggles. 'Don't laugh now, the poor old man was quite incensed. There were more than three cupfuls of wine left after Mass once, and he was almost on the floor by the time he had finished them. While Alejandro had disappeared off on one of his walks.'

'His walks?'

'Hush,' Blanche muttered in her mistress's ear. 'Hold still now, my lady.'

Elizabeth stood patiently and sucked in her breath while Blanche laced up her gown at the back.

When this fiddly task had been achieved, the princess exhaled sharply. 'Alejandro has taken to walking in the old palace grounds on his own, particularly when Father Vasco has gone to bed for his afternoon *siesta*. I see him on the hill sometimes from my chamber window, for Sir Henry Bedingfield no longer allows us to walk out beyond the river.' Her small mouth pursed angrily. 'Bedingfield claims his guards have grown lax these days and there are too many of my "creatures" staying down at the Bull for his comfort.'

Blanche snorted with indignation. 'He should mind his

tongue. My old husband Thomas is still in residence there, and he is not a "creature"!'

I could see Elizabeth was distracted, so I waited until she was dressed before asking if she would help my aunt. But all the while my heart was hammering with nerves, my brain repeating that it was too late, too late to save her.

'Please, my lady, will you write a letter to Master Dent for me, and beg him to release my aunt? She is too frail and sick to have committed these outrages they accuse her of, yet even now she may have been charged and be awaiting execution.' I bit my lip, determined not to let my tears spill. 'All I ask is one letter, my lady.'

Elizabeth looked at me pityingly. She had lost her own mother to the axe, even if she had only been a young child at the time. She must understand something of the pain I was suffering on my aunt's account, and certainly her small dark eyes seemed to say so.

'I am very sorry to hear of this injustice. But I do not think a letter from a suspected traitor and heretic will help her case.'

Though I could not remind Elizabeth of the services my aunt had done her, since Blanche was still in the room, yet I tried to speak with my face. As far as Blanche knew, her mistress had never met my aunt. But the truth rang clear in my voice. 'It cannot hurt, at least, and my father believes it may help. He and my brother sent me back here in the hope of a letter that might yet save her from the noose. Please, my lady, I beg of you.'

Elizabeth hesitated, then nodded briskly. 'Very well. Blanche, bring me pen and paper. I shall write a few lines to the magistrate in support of clemency towards this prisoner. But given that I myself am in prison, I fear it will do little good.'

'Thank you, my lady.' I kneeled and kissed her long white hand. 'Thank you so much.'

She wrote in a strong, black flourish on the paper, then signed her name, Elizabeth. Pausing there, she read the letter back over twice, then dipped her pen again, ready to score the empty spaces through at the end of her letter according to her usual custom.

But an urgent knock came at the door. 'My lady! There is a messenger below with a letter for you. He says it comes from the Queen!'

'A message from the Queen?' Abruptly losing all her colour, Elizabeth's hand faltered. 'Tell him I will be down in a moment. Give him wine!'

The princess laid aside the pen and gripped the cross at her neck. She seemed unsteady, her eyes suddenly unfocused. Blanche fussed about her with some powerful smelling salts in a small shaker, and pinched her cheeks until the blood ran there again.

'Enough!' Elizabeth waved Blanche irritably away, raising her chin. The excitement in her voice was as audible as her fear. 'I must go down and speak with this man. And read my sister's letter.'

She hurried from the room with Blanche following after, clutching at Elizabeth's train so the long skirted gown would not be dirtied on the rushes.

Looking down at the abandoned letter, I wondered whether I should score the end spaces through for her, to prevent anyone from adding further words. Intending to do so, I picked up the pen and dipped it in the ink, but did not quite dare to mark the paper. If the princess were to return and find me bent over her letter . . .

Yet I could not delay by waiting until the Lady Elizabeth had finished with the Queen's messenger. That could take hours, and my aunt might even now be in her cell, waiting to be taken out to the gallows.

Elizabeth would be furious, but I would have to face her fury if I wished to save my aunt. I checked the ink was dry, then rolled up the paper and sealed it with Elizabeth's own seal. Then I hurried down to the kitchen and called the servant who had carried messages between me and my brother over the summer. He agreed, though only for the costly fee of a shilling, to take the letter straight over to the magistrate.

'I have a horse stabled in the village,' the servant told me. 'Best not to take the main road though, for the guards on the gate may search me and find the letter. I'll head across the fields and ford the stream down below.'

I accompanied the servant as far as the old palace buildings. There I watched as the man hurried across the misty grounds, the sealed letter requesting clemency in his bag, until he was lost to sight among the trees.

I slid down the crumbling wall of the old palace and bent my knees up to meet my face. I was shaking as though I had an ague, my face hot, my body desperately cold.

I must have passed out.

The next thing I knew, Alejandro de Castillo was kneeling beside me with a leather-bound flask in his hand.

'Here,' he said, tilting my head back a little. 'Drink this and don't try to speak. You fainted. This is a strong Spanish wine, it will restore your strength.'

When I had recovered my senses enough to speak, I frowned up at him. 'Why,' I whispered hoarsely, 'does it always have to be you? Do you follow me about, waiting for me to collapse?'

Alejandro rocked back on his heels, watching me through narrowed eyes. 'Good, you're better,' was his only response. I tried to stand but he stopped me. 'Stay where you are for a few more minutes. Let the wine take effect. Here, have another drop. Trust me, it will help.'

'Is it holy wine?'

He grinned then. 'Not this stuff, no. But I can bless it if you wish.'

'I thought only a priest could bless wine.'

Alejandro paused in the act of restoppering the wine

flask. His smile had faded. I knew that he was remembering the insults I had thrown at him earlier. But I could see no way of making things better between us without inviting him deeper into my world of deceit and witchery. And once there, Alejandro would never be allowed to become a priest. Not when his masters realized how far he had fallen from grace.

'Who was that man I saw you with?' he asked.

There seemed no harm in the truth. I told him briefly of the letter of clemency I had persuaded Elizabeth to write, and how the servant had agreed to carry it to the magistrate for me.

Alejandro listened, a frown on his face. 'And you say he was going to the village first?'

'To fetch his horse, which is stabled there.'

'Hmm. I see.'

His eyes had taken on a faraway look, almost brooding in their darkness.

'What?' I demanded irritably. 'Say whatever is on your mind. For I can see that you are dying to.'

Alejandro straightened up and helped me back to my feet. 'We need to get back to the lodge. Can you walk?'

'Of course I can walk,' I replied impatiently, but kept my back firmly against the wall of the old palace. 'I'm enjoying the sunshine though. You go ahead. I'll follow in a short while.'

Snorting with disbelief under his breath, Alejandro picked me up and hoisted me over his shoulder as though I weighed no more than a cloth doll. Furious at this arrogant behaviour, I kicked and struggled against him, but Alejandro paid no attention, striding back towards the old lodge with me thrown across his shoulder like a cloak.

'What in Hell's name do you think you're doing?' I demanded, the blood burning in my cheeks. 'How dare you? Put me down at once!'

'In Hell's name?' he repeated, showing no signs of fatigue under my weight. 'You'd know all about that, I imagine.'

'What?'

'If you want me to put you down, you'd better turn me into a toad or something. Curse me so that I fall to the ground and froth at the mouth.' His voice grew almost teasing. 'What, can't you put even the smallest spell on me? What kind of witch are you?'

'Take off that cross and I'll show you!' I spat angrily.

'My cross?' He sounded genuinely surprised now. 'You believe the crucifix to be some kind of talisman against your power?'

Was there nothing this Spaniard did not know or could not guess about my powers? My frustration raged like a fire in my head while I slammed my fists against his back, hanging upside-down, my white cap fallen off, my fair hair tumbled about my face.

'Softly now,' he said, reaching the back door of the lodge. 'I'm going to put you back on your feet. Only don't attack me, you little termagant. There is something you ought to know first.'

Flushed and dishevelled, I staggered backwards as he planted my feet back on the ground. I was so angry that if I had been a man I would have killed him there and then. I looked at Alejandro and willed him to laugh at me. For if he dared to laugh at me, I would run upstairs, pull my dagger out from its hiding place in the straw mattress and stab him through the heart with it.

But he did not laugh. Indeed, his face was more sombre than I had ever seen it.

'What, then?' I demanded breathlessly, tidying my hair with my fingers. 'What is this thing you must tell me?'

'The man you sent with the letter,' he said flatly, watching my face. 'He did not go to the village. I was up on the hill behind the old palace and I saw him cross the stream, then turn right, back towards the bridge and the gates. There was another man waiting on the track there. The servant took a letter from his bag and handed it to this other man, took payment of some kind and then walked away into the woods.'

I stared, unable to believe what he was saying. 'No, you are lying!'

'I have no reason to lie to you, Meg.'

'Then he must have been giving the letter to that man to carry for him. Perhaps his horse was faster.'

'The man on the horse did not take the road to Green Hanborough. He turned left and carried on towards Woodstock village.'

'No, there must be some mistake,' I insisted, even while my blood started to run cold at the thought that I had entrusted Elizabeth's letter to a traitor. 'That letter was of great importance. It was written by the Lady Elizabeth herself. It must reach the magistrate today.'

'Listen to me, Meg,' he said urgently, and caught my flailing hands in his. 'I caught a glimpse of the rider's face as he passed below where I was standing. He did not see me, but I saw him as clearly as I see you now.'

My mouth was dry. I watched his lips move, but I did not want to hear the words. None of it was true. 'Who . . . who was it?'

'It was your father.'

FOURTEEN
Eternal Flame

I could not quite believe what Alejandro had said to me. Perhaps I was still asleep in bed and had dreamed all this: my aunt's arrest, Elizabeth's letter, what Alejandro claimed he had seen from the hilltop. Or perhaps I was going mad?

'My father? He must have been coming here for the letter, then.' I nodded, almost convincing myself. 'He will have met the man on his way here, heard what he was doing and offered to carry the letter to Marcus Dent himself.'

Alejandro rubbed my cold hands. 'No, your father turned his horse towards the village and the London road. He took the letter and rode in the opposite direction, not back towards Marcus Dent.'

'I don't believe it. Are you even sure it was my father?'

He nodded grimly. 'It was the same man we passed on the stairs at the Bull Inn when Elizabeth went to visit John Dee. You remember that night?'

Only too well, I thought bitterly.

'But this makes no sense,' I continued aloud, bewildered by Alejandro's tale. 'Why would my father do such a thing? He told me he was on his way to the Low Countries with my brother and cousin, to escape the shame of my aunt's arrest. Besides, he must know that by stealing the letter he condemns my aunt to death.'

I recalled conversations I had overheard between my father, Will and Malcolm, the whispered discussions after supper that had fallen into silence at my approach. Had they planned this all along, the three of them together, my father, my brother and my cousin? Had I been the unwitting fool who had been sent to get the princess's signature on a document that could be used to rally men to their cause abroad?

'All this time . . .' I gasped, the truth crashing down on me. 'My father's insistence that I should serve the princess, my brother sending me back here for a letter with her signature on it . . . What a witless idiot I have been!' I broke from his grip and stumbled away. I felt sick and dizzy. My head was throbbing again. I had to get inside, back to my bedchamber, to where the dagger was hidden. It was all I could focus on.

Alejandro followed me into the house and up the stairs. 'Let me help you,' he kept saying, but I just waved him away.

He watched anxiously from the doorway as I fumbled for the dagger hidden deep inside the straw mattress, and pressed its cold blade down my bodice, close against my chest.

'Meg, you need to rest. Your head—'

'No longer hurts,' I lied, and dragged away the cloth binding that Blanche had wrapped about my temples. The cut stung and I saw fresh blood on the cloth. A wave of nausea followed, but I fought against it. 'I'm going straight back home. I have to see Marcus . . . talk to him.'

'At least wait a few hours until you have eaten and are feeling stronger.'

'No,' I insisted doggedly, searching for my outdoor shoes and coat. 'I don't have time to sit down and eat a meal. Don't you understand? If I don't speak with Marcus today and make him change his mind, then my aunt will be condemned to hang.'

'I see.' Alejandro handed me my missing shoes and watched me sit on the bed to slip them on. 'And how precisely do you intend to make Master Dent change his mind?'

'I'm going to agree to marry him.'

There was a tense silence in the room. It seemed to me that I could hear ringing in my ears, or maybe it was just the after-echo of my own voice.

Then he nodded. 'I was afraid you would say that,' he murmured. 'Wait here for a few minutes. Don't leave the room. Don't go anywhere, do you hear me?'

I ignored him and continued looking for my heavy winter cloak. It was not particularly cold outside, being a sharp and sunny March day. Yet I was shivering nonetheless. When at last I found the cloak, I swung it about my shoulders, searched for my purse in the travelling bag, then stood there in silence, not sure what to do.

I was ready to go home, and knew there was no time to

lose. Yet something in me balked at the appalling message I must bear to Marcus Dent, that I had changed my mind and would marry him after all.

What choice did I have though in this game of flinch? I had played my hand, then he had played his, and I could not trump his card in any other way but to capitulate and marry the man. With Elizabeth's letter, I could have forced him to back down. I could have saved Aunt Jane. But without it . . .

Alejandro came back into my bedchamber before I could fall to brooding over my father's betrayal. He too was dressed for travelling, with a sombre black jacket over his shirt and his sword by his side. The only concession to his calling was the silver cross that still hung about his neck.

'No,' I exclaimed, and shook my head, guessing his intention at once. Marcus would be furious if he discovered I had gone to him in the company of another man. 'I must do this alone. One of the servants can drive me over and wait to bring me back tomorrow.'

'You can travel on the cart with my man, Juan. I will ride alongside. Do not worry, I shall not try to stop you throwing your life away on Marcus Dent.' Alejandro studied my face, his own expression unreadable. 'Have you spoken with the Lady Elizabeth yet? She is still your mistress, you must ask her consent to leave Woodstock.'

'Have you spoken to Father Vasco? Have you asked for his consent?'

'Father Vasco was no longer in his room. I left a note for him. He may be angered but he will understand the reason for my departure. Here in England, it may be considered no great thing for you to wander about the countryside alone, or in the company of a servant only. But in Spain we understand the need for an unmarried woman to be accompanied by a man of honour wherever she travels.'

I glanced at the sword by his side. 'There will be no need for *that*,' I said bitingly. 'I go willingly to Marcus Dent. It is the only way.'

I had not imagined the contempt in his voice before. 'What, are you the virgin sacrifice?'

Heat flared in my face and I brushed past him angrily. 'I must speak to the Lady Elizabeth.'

'What you must do is recover that letter,' he told me, 'and swiftly, before it can be used against your mistress.'

I turned in the doorway and stared back at him, frowning. 'Used against her?'

'A letter with her signature on it? Of course it could be used against the princess, and in any manner of ways. Some men are so skilled with such work they can take even the most innocent letter, change a few words and make it sound like treason. What was in it?'

I blinked, unsure. 'I don't remember. The messenger arrived just as she finished signing it and . . .' My stomach clenched. 'She didn't . . .'

I couldn't breathe. I shuddered at what I had done, how

easily I had wrecked everything, and raised my gaze to his without bothering to hide my horror.

'There was still space left on the sheet at the end of the letter and she forgot to score through it – she was in such a hurry to receive the Queen's messenger. Whoever possesses that letter could add whatever they wished and make it look as though Elizabeth herself had written it.'

Alejandro stood for a moment in the same horrified silence that had engulfed me. No doubt he was also thinking it would be the work of a few moments to turn an innocent letter of clemency into a treacherous document. Such a letter would condemn the already suspected princess and lead her to an ignominious death.

'Then you must go to her ladyship, and lay the truth before her. There is no other honourable course of action.' He seized my arm, squeezing it reassuringly. 'I will come with you, *mi alma*. Then we will ride to Marcus Dent, save your aunt and retrieve the letter from your father.'

'You make it sound so easy,' I said bitterly, though in truth I was secretly grateful to know he would come with me to see Marcus.

'It will not be easy. It may even prove impossible. But these are great matters, and there is no disgrace in feeling fear. Only the simple-minded are not afraid when they ride into battle.'

'Is that what we are doing? Riding into battle?'

We had reached Elizabeth's closed door. The burly guard on duty there glanced first at me, then at Alejandro, then with more interest at the sword by his side. But he made no comment and did not attempt to bar my way into the princess's bedchamber. The guards were too used to our comings and goings for such a visit to be anything out of the ordinary.

I looked over my shoulder at the young Spaniard. 'I need to do this alone,' I whispered, and was relieved when Alejandro nodded his understanding, withdrawing into the shadows.

I drew a steadying breath, then scratched gently at the door, wondering if her ladyship was still reading her sister's letter. Indeed, I did not even know what news the messenger had brought from court. To own the truth, I was burning to leave, to rescue my aunt from her accusers, but Alejandro was right. The Lady Elizabeth had a right to know that her letter had been stolen, and to punish me for my stupidity in trusting such a precious document to the hands of a servant I barely knew – assuming that was her will once she had heard the full sorry tale.

Elizabeth was standing by the window, the letter she had been reading abandoned on the bed. She turned as I entered, and I could tell that she had been crying, her eyes red-rimmed, her lips trembling.

Blanche Parry was nowhere to be seen, and I guessed she must have sneaked out to the Bull Inn to see her husband there, perhaps to ask his advice on whatever the Queen's letter had held.

'My lady, what is it?'

'I am to be questioned again. What else can this be but another failed rising against the Queen? And my name linked to the conspirators.'

For a moment, I thought she meant my cousin's plot, and felt my heart contract with painful fear. Then it jolted back into life as she continued, blind to my guilt.

'This is just one more attempt by the council to blacken my name and turn my sister against me. I do not know how much longer I can evade their torturous traps. There are many at court now who would gladly see my head on the block and the line of succession cleared for Catholics.' Elizabeth indicated the letter with an angry, fatalistic gesture. 'Lies, all of it. And yet my sister's advisors would have me dragged back to the Tower and interrogated again, if they are permitted to have their way.'

My blood ran cold at this.

It was the worst news imaginable, given that her letter was out there somewhere, perhaps even now being doctored to make it look as though she wished to conspire against the Queen.

'My lady,' I forced myself to say aloud, though the words stuck in my throat like fishbones, 'I fear the letter you wrote for my aunt's sake may have been stolen by . . . by my father, to be used as evidence of your support by those in the

Low Countries who would rise against the Queen.'

She stared, and her narrow mouth quivered. 'In the Low Countries? What nonsense is this?'

'My cousin Malcolm has been in the Low Countries these past five years, stirring rebellion in the hearts of exiled Englishmen.' I barely dared continue, watching her face. But it was too late now to hide the truth. My voice dropped to a cautious whisper. 'My cousin knows many Protestants there who would willingly cross the Channel, remove your Catholic sister from her throne, and crown you Queen instead.'

'And my letter?'

I straightened my back, looking her full in the face. 'My lady, I very much fear my father has taken your letter of clemency to my cousin. I entrusted it to a servant here who was seen to hand it over to my father, instead of taking it to the magistrate as he had been instructed. If some words of support for the rebels were to be added below your signature, in a similar hand, it could be taken abroad and used to foment revolt.'

Elizabeth felt for the carved wooden bedpost and leaned there, steadying herself. Her face appeared drained of blood, her breathing laboured. 'Do you know what you have done?' she demanded hoarsely, though always careful not to raise her voice. 'This folly could bring me to the block.'

She seemed to think for a moment, not waiting for an answer. Her lips worked desperately, though no sound came out. I guessed she must be going over what she had written in the stolen letter and considering how her words could be misread, twisted to find a more sinister meaning. Then she turned and walked restlessly to the window.

'You must retrieve this letter,' she told me succinctly, throwing the words like knives back at me. 'And prevent it from falling into the hands of my enemies. It cannot yet have been removed from the country. Do you know where your father may have taken it?'

'To my cousin,' I admitted, deeply ashamed of my family's treachery. 'Or perhaps my brother. Though they may be together, I don't know.'

'And thence to the Low Countries?'

'I fear so, my lady.'

She nodded, remaining admirably calm in the face of this possibility. 'Then you must discover where your cousin is lodging and follow him. Wrest the letter back from him by any means at your disposal. Is there any servant here whom you do trust?'

I flushed at the irony in her tone. 'No, my lady,' I said, but hesitated. 'Only . . .'

'Speak!'

'Alejandro de Castillo knows of this matter and . . . he has offered to accompany me.'

She was startled then. 'The young Spaniard would help me?'

'Yes, my lady. He would not see you suffer any injustice from this.'

Her small dark eyes examined my hot face at length, making me squirm at the thought of what she might be seeing there. Then she nodded sharply. 'Let de Castillo accompany you, then. He is to be trusted. And they are all knights, of course, in the Order of Santiago. He will be a good man in the event of a fight.'

She dismissed me with a violent gesture. 'Go, find this letter and bring it back to me so I can see it safe. Or else use it for its proper purpose and save your aunt from the gallows. But do not allow it to fall into the hands of my enemies. For they will swiftly become your enemies too, if that were to happen.'

I bowed low, leaving her chamber. Alejandro was still waiting in the shadowy alcove along the corridor. As I approached, he stepped out, his dark gaze searching my face.

I nodded, keeping my voice low, for the guard stood but a few feet away. 'She is furious, and rightly so. We are to find the letter and return it to her,' I told him, and the bitterness in my mouth destroyed all my hope. 'Unless it can be used to save my aunt. But I fear we may be too late by then.'

'Do not be disheartened, *mi alma*. It may be that we can persuade these men who hold your aunt of her innocence and the Lady Elizabeth's support.'

Alejandro hesitated, then made the sign of the Cross. There was pity in his face.

'If not, may the Lord have mercy on her soul.'

* * *

I sat up on the jolting cart next to the Spanish servant, Juan, whose grimaces and nods I could hardly understand, while Alejandro himself paced beside us on his restless black horse. We took the shortest route to Green Hanborough where the magistrate lived. I guessed they would be holding my aunt there too. It still took several hours before we reached the crossroads and turned down the shady, tree-lined approach into the small market town. It was late afternoon by then, and I was hopeful that whatever trial might be taking place would have adjourned for the day.

But as we came into the town, we found the narrow streets deserted. I did not understand why until I saw a thin stream of smoke rising above the houses. Juan shouted something in Spanish, whipping the horse to quicken its pace. We jolted over the cobbles into the small market square. There, a stake had been raised on a wooden platform in the middle, its sides piled high with brushwood and already smoking. A crowd had gathered around this sinister construction, shouting and jostling each other to get closer to the stake. Above their heads, I could see a figure in sackcloth tied to the stake, dishevelled and with shaven head, but at this distance it was impossible to say whether it was a man or a woman.

I stared, horrified beyond speech as I realized that a burning was about to take place.

Alejandro glanced across at me, a heavy frown in his eyes. 'Do not alarm yourself. This cannot be for your aunt. You told me they do not burn witches in England, that she will be hanged if found guilty.'

I nodded, trying to take comfort from his reassuring words. Yet my palms sweated and I felt sick, wondering who the stake was for.

Some poor soul whose death I did not wish to witness, that was for certain.

To be burned at the stake was the punishment for a heretic, for those who refused to follow the Catholic faith. It was a hideous way to die. I had been told that heretics roasting in the market square were a common sight in Spain, and a cause for celebration there. Yet surely few Englishmen would sentence their fellow townsmen to such an agonizing death? These were not the barbarous shores of Spain, for all my brother's doom-mongering.

A cheer went up in the square as the fire began to take hold.

I could see the man standing to one side of the platform, on a kind of makeshift pulpit. It was Marcus Dent, holding aloft a great black Bible, his face contorted with an almost demonic satisfaction.

'So perish all heretics and unbelievers!' he was shouting across the noise of the crowd. 'Behold the foul witch, roasting in the fires of Hell for all eternity! So all should burn who abandon the Holy Book to follow the Devil's teachings.'

I jumped down from the cart, ignoring Juan's protest as it rocked from side to side, and stared wildly up at the figure bound to the stake. I could see now that it was a woman, her body thin and wasted. The creeping sense of horror redoubled and I shook my head, barely able to comprehend what I was seeing.

At that moment, the woman's head twisted back towards me, recognizable even through the grey blossoming of smoke.

It was Aunt Jane. Her face was bruised and filthy, her yellow hair shorn close to her head. Her wide eyes stared desperately about the square, as though searching for someone who might save her from this terrible death.

Something collapsed with a crash in the stack of smouldering brushwood. Suddenly, a bright column of flame leaped out and up, licking at the coarse sackcloth of her robe, smoke billowing out as the material caught and quickened easily into flame. I heard my aunt scream, and knew that she was on fire.

'No!' I shrieked, but my voice was lost above the jeering shouts of the crowd. 'Aunt Jane!'

The horse whinnied loudly behind me, clearly panicked. Then I heard a clatter of wheels and guessed the animal must have bolted with its cart still attached.

Alejandro rode after me, calling out urgently. He leaned over as he reached out for me, holding the horse steady with his knees. 'Take my hand, Meg, you can ride with me. It's too late to save her. We have to get out of here before they see you!'

I ignored his outstretched hand. It was all I could do not to retch as the brushwood burned higher and clouds of smoke thickened about the stake.

Within only a few minutes, quicker than I could have imagined was possible, my aunt's wasted body had been engulfed in a white-hot wall of flame. The wind shifted, and now the unmistakable stench of roasting flesh blew across our faces.

'Aunt Jane,' I whispered, and fainted.

FIFTEEN

Invisible

I opened my eyes to a gently darkening sky and could not for a moment recall where I was or what had happened to bring me here. I was half sitting, half lying, with my back against a hawthorn hedge in a quiet grassy lane. Birds were singing unseen all around me, and the green verge was lush with daisies, bluebells, darkly budding strands of honeysuckle. For a few dizzying seconds, it seemed a perfect spring day. Then I remembered.

The stench of my aunt's poor tortured flesh was still thick in my nose and throat. My eyes stung with fresh tears. I turned my face into the grassy soil, retching weakly.

Slowly, Alejandro came back towards me. He had been standing at the end of the narrow lane, staring into the smoky, crowded marketplace.

I looked up at him groggily as he approached. His face was tense, his hand clamped over the hilt of his sword.

'Is it . . . is it over?'

Alejandro nodded curtly, not bothering to ask what I meant. 'You fainted. It was all I could do to keep you on the saddle until we were clear of the square. As soon as you feel able to ride, I'll fetch the horse and we can move on. I've tied him out of sight among the trees back there, for he was half maddened by the smoke and noise, then by having your dead weight about his neck.'

'I'm sorry,' I muttered, wiping my dirty face with my sleeve.

'We must get back to Woodstock before dusk falls. There is nothing we can do here now. We'll take this lane' – he peered into the distance – 'and hope to meet up with Juan in a mile or so. I don't like the look of the crowd that's gathered in the marketplace.'

'Where is Juan?'

'I'm not sure. His horse was scared by the flames too and must have bolted with the cart. He's been gone a while though, so either the cart has been overturned or he has his hands full trying to stop the horse kicking it to pieces.' He stared broodingly back down the road we had taken into the village. 'Unless Dent's men have taken him.'

Marcus Dent.

At the sound of that hated name, I knew that I wanted to kill Marcus Dent. Now that the sickness had cleared, my head steadied and sharpened to a single purpose: revenge. My aunt might be dead but I was still alive, the last of the Canley witches, and I knew what I had to do. The power filled me like the wind filling out the sail on a barge. I struggled to my feet without waiting for Alejandro's help.

'Where is Marcus Dent?' I asked hoarsely. 'Still in the marketplace?'

He caught me hard by the shoulders, turning me to face

him. 'Don't be a fool. In this mood, they'll take you too.'

'I don't care.'

'You don't care if you burn too?'

I lifted my chin. 'Do you?'

His eyes studied me grimly but he did not answer. He was angry. I had seen Alejandro angry before, but this was something new. He was holding himself in check, his body taut as whipcord, his gaze restless. I sensed there were words in his head which he had forbidden himself to speak. Not that I would have listened anyway, not with the rage and hatred burning through my veins, the desire to strike Marcus Dent down and crush him under my heel.

My aunt's face came into my mind, and I tried to block it out. I did not want to remember her bound to the stake in the marketplace, her robe on fire, her mouth twisting in an agonized scream. Nor did I wish to imagine how the heat must have felt, her skin blistering and peeling off in the white-hot inferno all around her, her tortured flesh melting down to the bone. Yet I could not seem to shake off those horrific imaginings.

I jerked free of his hands. There was venom in my voice. 'I have to kill him. Even if it means dying too.'

'You're not thinking clearly,' he told me, his voice still low, carefully restrained.

'My aunt is dead and Marcus Dent killed her . . . in the most hellish, barbarous way. What is there to think about?' I whirled on my heel and stared back at him furiously. 'If you were in my position, what would you do?'

'If he had killed someone I loved?' he asked tersely. His hand dropped back to the hilt of his sword, his knuckles whitening. 'I would spit him on my sword like a rabid dog and watch him bleed out his heart's blood. Though just killing him would not be enough. I would want to make such a man suffer before I rid this earth of him.'

I drew a shuddering breath, fighting to control my grief and rage before it overwhelmed me. 'Yes . . .'

An odd rustling noise in the hedgerow made us turn like deer at the sound of the hounds' furious baying, poised to flee. Further down the lane, peering through a thorny gap in the hawthorn hedge, someone was watching us.

The face was filthy, pale under the dirt, cut and bruised. But I recognized it immediately.

'Will?'

My brother staggered out into the lane and across to us, collapsing on his knees beside me. His right hand was cut, his knuckles bleeding. There was dried blood smeared across his forehead. He grabbed at the skirts of my gown like a child, his face contorted. 'I'm sorry,' he croaked. 'You must believe me. I tried to stop them but there were too many.'

'Where is the Lady Elizabeth's letter?' I demanded.

He stared. 'She wrote a letter for you?'

'Don't play games with me, Will,' I said furiously. 'Alejandro saw our father take the letter. He was heading south, not here to save Aunt Jane.'

'On my life,' my brother stammered, 'that was not what I wanted. My plan was to take the letter to the magistrate first and get Aunt Jane released from those butchers. Then we would steal the letter back afterwards and take it to the Low Countries, as proof of the Lady Elizabeth's support. But Malcolm did not want to take the chance it might be destroyed. He persuaded our father not to wait. They planned to intercept the letter on its way to the magistrate and ride with it straight to the coast.'

I did not know what to say. This was my brother. How could I not forgive him?

Yet my heart seethed with anger as I remembered my aunt's horrific death, the fear and agony she must have suffered in the last moments of her life. Will and Malcolm – even my father too, it seemed – had manipulated me into getting Elizabeth to write that letter.

Had they arranged for my aunt's arrest too, forcing my hand when I refused to help them get to Elizabeth?

Alejandro looked down at him with dislike. 'Why did they burn her? Are not witches hanged in this country?'

My brother nodded, a dull anger in his face. 'That was Marcus Dent's doing. It seems he is a friend of the magistrate and pushed for her to be burned. They brought her in on a charge of devil-worship, which Dent argued made her a heretic. And heretics *can* be burned.'

'Foul, worthless monster,' I muttered, more than ever

determined to kill Marcus Dent for what he had done here today.

But Alejandro had not yet finished with my brother. Frowning, he gestured to his cut and bruised face, the sorry state of his hands. 'How did you come by those hurts?'

'I fell,' he muttered obliquely.

'I want to hear the whole story,' I insisted, and knew my voice must sound wild and uncontrolled. But my brother could not be allowed to lie. Not about this. 'From the beginning, Will.'

There was a shout from the marketplace. The smoke and the stench had abated a little, and from the sounds of thwacking and beating I guessed they were putting out the fire that had consumed my aunt's pain-racked body. I shuddered at the thought of what must be left of her, and tried not to dwell on that.

In trepidation, Will stared up the narrow lane towards the marketplace. No doubt he feared being caught, as did I. He wiped a hand across his forehead, and I saw that he was trembling.

'Let's get out of sight,' he muttered, and we followed him silently through the gap in the hawthorn and into the freshly ploughed field behind the hedge. We were standing in deep and dry mud ruts, but at least the air was cleaner there, less smoky and horrifying.

'Tell us what happened,' I prompted him.

'I woke just before dawn to find that they had already

gone. Malcolm must have persuaded our father to leave me behind in case I made trouble over Aunt Jane,' he told us bitterly. 'I decided to come on my own, try to talk Dent into letting her go. I had some suspicion he was only doing it to hurt you, and I thought . . . Well, I thought if I offered to talk you round into marrying him, he might drop the accusation of witchcraft against Aunt Jane.'

'Talk me into marrying him?'

He spread his hands, his expression miserable. 'I know, I know, but I couldn't stand by and do nothing. Anyway, they'd taken the horses, so I headed for the village on foot across the fields. It wasn't hard to listen in on our aunt's hearing, for they held it outside in the square.

'Though it wasn't a proper trial,' he added resentfully, his voice dropping to a hoarse whisper as shouts rang out above us in the village. It sounded as though more horsemen had arrived at the busy inn. 'The whole thing was fixed from the start. Dent's pride was involved, and I could tell he wouldn't settle for anything but her death. And the bloodier, the better. He persuaded them that she was a heretic, not merely a witch. Aunt Jane never had a chance. They were already setting brushwood round the stake when the magistrate sentenced her to burn.'

I shuddered, trying not to think of my aunt's blackened corpse still smouldering in the village square, and fixed my gaze on my brother instead.

'I tried to get to the front so I could speak on her behalf,' he went on, 'but Dent's men were everywhere. I fought them off with my dagger – a few went down, I don't know if I killed any. But in the end there was nothing I could do to save her from the stake, and I . . . I ran away before they could kill me too,' he finished, shame-faced.

It was hard not to blame him for my aunt's death, but it would do no good to confront my brother over what had been done. Aunt Jane was dead and beyond anyone's help. But the Lady Elizabeth was still in mortal danger. 'So you don't know where our father is, with the letter?'

Will shook his head. 'Father intended to head straight for the south coast as soon as they had the letter. That was why we argued, because he would not wait to see if Aunt Jane could be freed first. But I know Malcolm planned to make one final stop before leaving Oxfordshire. I'm not sure where though.'

'We need to move,' Alejandro prompted us, standing at my shoulder. 'The crowd is beginning to break up and go home. The longer we stay here, the more likely it is we will be seen and arrested.'

My brother glanced up at him resentfully, a look which told me he did not trust the young priest-to-be. But he gave a shrug. 'We can't go back to Lytton Park. Dent's men recognized me, so for all I know I'm to be hauled up in front of the magistrate for fighting. And it's too dangerous to travel during daylight hours in case we are seen. I suggest we lay low here until nightfall, then head north.

We have cousins in Staffordshire who might take us in.'

I shook my head and stood up, dusting off my gown. 'No, I have to find that letter and return it to the princess at Woodstock.'

'Meg, are you mad?'

'If that letter is altered and falls into the hands of the Queen's spies, the Lady Elizabeth could face arrest and execution as a traitor. Don't you care?'

Will looked away, sullen. 'Every prince faces danger on the road to their throne. These things are beyond a woman's understanding.'

'That's my father talking, not you,' I told him. 'You don't truly believe any of that. Or you would never have risked your life by coming here today in the hope that they might pardon our aunt. Besides, Elizabeth is a woman. Is this beyond her understanding too?'

I turned to Alejandro, realizing with a start that he was the only man I could trust in all this.

'I don't know where to begin looking for them.'

Alejandro looked at me thoughtfully. 'It seems to me that all roads lead back to the Bull Inn at Woodstock.'

'You think they could be at the Bull?'

'Sir Henry Bedingfield has more than once called the Bull Inn the Lady Elizabeth's "court". Where better to find those who would put her on the throne in place of her sister?'

'Yes, the Bull's a good place to start looking,' Will agreed, and looked at Alejandro with a grudging new respect. 'Our father has often visited the Bull these past few months, listening for news of the princess, and knows many of the fellows who lodge there permanently. Even if he is not still there, the landlord may have seen him and be able to set you on the right road.'

'Then it's decided; we'll ride back to the Bull Inn before it gets too dark,' I told Alejandro firmly, then turned to my brother. 'We only have one horse, but you're welcome to travel with us.'

'Back to Woodstock?' Will shook his head, and I could see fear in his eyes. 'I'd rather take my chances on the road north, thanks.'

'Then this is farewell.'

We kissed and parted, my brother slipping through the gap in the hedgerow first. I watched his shadowy form move past us in the gathering dusk, following the narrow lane away from the village and towards open countryside where he planned to head north.

He had not been gone a minute when a shout was raised from the marketplace end of the lane. 'You there! Hold up!' Then came the sound of booted feet.

I had moved instinctively to shout after Will through the darkening gap in the hedgerow. I don't know what I meant to say. I probably meant to urge him to run, to escape as fast as he could from those pursuing him.

But Alejandro clamped a hand over my mouth and

dragged me hard against him, silencing me. He said nothing, and did not need to. I realized my folly at once, even though the urge to cry out after my brother was still strong. What would be the point in all three of us being taken? We might have done nothing wrong in coming here today, but Marcus Dent would soon find some excuse to detain us – and probably put me on trial as a witch too. I had intended to offer myself to Dent today in exchange for my aunt's life. But her callous murder had changed everything; I would rather suffer the same horrible death at the stake than agree to be such a monster's wife.

Dent would not dare touch Alejandro, of course. Only a fool would attack a Catholic novice now that the terrifying priests of the Spanish Inquisition had arrived in England. But I had never been important. The cruel and wealthy Marcus Dent could enjoy taking his leisurely revenge on my body for refusing him, and no one in Oxfordshire would raise a finger to stop him.

They caught my brother Will a few moments later. We heard a brief tussle between men further up the gloomy lane, then the distinct rasp of a blade being drawn, and I feared for my brother's life.

Someone called up the lane to 'Fetch Master Dent!' and the message came back – rather insolently, I thought – that Master Dent was in the ale-house with the magistrate, and to bring the Lytton boy there. The men dragged him back up the lane, Will protesting loudly all the way that they had got the wrong man, that he was innocent of any crime.

We stood in the mud ruts and listened to his struggles as they came towards us. So long as no one thought to look into the field that bordered the lane, we should be hidden by the friendly dusk and this hedgerow at our backs, its spiny branches peppered with white blossom. But my clothes were not dark enough, nor was my pale face. I would stand out against the hedgerow if anyone thought to glance over it, and then the men would have two more prisoners to show Master Dent.

I leaned against Alejandro and tried to weave my spell without making any sound, mouthing the words with only a thread of breath.

'*Obscure! Lady of the Night, cast your black cloak over us . . . Make us invisible to men . . . Invisible . . .*'

Grass grew coarse at the edge of the field, thrusting up as high as my waist in places. Its greeny-brown seedheads swayed and rustled gently in the breeze. I stared at the tall grasses as though my life depended on them, letting the spell fill the dark air around us.

The men were almost level with us. I could hear the scrape and thud of their boots on the mud track.

'*Obscure!*'

I closed my eyes, willing us to be invisible to them. A wood-pigeon cooed from a nearby copse as though calling for its mate; its deep throbbing note buzzed right through my body. I could not hold my breath any longer. But the spell held, at least. The men in the lane passed by without even bothering to make a search, still discussing what reward they might receive for my brother's capture. Their brutish voices faded as the men turned into the market square and headed away across the village.

I looked down at my hands and could see nothing. Not even my gown against the hedgerow. Nor Alejandro, his body warm beside mine.

We were both invisible.

I heard Alejandro's sharp intake of breath and hurriedly broke the spell, not wishing to alarm him.

'*Reveni!*'

Visible again, I felt light-headed, burning with anger as though with a high fever. I did not know what would happen if Alejandro were to let go of me, but I was glad he was there. Very glad indeed.

Part of me wanted to break away from Alejandro and run after those men like a howling banshee, screaming my beloved aunt's name in the darkness until they scattered in terror. But another part of me was afraid of those men, deeply and horribly afraid. The image of Aunt Jane's tortured face through the smoke and heat came back to haunt me, and it was all I could do not to faint again.

Held up by Alejandro's restraining arms, I did not move even after the men had gone. Perhaps I suspected that if I moved, I would fall to the ground like a puppet whose strings had been cut, my legs no longer able to support me.

'Well done,' he whispered in my ear.

I shook my head and felt his hands drop away. Tears of frustration pricked my eyes, though to my credit I managed to stay upright. I was ashamed of my fear and weakness. And something else: I was ashamed that I had been thinking about Alejandro while my brother was being dragged away.

'The letter . . .' I wiped my eyes with the back of my hand, unable to finish.

Alejandro nodded, an odd tension in his face. 'The letter,' he agreed grimly, and looked up at the first pale pinpricks of stars against the approaching blackness of night. 'It's time to find my servant Juan.'

We met Juan on the road and reached the Bull Inn just after midnight. As we entered the village, the Watch came round the corner, calling the hour aloud, and we had to duck back into the shadows until the old man with his swaying lantern had passed on his rounds.

Alejandro had helped me down from the cart just outside the small village of Woodstock, and told Juan to wait for us at the crossroads with both horses, safely out of sight behind a thick hedge of elder. We would continue on foot, so as not to alert anyone to our presence in the village.

I was exhausted, stumbling on towards the first houses like a drunkard, but what he had said made perfect sense. For all we knew, Dent was expecting us to call at the Bull Inn and might well have posted some of his men there, to watch for us.

I had done nothing treasonous. But if they could arrest one Lytton for fighting in the street, they could certainly arrest another for refusing to marry a man as influential as Marcus Dent.

Alejandro knocked softly at the bolted side door to the inn, and spoke to the landlord when he arrived. The man was irritated at being disturbed so late, but accepted a few coins in return for allowing us in off the street.

'You can't sleep here tonight,' he muttered, looking us up and down once he had finished bolting the door again. 'Not inside the inn, at any rate. There may be room in the stables for you,' he admitted, addressing Alejandro, 'but not the girl. It's a rough, dirty place, not suitable for a female.'

'Is Master Lytton here?' I demanded, ignoring the man's quick frown.

'What's it to you, girl?'

I threw back the hood of the travelling cloak Alejandro had given me to keep out the night's chill. 'I'm his daughter and I wish to see him.'

The landlord hesitated, licking his lips, and I knew with a thrill of certainty that my father was here.

I raised my hand and pointed at his face, speaking slowly and with power. 'We need to speak with Master Lytton tonight. You will show us where he is, and quickly. Take us to him now!'

SIXTEEN

Rebels

A few steps up the back stairs of the Bull Inn brought us to a tiny room set below the eaves, the ceiling as low as the door, the whole place in darkness. There we found my father slumped over a book by the light of a single candle, an empty flask of ale at his elbow, his shoes off, his clothes awry.

My father jerked upright as we entered, clearly alarmed at the intrusion. Then his face changed, and he sneered when he saw who it was.

'Get out, you weak-minded fool,' he told the landlord, and repeated this in a loud voice until the man stumbled away in confusion, dragging the door shut behind him.

My father was drunk, his words slurred.

I stood and looked at him, my temper flaring. My lips tried to form the word 'Father,' but I couldn't bring myself to breathe sound into his name. 'Where is the letter?'

'Which letter would that be?'

So he was going to play the ignorance game. Why was I surprised?

I stared across into my father's glazed, bloodshot eyes and knew him for the worst sort of cowardly traitor – a man who would not stir to help his own blood. The heat of my fury was as white-hot as the fire that had consumed my aunt.

'The letter you stole instead of allowing it to reach the magistrate,' I said delicately into the silence. 'The letter written by the Lady Elizabeth at your suggestion, begging for my aunt to be released and for the charges against her to be dropped.'

My father was surprised by how much I knew: it was in his eyes. But he kept smiling as he struggled to his feet. His chair fell backwards with a crash. 'I see, I see. And why on earth would I do that, eh?'

'So you and my cousin could take the letter abroad to persuade the Queen's enemies of Elizabeth's support.'

My father laughed then, rather wildly, and swayed, almost falling.

'You always were a clever child, Meg. Far cleverer than your brother, that's for certain. A pity you were born a girl. You could have had a promising career at Oxford or Cambridge.'

I stared at him, and struggled hard against the impulse to tell him precisely what I thought of him. He was still my father, and I had to love and respect him.

Honour thy father and thy mother.

I wondered why God would enforce such an impossible commandment when He must know how many unworthy fathers crawled on the face of the earth.

'You left her to burn,' I said hoarsely. I shook my head, utterly at a loss. 'My mother's sister, the woman who raised me from a baby. Why would you do such a terrible thing?'

'Your aunt died so that England can become free,' my father told me, throwing his shoulders back as though proud of what he had done. 'Yes, that letter will rally the Queen's enemies to our cause. Believe me, Meg, I didn't want your aunt's death on my conscience. But there was no other way. If Malcolm had succeeded in persuading you to allow him five minutes alone with the princess, he could have taken some other token of her support to the Low Countries. But when your aunt was taken by Dent, we suddenly saw what could be done with a letter of clemency from the Lady Elizabeth.' He smiled. 'You played your part in that well, Meg. I was proud of you.'

'You tricked me. You left Aunt Jane to die.'

'She was a proven witch!'

I looked at him steadily. 'I am a witch too, Father. Aunt Jane taught me her craft. What do you say to that? Would you have left me to burn too?'

He seemed unsteady on his feet, and leaned against the desk, staring at me. 'You . . . a witch?'

'Did you never suspect?'

His mouth moved silently, as though praying. 'Sweet Jesus. These last few years, yes, there were signs that you were no longer the good child I remembered, so innocent . . . I guessed your aunt must hold some strange influence over you. She was always a dark, secretive creature; she and your mother were forever whispering in corners. But I did not know how far it had gone between the two of you.' He sat down heavily, a frown knitting his thick brows. 'Does Dent know what you are?'

I nodded, and saw my father's face grow pale.

'You little fool,' was all he managed, not looking at me, but I could see that he was troubled.

'And what of my brother?' I asked angrily. 'Why did you run away in the night with Malcolm, when you knew Will would try to save Aunt Jane?'

My father hesitated. I could see remorse in his face, but also the dogged belief that he had done no wrong. 'Your brother weakened. He would not see that his aunt's death was a noble sacrifice to the cause. Yes, Will wanted to use the letter to save her life. But that would have lost us the chance to rouse the princess's followers and lead an army against the Queen. So Malcolm and I decided to leave Lytton Park without him, and intercept the letter ourselves. Besides, Will is safer at home.'

'Will was arrested earlier this evening. He had gone to see if he could change Dent's mind about condemning Aunt Jane, but he was too late to save her. As I was too.' My voice cracked a little with pain. 'We saw him dragged away by Dent's men. I don't know on what charge.'

My father ran a hand across his forehead. 'Dent will not harm him,' he muttered, but I could see this unexpected news had left him uneasy. 'He is a witchfinder, and my son at least is innocent of that foul charge. You had better pray you do not fall into Dent's hands though if he knows you took some knowledge of the dark arts from your aunt.'

We sat a while in silence. I was so tired I could hardly speak, nor think what was to be done in this unholy mess.

My father stood and went to the washbowl. He wiped his face with a damp cloth and straightened his clothes, the effects of the ale slowly beginning to fall away. But he could not disguise any more what he had become over the years – a drunkard and a coward. My father's once handsome face seemed dissolute to me now, fallen into deep lines and creases, his breath reeking from the ale he had been drinking.

Suddenly, Alejandro slammed his hand down on the table, making us both jump. 'The princess's letter,' he reminded my father fiercely. 'Where is it? We have wasted enough time here with the princess's life at stake.'

My father straightened, staring at him. 'I do not know you, sir,' he said with cold dignity. 'Nor why you come here in the company of my daughter. But I do know a Spaniard when I smell one.'

Alejandro's eyes narrowed on my father's face, but otherwise he seemed unmoved by the insult. 'My name is Alejandro de Castillo, Master Lytton. The rest need not concern you, though you may rest assured that your daughter is perfectly safe in my company.'

My cheeks were tinged with heat, my temper quickly rising. How dare my father speak like that to Alejandro? I was desperately ashamed of my own kin and wished I had not seen my father in this state. But I also knew what I had to do.

'Just give us the letter and we'll leave you in peace,' I told my father angrily, impatient now to be out of that stinking little room. 'If it should be used in any uprising against the Queen, the princess will be charged with treason. I should never have asked the Lady Elizabeth to write it, for it did no good and may yet do great harm.'

There was a silence. My father walked to the chamber window and back, his gait still unsteady.

'I don't have the letter,' he said at last.

Alejandro raised his dark brows. 'And you expect us to believe that?'

'It makes no odds whether or not you believe me,' my father said bluntly, and I knew from his face that he was speaking the truth. He indicated his jacket on the bed, his book and papers on the table. 'Search me, if you must. Search this room. You will not find the Lady Elizabeth's letter.'

Alejandro took him at his word and searched the room rapidly but with meticulous care. He glanced across at me afterwards and shook his head.

'Where is it, then?' I demanded.

'Since there is little harm in it, I shall tell you. We had just turned south towards London and the coast when we heard a troop of soldiers coming towards us on the road to Woodstock Palace.'

I stared, horrified. 'Troops, heading for Woodstock?'

My father shrugged. 'I do not know what their business was there. We turned aside into the woods to avoid being seen, but my horse stumbled in a rabbit-hole. Once we saw that he was lame, we knew my part in this mission was finished. Malcolm rode on alone with the letter while I led my horse back here,' my father admitted, and smiled when I stood, looking at Alejandro with fresh hope. 'Do not waste your time. As soon as he reaches the coast, your cousin intends to buy a passage on the first ship to the Low Countries. In a few days' time, both Malcolm and the letter will be safely abroad.'

I felt sick with disappointment. 'I do not understand. Why . . . why do this, Father?'

He did not meet my gaze, fiddling with the papers on the table, though his voice hardened. 'Someone had to do *something*,' he muttered angrily. 'This country has been sold out to a foreign power. Our too-pious Queen has married a Spanish Catholic and brought England to its knees. Already we are overrun with these Spaniards and their idolatrous priests. The Inquisition roasts heretics in our streets every day. The whole world is afraid.' He shook his head. 'You weep for the princess. Yet her life, my life, even your brother's life . . . none of these are worth losing England for.'

I shook my head, sure beyond everything that his way was not the one to choose. 'You're wrong, Father. Elizabeth will be Queen soon enough, and to risk her life by trying to hurry that day . . . that is how you will lose England.'

'How can Elizabeth be Queen unless we rise up against this Spanish union?' my father scoffed. 'The Queen is with child!'

'There will be no child,' I said quietly. 'Not now, not ever. I have seen it.'

'Where? In the fire? In your aunt's crystal?'

My father was laughing at me. He thought I was a fool, an apprentice who had overstepped their place. My fists clenched at my side. I wanted to show him precisely what I could do, stifle that mocking laughter in his throat. How surprised he would be when he saw that my skills were no longer those of a mere apprentice. Though I would not allow my temper to get the better of me this time. He might be a traitor to his family but he was still my father, after all.

'I have seen it in a horoscope calculated by the hand of John Dee.'

'The astrologer?"

I should not have said anything and I knew it. I had promised the Lady Elizabeth that I would hold my tongue and tell no one of John Dee's visit to Woodstock.

Still, at least my father's mockery had been silenced. He stared from my face to Alejandro's, half disbelieving, half excited by this revelation. He might mock and loathe women's magick, but it was clear that he believed in John Dee's skill as an astrologer.

Alejandro touched my arm gently. 'Time to go.'

I nodded, and left my father's room without another

word. I did not know if I would ever see him again, and at that moment I did not much care.

We made our way down the narrow stairs in silence, only a single lantern at the bottom lighting our way. Reaching the last stair, I sagged against the wall, suddenly too exhausted to go on.

Alejandro put an arm about my waist to support me. 'You can't travel any further tonight.'

'I must,' I whispered, though in truth I could hardly keep my eyes open, the lids were so heavy. 'The letter . . .'

'Will have to wait until first light,' he finished sternly. 'There's no moon tonight and the roads will be treacherous. Your cousin can hardly be riding through a moonless night to the coast. No, he'll be waiting until morning too. Besides, you're barely able to stand, let alone travel. Let's get some sleep now and pursue your cousin tomorrow.'

I stared, too tired to follow his logic. 'But the landlord said the inn was full, that there were only stables left.'

'Then the stables it will have to be.' His mouth twisted in a smile at last, seeing my surprise. 'What? If a lowly stable was good enough for the Blessed Virgin Mary, it should be good enough for us.'

Slipping quietly between the horses, I made my way to the back of the stables and set the lantern on a dusty shelf there. I made a nest by its flickering light amongst broken and discarded saddle leathers and old horse blankets. There was straw and muck underfoot, and the whole place smelled powerfully of horseflesh.

But I was too exhausted to care about these smelly and dirty surroundings. Sleep was the only thing I could think about. Sleep, and Alejandro.

Shaking out the straw-soiled blankets, I tried to think back to those simple days before the Lady Elizabeth was brought to Woodstock. The days of my childhood with Aunt Jane at Lytton Park. But the memories were so hazy; they seemed to belong to another life, another Meg, who had long since forgotten and outgrown them. That haziness distressed me. I did not want to forget Aunt Jane, however painful the memories.

I shuddered. I would never forget her death.

Sorrow was throbbing inside me, raw as a fresh wound. But I would not allow it to drive me towards the same fate my poor aunt had suffered. Not least because I could hardly retrieve Elizabeth's letter if I was dead. And since my shameful family was to blame for its theft, it was up to me to get it back.

Alejandro came back just as I finished making my bed. 'Juan won't have to sleep under the cart after all,' he told me, clearly suppressing a grin. 'He's found himself a room upstairs in the inn.'

I was astonished. 'How did he manage that?'

'Oh, some serving woman who's already sampled his Spanish charms has given him her bed to share. That's what the old rascal told me anyway. So at least one of us will be warm and comfortable tonight.'

I felt my cheeks grow hot as I realized what he meant. I glanced down at the nest I had made, padded liberally with horse blankets, the coarse wool prickly with hairs but making a softer bed than straw and hard earth. There was more than enough room for two.

'Do you want to . . . to share my bed?' I struggled to find the right words, my face growing hotter as I saw him turn back from trimming the lantern, his eyes on my face. 'That is, you won't get much sleep lying on the hard ground. I have plenty of blankets here, and . . .'

Alejandro's expression changed and began to harden, as though I had offended him deeply. His whole body had stiffened while I was speaking, and now he seemed to be drawing back into himself, his jaw clenched against whatever he was thinking – once more refusing to speak his mind, as he so often did in my company.

Did he want to share my bed?

What a question to have asked, and in a poor lantern-lit stable with only these rough beasts for company. If I had leaped over and kissed him full on the mouth, I could not have thrown myself at him more wantonly. I wished myself a thousand miles away from the Bull Inn, seeing how his mouth had tightened, the brooding in his aristocratic face intensifying.

Yet despite my embarrassment, I heard myself finish

what I had intended to say. 'There's no need for you to be uncomfortable tonight, Alejandro.'

It was the first time I could remember ever having used his name.

Alejandro closed the lantern with a soft click and trod silently towards me, his face unreadable as ever. 'Meg,' he remarked quietly, looking away from me as though the would-be priest could not bear even this single moment of intimacy between us. 'I'm flattered by this invitation to share your bed, truly I am.'

'No, indeed I—'

He hushed my breathless denial, holding up a hand. 'You and I had a difficult beginning, Meg. When we first met, I considered you an unsuitable companion for the Lady Elizabeth. You seemed so wild, headstrong, opinionated, even immoral. But I've come to understand you better over the past few months, and I realize now . . .' Slowly his gaze rose from the muck-strewn stable floor to my face. 'I realize you would never offer such a thing lightly.'

The longer he spoke, the redder I became. By the time he had finished his speech, my cheeks were so hot I could probably have outshone the lantern. Hurriedly, I tried to back out of the noose I had so provocatively thrust my head into.

'I just meant you could sleep here too,' I stammered. 'As in *sleep*. It wasn't meant to be an invitation to do something else.'

He had come so close now, we were almost touching. His body blocked out the light from the lantern. My heart hammered in my chest. I stared up at him, suddenly unsure. What did I want here? To beckon him on, and risk both his rejection and his disgust? Or to say no, and live with this turmoil in my heart?

Alejandro had stopped. He looked at my face for a long moment without speaking, perhaps seeing some shadow of my pain there. Then his hand came up slowly, as though approaching a wild animal, and stroked the loose hair back from my face, tucking it under my cap.

'Of course not,' he murmured. 'Pray accept my deepest apologies. I mistook your meaning.'

Far from reassuring me, this confused me even further. His touch sent my poor nerves skittering. I caught my lower lip between my teeth, and saw his gaze narrow on the movement. I was acutely aware that we were alone in the stable. There was no one else here to see or know if we kissed each other, to run and tell my father.

Nor even if we chose to . . . to go further.

With great daring, I placed one hand flat on his chest, next to the silver cross which hung there. I remembered making its silver burn his hand. Tonight it was cool.

Alejandro stiffened at my touch, but did not draw away. I cocked my head to one side and listened to the erratic thud of his heart under my fingertips. His heart was beating as fast as my own. Perhaps faster.

Alejandro might be a Catholic priest in training. But he was still a man, and he *wanted* me.

I looked up into his eyes. 'Alejandro.'

He made an odd sound under his breath, and his hand came up to cover mine. In the chill darkness of the stable, the warmth seemed to beat off him in waves. Then slowly, with deliberate care, Alejandro unpeeled my fingers from his chest, one by one, and lowered my hand back to my side.

My cheeks flared with shame. How could I have been so wrong *twice*? He did not want me, and my touch had embarrassed and offended him.

The cruel hurt of his rejection was like a punch to the stomach. Biting my lip hard, I turned my head away. I did not want Alejandro to see my expression. He must not know the pain I was in, thanks to my idiotic mistake.

He was to be a priest!

How could I have forgotten that?

'I'm sorry,' I muttered, risking a quick glance at his face.

His face was twisted in a grimace, his brows drawn together as though in pain. 'No, it is I who should be sorry. I told your father you would be safe in my company. Instead, I have allowed an unacceptable intimacy to take place. Now you ought to get some sleep. It's very late and we'll be leaving at first light.'

I stumbled as I turned away. *What had I been thinking?*

Alejandro caught my arm. 'No, wait. Let me explain.' His voice sounded tortured. I turned, staring up into his face.

'You do not understand, and why should you? It is not merely that I will become a priest soon, for members of my order are permitted to marry, so long as they marry under the strict rules of chastity handed down to us in the Order of Santiago, where a husband may only spend a few nights of the year with his wife. But . . .'

I touched his cheek, unable to bear his pain. 'But you cannot be with a witch?'

Again, with the utmost gentleness, Alejandro removed my hand from his face and lowered it to my side.

'If it is a witch who does no harm to any living person and works only good magick, never killing nor conjuring the spirits of the dead—'

'I have always followed that path,' I interrupted him. 'And my aunt too. It is the path of white magick, the path of the hearth fire.'

'Hush,' he said, and shook his head. There was pain in his face. 'No, I could not be even with the purest of witches, a woman who works both magick and God's will. For you do not know my past. You do not know what I have done.'

'Then tell me,' I urged him, not understanding.

'When I was a young boy, about seven years old, I knew a woman named Julia. She was one of my father's servants. One day, I was walking in the woods near our country home, and I saw Julia . . .' Alejandro hesitated, then frowned. 'I saw her working magick, casting some kind of spell over a fire and making incantations. I realized then that Julia was a witch. A servant from our own household . . . a witch!'

My blood ran cold. 'What did you do?' I whispered.

'I ran straight home and told my father. Even at that young age, I knew witchcraft was evil. But I swear I had no idea how severe her punishment would be. There was a trial, at which I gave evidence of what I had seen that day, and Julia was condemned to burn as a witch.'

He stopped, and I saw a damp sheen over his eyes. Was Alejandro crying?

'It was a warm bright spring, all the new buds opening on the trees in the square. My father made me stand and watch her execution. I remember the smell of the smoke, the priests' faces, her cries for mercy . . .' His voice became low. 'There is one more thing to tell. Just before she died, Julia cursed me. She swore by all the demons in Hell that if I ever fell in love, the woman I loved would die in childbirth. And my baby son with her.'

I stared up at him, horrified, my skin creeping.

'So you see,' Alejandro finished, 'I can never allow myself to get too close to any woman. For death is the fate that would await both her and my unborn child.' He dropped my hand at last and took a step backwards. His gaze lingered on the makeshift bed I had made. 'Now you must get some rest. I will wake you just before dawn.'

'Thank you,' I managed, and could not believe how steady my voice sounded. As a child in Spain, Alejandro had informed on a witch and been the unwitting instrument of her death. I tried to hide my shudder. Would he do the same to me one day?

'Don't fret about this night's delay. We will get the princess's letter back even if we have to sail to the Low Countries to find it.' Alejandro gave me a sombre smile which I guessed was intended to reassure me, then turned away. 'Sleep well, Meg Lytton.'

SEVENTEEN
The Gift

I was woken by the sound of Juan's voice at the stable door, and sat up at once, still tired after a troubled night. Alejandro and his servant were conversing in low voices, though even if they had spoken more clearly I could not have understood, for they were speaking in Spanish. I climbed out of the blankets, shook out my crumpled skirts and did my best to make myself presentable.

The sky was still dark, though flushed with a glowing light along the far horizon. I stood at the door, hoping I did not still have straw in my hair.

Alejandro turned and saw me. He came towards me at once, his gaze searching my face. 'Did you sleep well?'

I nodded, and glanced at Juan over his shoulder. 'Are we ready to go? It's a long journey to the coast.'

'We're not going to the coast.'

'What?'

'Juan says your father was mistaken. Your cousin Malcolm has not gone directly to the coast.' Alejandro indicated his servant, who was busy saddling the stallion, and Juan gave me his odd, lopsided grin. 'Apparently he spent last night not far from here, at the home of one

Tom Dorville.' He saw my instinctive reaction. 'What is it? You know this man?'

I remembered the quiet young man I had met here at the Bull in my brother's company, and whose watchful gaze I had mistrusted. His name had been Tom.

'I think so, yes,' I agreed. 'One of my brother's friends from Oxford. Where did Juan hear this?'

Juan grinned again, said something incomprehensible and pointed to the upstairs windows of the Bull Inn.

Alejandro hesitated. 'From Anne, the serving woman he was with last night. She heard your cousin talking to this Tom Dorville in the taproom. He was trying to persuade the young man to lend him a faster horse than his own.'

'That sounds like Malcolm,' I said drily.

'Anne has given us directions to Dorville's house,' Alejandro told her.

'Then let us waste no more time, but go there at once. All I need is a moment to freshen myself, then I will be ready.'

Abruptly, Alejandro nodded to his servant to fetch the cart. He had a stubborn look about his eyes. 'You should stay here while we follow him. I fear there may be trouble, and it will be safer for you to wait here. Anne has offered you her chamber if you wish to rest and take your breakfast away from prying eyes. It is only a small room, Juan says, but private.'

I realized with a shock that he meant to leave me behind,

to take no further part in this chase. 'But he's my cousin. It's my fault the letter was written in the first place, and that it was stolen.'

'No, I was mad to let you come this far. It is too dangerous for a woman. You must go back to Woodstock Palace and wait with the Lady Elizabeth. That is where your place is now, not riding about the countryside in search of spies and renegades.'

'And what if I refuse to go back to Woodstock without the letter?'

'You have no choice. I will not take you with me, and that is final.'

'Then I will go alone,' I said obstinately. 'On foot, if needs be.'

'Don't be a fool!' His face tightened in anger. 'Do you not see how impossible it is for me to take you along? You could have been killed yesterday. I will not have your death on my conscience too.'

'*Too?*' I echoed, not understanding, then saw his expression, the despair behind his anger.

'Like the woman I betrayed when I was young,' he muttered.

'You were only a boy, Alejandro. You made a terrible mistake and a woman died for it. That does not make her death your fault.' I drew a sharp breath, determined not to give way. 'Whatever happens today, you will not be to blame. I go with you of my own free will.'

'I can't allow—' he began raggedly, but I interrupted.

'It's done, I'm coming,' I insisted, my chin held high, and hurried back inside to fetch my cloak before Alejandro could leave without me.

I ignored the little voice at the back of my mind that told me I was growing too close to Alejandro, and he was right to be so cautious.

Alejandro was cursed. He had freely admitted that he had no intention of ever falling in love with a woman – let alone a suspected witch like myself. And I was not foolish enough to look too deep into the eyes of a would-be priest. So what danger could there be?

It was less than an hour later when we reached Tom Dorville's house, which lay not far from the Bull Inn in the next valley. The narrow road clung to the river for a while, crossing it occasionally, then moved back into heavy woodland. The house stood back from the road, only reached by a shady track which we almost passed without seeing.

Alejandro reined in his stallion and sat a moment with his hand raised, listening. Juan pulled the cart in behind him and waited patiently.

It was still early. The sun had slowly risen, bringing a gentle mist to the dew-damp grasslands and verges. The morning was quiet, only birdsong above us and the gurgling rush of water from the nearby river. Nonetheless, Alejandro seemed to have heard something out of the ordinary.

'Horses,' he said, with quiet authority, and pointed down the track. 'We're in time. They haven't left yet.'

The hairs rose on the back of my neck and my stomach pitched, queasy with nerves. It had been one thing to talk of confronting my cousin and demanding the return of Elizabeth's letter, but now that we were here, I was suddenly unsure. Alejandro had warned me there might be trouble, that this could be dangerous. Was I ready to see Alejandro fight my cousin over this?

But I was here for a purpose, I reminded myself sternly. I was not some helpless girl, an onlooker with no real power. I did not want to see either Malcolm or Alejandro hurt. But if using my gift meant risking my cousin's life, then so be it. He had made his choice when he accepted the stolen letter from my father and agreed to carry it to the Queen's enemies in the Low Countries.

Juan scrambled down from the cart and ran, half crouching, along the track towards Tom Dorville's house.

He returned a few minutes later and went straight to his master, clutching Alejandro's stirrup as he whispered hoarsely up at him, 'Four men. The two younger getting ready to mount up, the others remaining behind.'

Alejandro nodded. 'We can't take them here then,' he mused. 'Not with those odds.'

'An ambush, further along the road?'

'Yes,' Alejandro agreed. He glanced thoughtfully at the sheep in the field opposite. 'Unless we have mistaken their purpose, they will be taking the road south. If you drive on ahead, as fast as you can, and set your cart across the road at some narrow point, I will endeavour to slow them up. Then I will follow cross-country and hope to rejoin the road behind you.'

'What are you going to do?' I asked, trying to keep the anxiety out of my voice.

'What all good country boys know should never on any account be done,' he told me, and grinned, turning his reluctant horse towards the field. 'I'm going to drive that herd of sheep across the road. That ought to give you five minutes at least.'

Before I could make any answer to this, Juan had leaped up on the cart beside me and lashed the whip several times over the horse's flanks, shouting in Spanish.

It may not have understood his words, but the tone of urgency and the whip being laid repeatedly about its sides left the animal in no doubt. The horse reared up in the shafts, then pitched forward at speed. The cart jolted along behind it, the high ruts in the lane shaking us violently from side to side.

I could not glance back for fear of losing my seat, but clung on grimly.

We continued at that pace for nearly a mile. The road there snaked down a sharp incline towards the rocky river bed, almost a stream at that point, and crossed through the water in a ford. In flood time, I guessed the road must be all but impassable here. But the weather had been so dry in recent weeks, the river had shrunk to a quiet current, little more than ankle-high to enter and reaching to the knee in the centre.

Juan lashed the horse through the ford, water spraying out from the cart wheels. I clutched at the skirts of my gown, drawing them close as we reached the middle of the ford, but we were safe enough up on the seat. The ground rose up there, taking us onto the other side, and that was where Juan drew the cart round.

He threw the reins to me and jumped down to drag on the horse's bridle. 'Hai! Hai!' he shouted, and clucked his tongue strongly, urging the beast across the road.

Soon the cart was across the lane, completely blocking the exit from the ford. The horse whinnied and plunged restlessly, unhappy with its position, but Juan stroked its muzzle and muttered in its ear until the animal stopped rolling its eyes and quietened down.

In the sudden stillness, I caught a distant thud of hooves behind us on the track.

Juan grinned up at me, apparently unconcerned by the realization that we were about to have company. 'Down, *señorita*,' he ordered in his thick Spanish accent, and gestured me to climb down from the cart. He glanced about, then pointed me towards a sunlit break in the trees along the high-banked verge. 'You hide now, yes?'

I did not bother to argue, though I was determined not

to stand idly by when Malcolm and his friend came thundering down into the waters of the ford, as I knew they must do at any moment.

Clambering up the bank, I bent under the low gnarled branches of a hazel and waited there, almost in a crouch, the soft brownish catkins dangling against my cheek and throat. I felt some sympathy for the horse as it stamped and sweated, shivering its flanks to brush off the flies as they landed. I too was restless and full of nervous energy, unwilling to stand passive in the face of approaching danger.

Two riders appeared on the bend, cloaked as though for a long journey and bent low over their horses' necks at the gallop.

As both riders came down the hill, they hauled on the reins to slow their pace, no doubt seeing the unexpected obstruction that blocked the road beyond the ford, and reached the water's edge at a cautious walk.

I stared hard at Malcolm through the green shade of leaves and catkins.

Did he have the princess's letter?

Malcolm stiffened at the sight of Juan and his cart drawn across the road. He reined in his horse and glanced sideways at Tom, who was also eyeing the swarthy old Spaniard with suspicion and distrust.

'What do you think?' he asked Tom, probably because his friend knew this area so well.

'Never seen him before. He's a stranger.'

My cousin nodded, his face tense. He flicked back his cloak to reach the hilt of his sword, though he did not draw it but merely loosened it in the scabbard.

'You there!' he shouted across the sunlit water. 'Why don't you move the cart? It's blocking the lane. What's wrong?'

Unable to make any kind of intelligent reply, and no doubt playing for time until the arrival of his master, Juan managed a series of odd grunts and grimaces of his weatherbeaten face that left the two young men in a fit of impatience.

Sitting on his horse at the water's edge, Tom pointed at the offending cart. 'Get that damn thing out of our way,' he ordered Juan. 'And at once, man. We're in a hurry, can you not see that?'

'Is he a simpleton?' Malcolm demanded. He glared about the shady lane, eyes narrowed, clearly on the alert for signs of a trap.

Not ready yet for him to see me, I shrank further back into the shade of the hazel tree and caught my breath in pain. I'd scratched my face on a branch. It stung and my cheek felt wet. Yet I did not dare raise my hand to check any bleeding, in case one of them spotted the sudden movement and realized that Juan was not alone.

'He's a foreigner.' Tom swore under his breath. 'A Spaniard, I'd stake my life on it.'

'*A Spaniard?* Here, in Oxfordshire?'

'I don't know why you should be so surprised, Malcolm. These filthy Spaniards spread themselves through our land like a disease.' Tom spurred his horse forward through the water with tiny splashing noises. 'If the fool cannot understand plain English, I'll make him understand with the tip of my sword instead.'

The pain of cutting my cheek had left me angry and on edge. Where was Alejandro?

I stared at Tom riding through the ford, and then at Malcolm, still arrogantly astride his horse on the other side, and let the anger fill me. Oh, I knew I should leave it to Alejandro to get the letter back his own way. But I disliked how Tom had called them 'filthy Spaniards' and likened them to a 'disease'. So what if Alejandro had not yet reached us? I did not need him – or any man – to fight Malcolm on my behalf. Not with this tingling from my scalp to the tips of my fingers.

The power stirred inside me, warm as the blood in my veins, and I stared, my lips dry, my ears ringing, my whole body tensed with the desire to work magick.

Juan had not flinched, though Tom was almost out of the water, his sword drawn now and flashing in the sun. The old Spaniard did not even glance over his shoulder, though he must have been wondering where his master was. His eyes very dark, he stood motionless beside the cart and waited.

I hissed, and Tom stiffened. His horse faltered, finding an awkward footing beneath the water.

With an ugly oath, Tom snatched at the reins and dragged the horse's head up.

'What is it?' Malcolm called.

'Nothing,' Tom replied, but he was frowning now, less certain of himself. His gaze searched the leafy banks in vain; the sun was in his eyes. Besides, I was crouched in the shadows. My cloak hid me amongst the rough trunks, and the dangling catkins hung darkly yellow as my hair, clustered thickly on the branches around me.

Again, I hissed.

The unpleasant sound reverberated about the trees, sibilant, seeming to come from everywhere at once. A ridge of cloud shifted across the burning face of the sun, and suddenly the lane was strangely dark. The horse's ears pricked forward, and its liquid eyes rolled uneasily.

Tom caught his mount's mood and swore again, angry and impatient. He slid down from the animal's back and stood there, staring first at Juan, then at the stranded cart blocking the road, and finally about himself in the shady lane. His hand wavered on the sword hilt, but he brought the weapon up and pointed it at Juan.

'Move the cart,' he instructed him clearly. 'Or die.'

There was sweat on my forehead. I stepped out slightly from between the trees. I heard Malcolm's exclamation as he saw me, but ignored him. It was too late now to worry about that. We had come here to get the stolen letter back, and that was all I could think about.

I lowered my head and raised my eyes, as I had seen my aunt do a hundred times before, standing within the protection of the circle to call on the spirits.

I spread my hands out, palms open, and fixed my gaze on Tom's astonished face. 'Throw away the sword,' I told him in a clear voice. 'You do not need it.'

'I do not . . . need it?'

'Throw the sword away, Tom. The weapon is burning your hand. Can you not feel the heat?'

Tom frowned, then stared down at the sword hilt in his hand. With a sudden gasp, he threw the weapon away from him. 'It burns!'

The sound of approaching hoofbeats was a maddening distraction I could have done without. Tom heard them too and stiffened. He blinked and glanced back at Malcolm in confusion, then down at his sword glistening in the water as if unsure how it had got there.

Malcolm shook himself with an effort. He too had been caught by my spell. Awkwardly, he urged his horse into the flowing water.

'Tom, it's an ambush!' he cried. 'That's Meg. She must be working with the Spanish now. We still have the letter, let's get out of here!'

Tom's face cleared as he realized what had happened. He turned and scrabbled for his horse, but it was too late. With a crash of undergrowth, the sun suddenly burning hot overhead again, Alejandro burst into the narrow lane opposite my hiding place, a stone's throw from the cart on the side of the ford.

EIGHTEEN

Liberty

Alejandro wheeled his sweating horse violently about to face the two other men. He would have looked like a devil in his black jacket if it had not been for the ornate silver cross swinging about his neck. Without taking his eyes from them, Alejandro drew his sword of Spanish steel.

'So you are happy to die for England, thief?' His voice was grim as he addressed Malcolm across the sunlit ford. 'Draw your sword, and meet me. Your wish is about to come true.'

'It will be a pleasure to spit you on my steel, Spaniard,' Malcolm growled in return and drew his own weapon.

Tom had pulled himself up onto his horse again. The animal was still nervous, floundering in the shallow water as he tried to wrench its head round and head back the way they had come.

I hissed again, using all my power, and saw the horse roll its eyes wildly, then rear up, unseating Tom and casting him with a loud splash into the water.

Alejandro's horse had whinnied uneasily at my hiss but he controlled it with a word and a squeeze of his knees. '*Dios!*' he muttered, and shot me a look which made my cheeks flush with heat.

Was he angry that I had used my power? I shook that fear away. The consequences of using it no longer mattered. The letter was all that mattered, and while Malcolm held it, Elizabeth and the future of the whole country lay under threat.

'Tom?' Furious, his face red, Malcolm drove his horse deeper into the ford. He leaned down to help a sodden, gasping Tom back to his feet, then raised his head to glare across at Alejandro. 'Bid your little pet be silent and keep her witch's spells to herself. Unless you cannot fight without a woman's help, Spaniard?'

Alejandro glanced at me on the leafy bank and I nodded my agreement, though reluctantly. I had done what I could. Now it was up to Alejandro to retrieve the letter from Malcolm. My cousin knew too much about my power; he had made himself proof against my influence. But he would not be proof against Alejandro's swordplay.

The two horsemen met in the middle of the flowing water, each as keen as the other to prove himself. I had never seen Alejandro look so fierce, his dark eyes shining, his cloak thrown back to leave his fighting arm free.

The loud clash of their swords sent birds flying up from the hedgerows. Malcolm swayed under that first blow, perhaps not having expected to meet such strength in Alejandro's arm. He parried the stroke well enough, but fell back slightly, swearing an oath under his breath as he was forced to give ground.

Alejandro followed him hard, pressing his advantage with a second blow, then a third. This time I saw Malcolm flinch under the violent clash of blades.

I felt sick with apprehension, not wishing to see either of them hurt. Yet if my cousin would not willingly hand over the letter we had come for . . .

The ground under the horses' hooves was treacherous and shifted constantly, slippery from the water. Alejandro controlled his horse with a relentless hand, and the stallion responded, knowing its master well. Malcolm had more trouble on his borrowed horse, and cursed as his mount faltered and slipped. Dragging its head up, he only just turned away in time as Alejandro's sword flashed down across his unprotected shoulder.

'Yield!' Alejandro insisted. 'Yield, and return the stolen letter you keep there.'

'Never!' Malcolm gasped, and twisted to avoid the lunge of Alejandro's sword. He was holding his ground, and bravely too, but I could see that my cousin was tiring more quickly than his more skilled opponent. Alejandro had been trained as a soldier in Spain, after all, and had been in the thick of a fight more than once. Malcolm had no such experience to draw on.

My skin prickled and my head swam, leaving me momentarily dizzy.

It was a warning. I looked down and saw Tom scrambling up the bank towards my hiding place, his clothes still dripping from the river, an unsheathed dagger in his hand. I could have called for Juan, who was watching the fight intently from atop the cart, but I did not wish to distract Alejandro. If he were to make a mistake now, look away even for a second . . .

Narrowing my eyes, I stared down at Tom and spoke softly. 'There is nothing you can do to hurt me. You feel too weak. Too weak to go any further.'

Tom hesitated, his face uncertain. Then he shook his head. His mouth twisted in a snarl. 'Keep quiet, witch! I know what you are trying to do. You think you can unman me with your foul spells.' He continued climbing. 'But I shall catch you, Meg Lytton, and make you wish you had never dabbled in the dark arts.'

I spread my hands wide, my fingers held long and strong, and asked the spirits of the trees about me for strength. I called on the damp earth, and on the power of the making. The fresh greenery and the birdsong, the blue sky and the babbling stream: all these filled me. My body began to vibrate, blocking out the clash of swords below us, the smell of human fear.

Tom straightened up, coming towards me. He licked his lips, and his eyes moved up and down my body. 'I cannot pretend not to have wondered what it would be like to see you unclothed.' His smile was cold, and I knew he was enjoying himself. 'By the time I'm finished, you'll be ready for the fire . . . just like your devil-worshipping aunt.'

He had looked at me in the same way that night in the Bull Inn, yet I had not then recognized Tom for what he was – a traitor to Elizabeth, and to his unhappy country. I had thought him quiet, when in truth he was scheming and two-faced.

Carefully, I pictured Tom in my mind's eye, just as my aunt had taught me. I sketched his face against the inner darkness, his cruel eyes, his sneer, the grasping hands. Then I made this inner Tom suddenly grimace and step back, as though encountering some dreadful creature. I widened his cruel eyes and pulled his sneer wide until it was a gaping 'O', then imagined a buzzing that grew in intensity until I could feel it rumble through every bone in my body. Only then did I whisper the words beneath my breath, finishing with his name, 'Tom Dorville.'

The spell was almost too late.

I smelled his reeking breath on my face, felt his hands on my shoulders, then abruptly Tom was staggering back, his face contorted, his hands flailing wildly about his head as though batting away a swarm of angry wasps.

Tom turned with a cry and ran, only to catch his foot in a briar and tumble down the bank. He landed headfirst in the shallow waters of the ford.

I heard Juan's startled exclamation. Then he was halfway up the bank, grinning and holding out a friendly hand. 'Come, *señorita*,' he urged me in his thick Spanish accent. 'Back to the cart.'

The other two were still hard at it. Both had dismounted and were fighting on foot, hand-to-hand, up to their knees in water. The horses stood together on the bank, wet-flanked and shivering. As Juan helped me up onto the cart seat, I saw Malcolm slip as he lunged. Alejandro's answering lunge passed through my cousin's feeble defence – a flash of silver in the shady lane – and suddenly Malcolm was standing still as stone, with the fierce point of Alejandro's sword at his throat.

'Yield,' Alejandro repeated, and now his voice shook with exhaustion.

Malcolm's eyes were desperate. 'Better kill me,' he said, 'for I have failed England.'

'That letter would have brought nothing but a traitor's death for the Lady Elizabeth and more sorrow to a country already at war with itself.' Alejandro gestured to Malcolm's sword. 'Throw it down.'

Malcolm obeyed and stood trembling in the water, his gaze narrowed on the one who had bested him.

'Now give me the letter, and you may go free.'

My cousin hesitated, looking from Alejandro's face to mine. 'What will you do with it?'

'I will take the letter back to the Lady Elizabeth so that she may satisfy herself it is no longer a threat to her life. Then I will personally ensure that it is destroyed.' His eyes flashed angrily. The point of his sword pressed more deeply into Malcolm's throat, so that a trickle of crimson blood ran down to stain his shirt. 'Now hand over what you stole, Malcolm Lytton, or I will run you through and take it from your dying body.'

Malcolm flinched. 'Here,' he said hoarsely, and reached inside his cloak, producing a folded and bound document. 'Take it, Spaniard.'

Alejandro took it, watching Malcolm's face. 'My thanks,' he said drily.

'What now?' Malcolm demanded, a barely suppressed anger in his voice. He glanced at Tom, who had emerged from his second dunking in the stream and was nursing what appeared to be a broken arm. 'Are we to die here like dogs, or will you be true to your word and let us go? Tom is hurt; I need to get him back to his house.'

Stepping backwards through the flowing current, his gaze held steadily on Malcolm's face, Alejandro nodded. 'You may go. But if I ever meet you again—'

'Yes, yes, you will chop me up and feed me to swine. I get the idea.' Malcolm shook his head in disgust, though I noticed he was quick enough to make a grab for their horses before Alejandro could change his mind. 'You think you are invincible together, you and your little witch. But you will meet your match soon enough.'

I stiffened, and jumped down from the cart. 'What do you mean?' I called out to my cousin across the noise of the water.

Malcolm was leading Tom's horse back towards him,

so he could help Tom mount up. He smiled coldly but seemed reluctant to say more. 'You will find out,' was all he would say.

Only once they had ridden slowly away down the lane, Tom nursing his injured arm as he rode, did Alejandro finally sheathe his sword. He mounted his horse and rode gently through the ford again, the bright surface of the water buzzing with flies.

On the other side he reined in and sat looking at me, his serious gaze searching my face as though he feared what he might see there. 'Are you hurt?'

'Not a scratch,' I insisted.

With a frown, Alejandro looked at Juan. His servant was beginning to turn the cart round, but slowly, taking care not to startle the already nervous horse. 'It will be quicker if I ride back to Woodstock alone. You can follow with Juan on the cart.'

'No!' I exclaimed, instantly furious.

'Meg, it is not safe. They could be lying in wait for us up the road here. I do not trust your cousin.'

'I don't trust him either,' I agreed. 'So let us go cross-country.'

It was Alejandro's turn to be furious. 'Cross-country? With a cart?'

'Then take me up before you on the horse and let Juan follow on the road.'

He shook his head. 'This is madness.'

'It was my fault the letter was stolen in the first place. I was the one who foolishly listened to my father and persuaded Elizabeth to write it. Then my own father stole it, my treacherous cousin nearly died for it.' I shook my head despairingly. Why did he not understand? 'I must be the one to give the letter back to her, to assure her that it can never be used against her. Can you not see that?'

He looked at me for another minute, then reluctantly nodded. 'Very well, you may come with me and Juan will follow with the cart. But first . . .' He held out the letter in his hand, still folded and bound. 'Make sure this is the letter you sought. In case I need to go riding after your cousin again and kill him this time.'

I unwrapped the letter and scanned it briefly. 'Yes,' I agreed, with a deep relief, 'this is the letter I saw the Lady Elizabeth write to Marcus Dent. Though something has been added.'

My voice had risen in outrage. Alejandro nudged his horse forward to read the letter over my shoulder.

'See?' I pointed to the space beneath the Lady Elizabeth's signature where a few bold lines had been added in a curiously similar hand. 'That was blank before.'

'What does it say?'

I read it out:

'*Whatsoever is done in the name of England's liberty and against all those who profess the hated Catholic faith is done with my blessing and that of Almighty God.*'

Alejandro stared at the letter, a creeping horror in his voice. 'What villains, to have added such a lie to an innocent letter! This would have signed Elizabeth's death warrant many times over in the eyes of the Inquisition, whatever nonsense came before it.'

I refolded the letter, trying to control my anger as I thought of how my family had used me for their wicked plots and schemes, without a care for who might suffer. 'We should destroy it now. It is a danger to the princess . . . and to us, carrying it.'

He shook his head. 'We cannot simply tear it up. The Lady Elizabeth must see it destroyed with her own eyes.'

'Then let's go at once. We must get this back safely to Woodstock immediately, and without being seen.'

He reached down for my hand. 'Climb up before me, and we will ride across the fields. Juan,' he addressed his servant, hauling me up onto the saddle before him, 'follow us on the road, but take no risks. There are still many here who would kill a lone Spaniard.'

Juan saluted and added something in laughing Spanish, to which Alejandro replied with a few sharp words. Then he urged the stallion up the grassy verge and through a narrow gap in the hedgerow. The open fields lay just beyond, green and sunlit all the way across the valley and back to the darker, forested slopes of Woodstock.

The pace increased once we were clear of the trees, land flashing past in a blur under the horse's hooves. Never much of a horsewoman, I began to feel queasy. As the black stallion launched into a powerful gallop, I clung to Alejandro's flapping cloak with one hand, the other clutching Elizabeth's letter like a talisman against danger, and turned my face into his chest.

I heard him chuckle. 'Scared at last, Meg Lytton?'

I shook my head. 'Sick,' I muttered indistinctly, and Alejandro must have caught my reply, for his shoulders shook and I knew he was laughing again.

It seemed Elizabeth's letter was less of a talisman and more of a beacon to show our enemies where we were, for no sooner had we entered the denser woodlands on the way to Woodstock than we heard voices ahead. Coarse shouts, like those of soldiers searching the woods.

Alejandro stiffened and led the horse carefully off the track. We rode in silence for a few moments. In a whisper, I started to ask if he knew a way round the woods, but he hushed me. I realized there was another group of men nearby, just out of sight behind a cluster of bushes.

We froze, listening to the men talk amongst themselves while Alejandro held the horse absolutely still, knowing that one movement could betray us. Alejandro's arms came around me to grip the reins, and I felt a secret pleasure in the strength and warmth of his body against me.

'Look, it's simple. We were told to keep looking,' one

man insisted in a stubborn voice. '*Keep looking until you find them*, that's what he said.'

'No, he just told us to keep looking. He didn't say who we were looking for.'

'The witch,' the first voice replied, clearly weary of having to explain everything. 'The witch and the young Spaniard, those are the ones we're looking for.'

A third man spoke up, his voice deep and perplexed. 'And they went this way? But I don't see why they should still be here when they left Woodstock . . . what, yesterday? The day before? It makes no sense to me.'

The first voice reprimanded him sternly. 'It's not our concern to make sense of his orders, just to carry them out. He knows what he knows.'

Man number three was still unimpressed. 'But *how* does he know what he knows?'

'I don't bloody know. Maybe God talks to him in his sleep. It's none of our concern, I tell you.' The first voice sounded almost fearful. 'Now stop arguing and keep your eyes and ears open. When Master Dent tells us to do something, we hop to it quick as we can. See? We don't stand about debating how Dent knows the witch and her paramour will be here, we just look where we're told to look.'

Master Dent. I was winded at the sound of that name, as though someone had just punched me in the stomach. Terror seized me and I could not even look up at Alejandro, though I felt his arms tighten about me. Through the back of my gown, the cool press of his silver cross made me shiver.

The second voice chimed in as they drew level with our hiding place. 'I'm sweating like a pig in this sun. Will there be ale when we get back to the Bull, do you think?'

'And who says we're going back to the Bull?'

'Aren't we?'

'If we find the witch, maybe. If not, we'll be lucky to be allowed our beds tonight, let alone ale.'

'Wait, what's that over there? Something moved . . . is that one of them?'

The three men paused, clearly all staring at something nearby amongst the trees. I held Elizabeth's letter firmly against Alejandro's chest and closed my eyes. The fear of discovery twisted in my guts until I could hardly breathe. I did not dare look up.

Had they seen us through the ivy-thick trunks?

Then finally, the deep voice of man number three said, 'No, it's a turkey. Must have got loose from old Woolley's farm.'

The men moved on and soon I could not even hear their voices. Alejandro let out a long-held breath and looked down at me. 'This is going to be rather more difficult than I thought. With men searching the woods, it'll be next to impossible for us to get back to Woodstock unseen. Unless we can find somewhere quiet to hide until nightfall, and sneak back under cover of darkness.'

I nodded, and was just about to suggest a good place to

hide along the edge of the woodland when more voices approached us. This time the men seemed to be on horseback like ourselves.

One man was shouting after the others we had heard, 'Have you seen anything yet?'

A faint shout of 'No,' came back.

There was a pause while the horses moved closer and stopped a mere ten feet from our hiding place. Then I heard a voice so chillingly familiar that I gasped and inadvertently sank my nails into Alejandro's arm.

It was Marcus Dent himself.

NINETEEN
The Devil's Mark

'She's here somewhere, with that young Spanish dog, and I intend to find her.'

The man's voice belonged unmistakably to Marcus. The last time I had heard that voice, it had been whipping a crowd of villagers into religious fervour while they watched my aunt burn.

'But these woods have already been searched, Master Dent, and not a trace found.'

'Then let them be searched again.'

The witchfinder sounded worryingly sure of himself. But how? Malcolm was no friend of Marcus Dent's. My cousin would never have told Dent where to find us, even in a fit of spite.

Besides, we had only left Malcolm and Tom Dorville a short while back. News of our whereabouts could not have reached Dent so quickly.

We must have been seen entering the wood. That was the only possible explanation.

Someone rode up at a smart pace and reined in beside the waiting men. 'Still no sign of them,' the newcomer admitted. 'What now, Master Dent?'

Dent's voice hardened. 'Go back to the village and bring

as many dogs and beaters as you can find. That should flush the pair out.'

'Yes, sir.'

Their horses moved forward a few feet while the men discussed how long this new tactic would take.

Under cover of that noise, Alejandro nudged his black stallion towards the gnarled oak he had been eyeing.

'Here,' Alejandro whispered in my ear. 'Climb up into this oak tree. We'll slap the horse's rump and let them follow it. Then we'll wait until nightfall before continuing on foot.'

His plan was madness, and he must have known it. Once the dogs arrived, they would be bound to sniff us out, even hidden up a tree. Besides, by staying together, we increased the chances of us both being taken.

I gnawed at my lower lip. Just possessing Elizabeth's letter, with its dangerously altered contents, would be enough to merit a charge of treason. But unless he was caught in my company, Alejandro was still innocent of all charges.

I looked at the gap between the horse and the tree's leafy branches, and shook my head. 'Can't do it,' I mouthed up at him.

'Try,' he mouthed back.

I pursed my lips and glared at him. 'No.'

'Meg,' he whispered in a warning tone, then sighed. 'All right, I'll go first and pull you up into the branches. Here, hold him steady.'

'Wait,' I whispered, then closed my eyes, thinking of the

two of us, the space around us dimming to a shadow, and spoke a single word of power. '*Obscure!*'

The spell of invisibility would not last, I knew that. My power was not strong enough. But it might give us both a chance to avoid capture.

Which gave me an even better idea . . .

Gingerly, I took up the reins as I heard Alejandro, invisible but warm beside me, pull himself up onto the lowest branch of the oak.

I knew how to ride side-saddle, but had never been terribly keen on horses. Huge snuffling creatures that moved unpredictably, particularly when you were trying to make them stand still. Nonetheless, I gathered the reins together and patted the great lumping animal's neck in what I hoped was a reassuring gesture. If I wanted to save Alejandro from a false accusation of treason, I would have to conquer my dislike of horses.

Once Alejandro was safely perched in the riotous green foliage of the oak, I heard the leaves rustle and saw the branch shake as he shifted position.

'Meg, give me your hand!'

With all my strength, I wrenched the stallion's head round and lashed him twice about the neck with the gathered reins.

'Forgive me!' was all I managed before the startled horse leaped forward beneath me and crashed through the undergrowth.

Birds flew up in all directions, fallen twigs cracked violently under the hooves, and the men who had been riding slowly away pulled up in confusion, shouting and pointing after my fleeing horse.

I was invisible now, though how long that state might last, I could not be sure. But no one would pursue me. Who would chase a riderless horse?

I let the stallion have his head – as if I could have prevented such a powerful animal from running away with me! – and we tore off through the trees at breakneck speed. Bent almost flat to avoid being struck by low branches, I clung on desperately, much as I had clung to Alejandro's coat, and hoped the horse at least would have the good sense not to collide with a tree. With my eyes clamped shut in terror most of the way, I had no idea in which direction we were going.

Nor did I particularly care, so long as I put plenty of distance between myself and Alejandro before they caught me.

Eventually, the stallion slowed to a panting trot, its flanks heaving with effort. I was exhausted by then, barely able to hang onto the reins, my fingers laced frantically into the horse's thick mane. There was the tinkling rush of a stream nearby, and the horse stopped abruptly, bending to the water.

The sunny woodland spun, my fingers loosened, and I fell to the ground with a thud. The horse lifted its head and eyed me resentfully, its long black muzzle dripping, before bending to drink again.

My hands tingled and I looked down, watching with horrified fascination as they returned to visibility. The rest of my body followed swiftly, though still a little shadowy.

The sound of pursuit reached me as I sat there on the bank of the stream, trying not to be sick.

Dent's men!

I could hear horses crashing through the woods about a quarter of a mile away to the east, and men on foot somewhere to their north. They were shouting to each other and it sounded as though they were beating the bushes and woodland hollows as they moved forward, casting a wide circle so I could not escape.

Far off, I caught a muffled bevy of barking as dogs were brought into the chase.

I did not much care any more if they caught me, which seemed inevitable now. All I cared about was not dragging Alejandro de Castillo into my private war with Marcus Dent. I just hoped Alejandro had the good sense to stay in that leafy oak tree until those pursuing me had moved on.

The letter was crushed into the bodice of my gown. I drew it out and looked at it.

Should I destroy the letter before they reached me, or risk Elizabeth being charged with treason on the grounds of what this letter contained?

Yet if I destroyed it, Elizabeth would never be entirely

sure that it was gone. She had said it herself: 'Bring the letter back to me so I can see it safe.'

I staggered to my feet and searched about for a hiding place near the stream. I found one some ten feet away. A huge old beech had been stuck by lightning, its fallen branch gathering moss now in the undergrowth. One end was hollow. I thrust the letter inside and concealed it as best I could with leaves and mud.

I spread my fingers and turned in a full circle as I muttered the words, laying a quick concealing charm about the place. It would not hold for ever, maybe until the end of the day, but there was no time to perform a more complicated spell. At least anyone who rode through here in the next few hours would not notice the fallen beech.

The letter safely hidden, I dragged Alejandro's stallion away from the stream and attempted to mount him again. It was time to find my way back to Woodstock if I possibly could. But the horse was having none of it. He seemed to sense that I was not only an inexperienced rider, but too exhausted to exert any influence over him. Every time I twisted my fingers in his mane and tried to hoist myself onto his back, the animal moved a few steps forward.

'Stand still, damn you!' I muttered, and fixed him with a stern eye. 'Let me up.'

The horse looked quizzically at me, but neither of us had time to find out who would have won that particular battle, for at that moment a shout went up amongst the trees.

'She's here! The witch is here!'

So Dent's men had found me at last. Did I have the energy to cast another spell and conceal myself from their eyes? I did not think so. My head was pounding and my legs could barely support me. Indeed, my capture seemed almost inevitable – as though fate had led me to this moment. I leaned my forehead on the horse's warm flanks and waited for my pursuers to close in on me . . .

Rough hands pinioned my wrists behind my back and turned me, pushing me to my knees.

There were five men staring down at me: four on foot, and one perched on the back of an ancient-looking mule. I looked up at their curious faces, wondering which one would be most susceptible to my voice.

'Cover her face!' The oldest among them glared at me with undisguised malice. I recognized him as a man from Woodstock village, one of the church elders. 'The witch can work magick with her eyes.'

'Says who?'

'Says Master Dent, that's who. Now ride and tell him we've got her.'

The man with the mule grabbed at the stallion's reins and led him away at a trot. One of the others threw a sack over my head, his eyes wide as though afraid I might smite him down before he could finish.

The inside of the sack smelled of old cabbages. I kneeled on the damp earth in darkness and listened to the men argue over who had seen me first. It seemed there was a reward for the man who caught me.

Before long, I heard horses approaching quickly. Then Marcus Dent's voice was above me.

'Well, well,' Marcus said, and I caught a hint of triumphant laughter in his voice. 'Meg Lytton brought to heel at last. Though we had better make sure this is the Lytton witch before we take her back to face trial. Pull off the sack for a moment.'

The abrupt sunlight dazzled me as the sack was lifted. I raised my head, and the men who had captured me took a few hurried steps back, as though in fear for their lives. Was I considered so dangerous?

Blinking, I stared up angrily into Marcus Dent's face. 'Why are you doing this?'

'Silence, witch!' He turned to the man beside him. 'Yes, this is the Lytton girl. What about the man she was with?'

'No sign of him, Master Dent.'

Marcus Dent narrowed his eyes but nodded. He looked back at me. 'It's about time we found out just how deep the rot goes in the Lytton women. First the aunt, now this girl—'

'You'll pay for murdering my aunt!'

He laughed at my furious outburst and put his boot in my face, pushing me to the floor. 'Gag the witch. Put the sack back over her head. Let's take her back to the village. I've sent ahead for a jury to be assembled. No more shilly-shallying – we'll settle this tonight.'

The man next to him muttered something urgently in his ear, but Marcus shook him off with disdain.

'Elizabeth? No one cares what that bastard whore says or thinks. It is only by the Queen's grace that she has not yet lost her head.' He nodded to the man behind me. Some filthy rag was pulled round my mouth as a gag, and the coarse hood of sackcloth was shoved roughly back over my head. 'Besides, when Elizabeth hears the charges brought against this one, she will not dare speak for her . . . unless she too is a witch.'

I was lifted bodily and thrown over a horse like a sack of wheat. Winded, I lay there groaning against the gag, my head and feet sticking out. Then the horses began to move, jolting me up and down, and I forgot the pain in my belly and focused instead on not being sick.

Soon Marcus Dent's revenge would be complete. I was going to die, and probably in the same horrible manner that my aunt had perished. But at least the princess's letter was safe. And they had not found Alejandro.

The 'trial' was a mockery of justice. The jury was a benchful of nervous-looking men, most of them little better than farmers dragged in off the fields, with Marcus Dent presiding in the absence of the magistrate. It was unclear on whose authority he was acting, but no one there dared question his right to pass judgement on me. Presumably they feared finding themselves next on his list.

They had chosen the nave of Woodstock church for my arraignment, since the landlord of the Bull Inn would apparently have nothing to do with this business. It was cold out of the sun, and the tortured body of Christ seemed to mock me from his crucifix, but at least I was in the right place to say a last-minute prayer not to wake up in Hell tomorrow.

I sat on a rickety stool in front of these good men, with my hands bound behind my back, and my fair hair loose about my shoulders – probably looking like a bird's nest after the past few days without being combed. My gag and hood had been removed so that the jurors could question me properly. But I had been threatened with the gag again if I should speak out of turn or attempt to curse anyone present. I considered trying to turn myself invisible again, but the spell would not last long enough for me to escape with my hands bound.

Marcus Dent was holding up a leather-bound Latin book with the same reverence he might have shown to the Holy Bible. I read the name in gilt lettering on the spine and shivered. It was the *Malleus Maleficarum*, a book my aunt had warned me of many times. The Latin name meant *The Hammer of Witches*, for it was an evil and ignorant tract against the occult, telling men how to test and execute witches in their towns and villages. I looked at the book with loathing, certain that thousands of innocent women across the wide continent of Europe must have met an agonizing death through its teachings.

'You are charged with the foul and unnatural practice of witchcraft, Meg Lytton,' Marcus Dent thundered, his voice echoing through the church. Some of the local men sitting in judgement on me shifted uncomfortably on their stools and would not meet my gaze. 'How do you plead?'

'Not guilty.'

'Why did you choose to turn your back on Christ and become a witch?' he demanded, as though he had not heard my previous answer.

'I am *not* a witch,' I replied clearly, and thought nothing of the lie, for I knew Dent meant to see me hanged or burned if I was found guilty.

'No one is fooled by these empty answers. You have been seen in company with a known witch, and often secretly closeted with her. One of your father's own servants testified only two days ago at your aunt's trial that he has often seen you wandering the woods with your aunt and gathering plants together.'

'Is it now a crime to pick herbs?'

He smiled coldly. 'Tell me about when you became a witch and renounced the Holy Catholic faith.'

'I have renounced nothing.'

'Did your aunt, Jane Canley, initiate you into the foul sin of witchery before she was burned for heresy?'

Marcus Dent peered at the book in his hand, then came closer. He had opened the *Malleus Maleficarum* and seemed for a moment to be searching for one particular page. Then he circled my stool, staring down at me with burning eyes. His questions followed rapidly on from each other while he ignored my stubborn, repeated denials.

'With which demons and familiars have you been consorting?' he demanded, reading aloud from the book. 'Did you take any demon as your lover? What sabats did you celebrate with your witch-aunt, and where did they take place? Who are your accomplices in this evil?' Then, violently dragging down the left shoulder of my gown to reveal the swelling of my breast, he shouted, 'Is this not the Devil's mark?'

Half the men on the jury rose from their bench to peer in fascinated horror at my bared flesh. The others looked away uncomfortably. I did not need to glance at my left breast to know what was there, always hidden just out of sight by my bodice.

It was my birthmark, about the size of a thimble. Marcus Dent had seen it that day at Lytton Park when he attacked me. Only now did I realize how deep his planning went. He must have been dreaming of this day, this trial, ever since I refused him.

I looked up at him, my voice steady even though my heart was boiling in my chest.

'I'm amazed at what you're prepared to do for revenge when a woman refuses to marry you, Marcus Dent.' I lowered my eyes demurely. 'If I had known how strongly you felt, I would have said yes the first time you asked.'

Some of the watching jury laughed behind their hands. I enjoyed his humiliation for only a few seconds though, for Marcus's fist swept down in a vicious blow and knocked me from my stool. With my hands still bound, I was unable to save myself. My head and shoulder cracked painfully against the stone flags of the church floor.

'We need no further proof of her guilt,' Dent shouted to the assembled villagers. 'You have all seen the Devil's mark on her breast. You have heard the servant's testimony that she was always in secret company with her aunt, a known Satan worshipper. I call for this girl to be hanged as a witch without further ado, and as many of her evil accomplices too as we may find over the following days.'

The small church was in uproar. One man stood up to shout that there was no proof at all, but several of the others hushed the man and pulled him back down.

'At least give her a chance to confess and die in a state of Grace!' someone called out from behind the pillars.

'No, let the witch hang unshriven,' another insisted – a weaselly little man, his eyes gleaming on my bare shoulders. 'Her aunt and her familiars await her in the fires of Hell. Why disappoint them?'

'Wait!' Marcus Dent exclaimed, and held up his hand for silence. When it had fallen, he prodded my fallen body with his boot. 'I am not an unjust man, and this church is sacred to Mary Magdalene, whose sins were many but who was saved by our Lord. To hang or to burn is fit only for those witches most proven in their guilt. So let us invoke Saint Mary Magdalene to save this woman's soul if she is innocent.'

'How will we prove her guilt?' one of the men demanded.

'By one of the oldest methods in these isles, that of swimming the witch.' Dent smiled brutally. 'Meg Lytton will face trial by water. Bind the witch's arms and legs, lower her into the village pond, and if she drowns she is innocent. If she survives, she will be hanged and may the Lord have mercy on her soul!'

There was little argument this time, only a few muttered protests from those who seemed to dislike Dent's high-handed methods more than anything else. It seemed my fate had been decided, and no tears would be shed over my dead body. I would either be drowned or hanged while the villagers looked on. Either way I would die today. The clerk scurried forward with a hefty book for Marcus Dent and the other members of this mock courtroom to sign, stating their names and the agreed verdict and sentence.

I lay for a few moments in a stupor, trying not to imagine how it would feel to drown. Then I was lifted roughly under the arms and half dragged to the altar by a priest in a hooded black robe, whom I had seen before in the shadows, watching the proceedings from one of the side chapels.

The priest cast me down on my knees before the crucifix and the vast statue of Mary the Virgin that stood to one side of the altar.

'Child, you have been sentenced to death. But whether you reach Heaven or Hell afterwards is your choice.' The priest stood beside me, staring down from the dark cowl of his hood. 'Do you confess your sins freely to Christ and beg His forgiveness?'

His voice was rough, muffled by the hood. Yet something about it made me glance up at him, catching a familiar echo . . .

'Don't look at me, you fool,' he whispered urgently. 'Look at the altar!'

Obedient, my heart thundering, I turned back to stare at the lean, writhing body of Christ on the cross.

'Are you mad, Alejandro?' I demanded, also in a whisper. 'If they catch you—'

'They will not catch me,' he said confidently.

'But what are you doing here? You can't hope to rescue me, there are too many of them.'

'I admit, the numbers are not ideal. But Juan is here, waiting for us with horses on the north side of the church. Once you are outside—'

'You there, priest!'

Alejandro stopped at the shouted command and turned his head slightly. 'It is Marcus Dent,' he whispered cautiously, then held up his hand, raising his voice. 'I fear this girl will go unshriven to her death. Maybe another five minutes?'

'The witch already had a chance to repent her sins and

did not take it. Now it is time for her to join her aunt in Hell.'

Afraid that Alejandro would do something reckless and get himself killed, I stumbled back past the roodscreen to where Marcus was waiting and let him take me.

Marcus Dent smiled, dragging me to the church door. Outside, I could see his men carrying planks and rope to the village pond for my execution. First though, he hissed in my ear, I had to be prepared. He pulled my bodice even further down so the gathering villagers could ogle me and the proof of my 'Devil's mark'. Then Marcus seized my long fair hair and sawed through it with his knife, leaving a ragged edge that reached only just below my ears.

I suddenly remembered the vision of the future in the scrying mirror, of me on a cart bound for London with my fair hair cropped short as a boy's, its shame hidden under a cap.

Did that vision mean I would survive this?

The tiny glimmer of hope in my heart was abruptly extinguished. My aunt had told me once that the scrying mirror did not always predict the future clearly. Sometimes it told a future which might come to pass if certain conditions were met. In this case, that I neither drowned nor was hanged today, but survived to return to Elizabeth's service. And what were the chances of that?

'You won't need to look beautiful where you're going,' Marcus whispered. I felt his breath on my bare neck and shuddered. 'It's a shame, Meg. But you should have agreed to marry me when you had the chance. You thought I was helpless in the face of your refusal, that I could do nothing. Now do you see how powerful I am?'

Powerful? I wanted to hurt him. I wanted to hurt all of them, these vile cowards who felt such a need to crush what they could not understand. But if I raised my eyes to his face now, if I spoke a single word of power, I knew Alejandro would not be able to stop himself from taking advantage of the moment and attempting to rescue me. Then they would catch Alejandro and kill him too.

If I was to die today, I was determined to do it alone.

'I shall tell them to bring your brother Will out from his prison to watch your execution,' Marcus Dent added, and turned me round so he could smile down into my face. 'For it will be his turn next. Your brother attacked my men when they were doing their holy duty by burning a proven witch and heretic, and his punishment is death. You can show him how to die.'

I gritted my teeth and resisted the urge to bring my knee sharply up into his groin.

Marcus would only make my death more painful and torturous if I annoyed him. And that might tempt Alejandro de Castillo to act like a hero instead of doing what I wanted him to, and running away.

TWENTY

Blown Away

Dent's men pushed and prodded me down to the village pond, a deep stretch of water straddled by an ancient willow. There, they jeered at me, stripping off my gown until I stood all but naked in my underclothes. My face burning with anger, I tried not to listen to their whistles and impertinent comments.

Someone came running with some spare lengths of rope. The owner came after him a moment later, demanding their return immediately following my death, and was promised he would not have to wait long. One of the men ordered me to touch my toes, then clumsily bound my wrists to my ankles so that I was bent double in my flimsy undershift. Then a rope was passed twice about my waist, pinching my skin cruelly.

Several men in sombre black suits came to inspect how well I was secured, their faces full of contempt.

'How do you like your punishment, witch?' one of them asked, checking that the ropes were tight.

Not very much, I felt like replying, but did not wish to draw this out any longer. My shoulders and hamstrings ached desperately and my back was in torment. Drowning would at least stop the pain.

During all this meticulous knotting and checking of my

bonds, Marcus Dent stood on a table at the edge of the pond, higher than everyone else and making the most of his moment of triumph. He called lengthily on Saint Mary Magdalene to guide them, and preached to the crowd until I wondered if he would have been happier as a priest than a witchfinder.

Suddenly there was some commotion, and I saw Dent turn his head. His eyes were no longer fixed on me but on the narrow, grassy road that led to Woodstock.

Straining to turn my head, I caught sight of my brother, his hands manacled, his face very pale and dirty, walking between two of Dent's men.

'Ah, young Will Lytton!' Marcus Dent exclaimed, his triumphant smile broadening. 'Bring the boy here. He has come just in time to witness his sister's death.'

Two men took up the ropes and walked me out into the duckweed-infested water. Then there was a hard tug on the rope, and I tumbled over into the pond – not surprisingly, given that my wrists were bound to my ankles. Two of the men lifted me into position in the deepest part of the water, which was when I suddenly saw a hooded figure fleeing across the village square.

Alejandro!

So Alejandro had finally taken my advice and was on his way back to the relative safety of Woodstock Palace before he too could be seized by the vengeful Marcus Dent and his men.

My mind stuck hard on the thought of being parted from Alejandro. It was like a bone wedged in my throat, stopping me from breathing. But not from thinking. Anger filled me. All this was because I had refused to marry Marcus Dent. He had never felt anything for me, of that I was sure. But perhaps he had sensed my power and decided to control it by marrying me, by making me one of his possessions, like the cruel book of hatred to which he clung so fervently. What a worthless man Dent was, obsessed with his own lack of power, forever trying to frighten people into obeying him.

'Do you think it ends here?' I flung at Marcus Dent. 'That I can be so easily removed from this world?'

I noted with satisfaction how Dent's face paled and his pious speech died away. 'Put her in!' he demanded instead. 'Dunk the girl. Let's see if she floats.'

The men began to lower me in a sitting position, still bound hand and foot, into the chill dark water. The greenish scum on the surface parted to admit my limbs. I shivered, seeing my own helpless reflection in the water, and threw back my head as far as the ropes would allow me so I could still see Marcus's face.

'This is what you wanted all along, isn't it?' I shouted defiantly as the water began to cover me. 'To see me die just because you didn't get your way. But I shall come back, Marcus Dent, and have my revenge. My spirit will haunt you night and day until you run mad and your own men turn against you.'

Dent's eyes narrowed at that. 'Shut the witch up!'

At his furious command, one of the men shoved my head under the water. I shut my mouth tight and held my breath. It was dark and chilly beneath the surface. No wonder pike were such silent, mournful-looking creatures, I thought.

I struggled against the desire to breathe, flailing and churning up the mud and weed.

This was so cruel and unfair.

I had felt childishly secure in my gift, able to twist any man to my will. Yet I had not been able to influence Elizabeth, nor Alejandro, nor even Marcus Dent when it mattered.

It was time to stop pretending and face the truth. I possessed no special power at all. My 'magick' had been nothing but the tricks of a village witch, and now I would die for my arrogance.

If she sink, she be no witch and shall be drowned.

If she float, she be a witch and must be hanged.

Would this be considered sinking? Yes, I thought simply. I am no witch and I am sinking. Let them drown me and prove me innocent.

Slumped in my bonds, I opened my mouth wide and breathed the dark greenish water. It burned and seared my throat like a flame and I enjoyed the agony of its caresses. It would be the last sensation I ever felt, so I clung onto it lovingly. Pain, pain, pain. Sweet, mortal pain.

'Meg!'

The voice tugged at me, like a bird tugging at a worm.

'Meg, don't leave me!'

Damn it.

It was my brother's voice. Will was in trouble and he needed me.

His voice came again, waking me from my nightmare of dying. My heart was bursting and I was no longer content to perish at the hands of these ignorant men. The pain in my lungs was not beautiful; it was cruel and intolerable. I had to get out of the water. I had to breathe again, to survive this torture.

My mind spun these thoughts, then my eyelids shivered open on the dark underbelly of the pond.

Through the rippling water, faces seemed to swim against the light: Dent's, contorted with triumph; the pale-faced men who were holding me down, talking to each other over my submerged head; a crowd of villagers, gathered about the water's edge to watch me drown.

I remembered my aunt's death, her pleading eyes across the smoke of the bonfire.

Help me, Aunt Jane. I could not help you, but is there any way I can help myself?

The words came to me suddenly, clear and sharp as the sound of a bell. Had her unquiet spirit put the spell into my mind or had I seen the words in one of her books? I did not consider the question long, but thrust my head up above the water as hard as I could, dislodging the hands that held me.

As soon as my mouth broke water, I cried aloud in Latin, '*Lift me, Dark Mother! Free me from my bonds, O Queen of the Night!*'

The men fell back in horrified surprise, staring down at me as though I had grown two heads.

A sudden panic in his voice, Dent shouted, 'Push the witch back in! Hurry, before she curses us all!'

But I was too quick for him. Before the men could recover their wits, I intoned the Latin charm three times in a voice of power.

I began to rise from the village pond, my legs dripping and covered in green weed. Slowly and majestically, the sodden rope unravelled itself from me and fell back into the water. I straightened my aching back and stretched out my hands towards the villagers, continuing my spell of protection.

I was free, and the pond was several feet beneath me as I rested on the air, floating on nothing.

'Let the waters rise,' I said clearly, 'and the winds blow the evildoers from this place. Lady of Darkness, I beg protection for your faithful servant.'

Marcus Dent had climbed down from his table and was glaring at me, his face red with fury.

'Bow to your fate, witch,' he commanded me coldly, 'and cease this demonic prattle.' He gestured angrily at the men guarding me. 'Don't just stand there, you fools. Pull the witch down from there. Gag her to stop her spells.' When they did not move, Marcus Dent looked about the crowd of staring villagers and raised his voice. 'Pay no mind to these tricks and illusions. They are nothing that need concern good Christian men like ourselves.'

'But the witch . . . she's floating in mid-air! This be no illusion, Master Dent,' the younger man stammered, then turned and fled.

At his heels the wind I had called began to rise. Dusty and inexorable, it whipped at the aprons and skirts of the housewives, and blew the men's caps away. Below me, the water had begun to circle in a whirlpool; now it rose from the pond until it floated in a wobbling line just below my feet, a muddy, wet, impossible floor on which I set my bare toes and laughed.

Dent was shouting at the crowd now, insisting that God would protect them if they dragged me down and hanged me. I begged the wind for more force, and the willow tree creaked and bent, its delicate green tendrils thrashing the air. The sky darkened as though it was night, all the trees and hedgerows around the village green shaking violently. Then the church bell began to toll behind me, swinging in the wind I had raised.

The girls' hair flew about their faces and they screamed, hanging onto their mothers' dishevelled skirts. The women seized their children and dragged them home, almost blown there by the wind that pursued them. Their men ran behind with shouts and curses, struggling to secure their doors and windows against the unearthly gale.

Dent was hanging onto the willow, both arms clasped about its trunk. His rage was palpable. 'You will suffer for this, witch! I shall not forget.'

I muttered a single word in Latin under my breath and watched in satisfaction as Marcus Dent was lifted from his feet. The witchfinder clung to the willow with desperate hands, but the wind was too strong for him. Seconds later, it took him like a piece of clothing snatched from a clothes line. With a last furious cry, Dent flew backwards and was consumed by the dark whirling chaos of the storm.

At the very instant that he disappeared, something small and white came spinning towards me out of the storm. Instinctively I reached up and caught it, one-handed. It was my little white charm-stone, the one my aunt had given me as a protective amulet. Dent had taken it from me at Woodstock and now it had returned to its rightful owner.

At once the village green was calm again. Empty, calm and eerily still.

'Meg!'

Lowering myself slowly back to the damp, blossom-strewn earth, I embraced my brother Will. The enchanted wind had not touched him, but had swept everything from around him like a stream racing around a rock.

'Are you hurt?' I whispered.

I could see astonishment in his face as he stepped back. No doubt he had found it hard to witness his younger sister floating on the air and whipping up a dark storm to blow our enemies away. Yet my brother did not seem shocked by what he had seen here today. It was as though Will had always known in his heart that I was no ordinary girl. I only hoped he had not lost his love for me now that I had openly marked myself out as a witch.

He shook his head. 'Not a whit,' he replied.

'I'm glad.'

'That was some performance. You must be exhausted. Come, your Spanish friend is finding us horses.' He slipped an arm about my waist as I staggered.

I suddenly remembered seeing Alejandro out of the corner of my eye, a dark figure fleeing the village green as I was lowered into the water.

Or rather, going to fetch horses.

'How did Alejandro know . . .?'

Will smiled grimly and showed me the pistol under his jacket. 'Oh, we had a plan to rescue you. In the end though, we didn't need it.' He sounded almost admiring.

'Trust a Lytton to have a plan,' I managed.

Will laughed, then pointed ahead. Alejandro had appeared in his priest's robes at the mouth of the lane, leading two frightened-looking horses. Behind him came Juan on the cart, who stood and waved his whip at me with some jubilant but unintelligible cry in Spanish.

'What did his servant just say?' Will whispered in my ear.

'I have no idea,' I replied, but waved back cheerily enough

at the swarthy Spanish groom. 'Though "You're alive!" seems like a good guess.'

Despite the pains in my legs and back, I felt like grinning triumphantly myself. One minute I had been facing my death, the next I had been putting my enemies to flight. I had not understood the extent of my power until that moment when I had felt the icy grip of death and chosen to shrug it off. So the game continued, and this round had gone to me. Though I had no doubt that if Marcus Dent had survived being cast into the heart of my magickal storm, he would be back soon enough. And intent on revenge.

I would have to find some way to silence him and his men, I realized. For in ruining me, Marcus Dent would ruin my mistress too. When it came to her ears that Elizabeth was harbouring a witch in her household, the zealous Queen would be quick to have both me and her younger sister interrogated by the Spanish Inquisitors whose methods of torture and interrogation had so terrified the entire country.

We reached Alejandro and the horses. He had thrown back his hood, his expression forbidding.

I looked at him, unsure what to expect. 'Alejandro?'

'Short hair suits you,' he remarked, and smiled when I ran a hand over my shorn locks. I had forgotten that Marcus Dent fancied himself as a barber. 'Just don't ever try to pass as a boy. There are a couple of things that might get in your way.'

'Be quiet,' I managed feebly, then wondered why my lips felt so numb and my legs were shaky.

Alejandro gave me an assessing look, then pulled his priest's thick robe over his head and handed it to me. 'No, put it on,' he insisted when I tried to protest. 'I stole it from the local priest. Anyway, your need is greater than mine. You look half dead.'

'That's not funny. I nearly *was* dead.'

'And whose fault is that?' With a frown, he watched me hand back Will's now very damp jacket and drag the priest's robe down over my head instead. 'Why did you ride away from me in the woods, Meg? You must have known Dent's men would catch up with you.'

'The horse bolted under me,' I lied, avoiding his gaze, and knew he did not believe me. But it was the only answer I had for him.

His gaze searched my face, his voice terse. 'I didn't think you were going to make it.'

'Not . . . your . . . fault,' I managed, shivering so violently now that my teeth were chattering.

'It was harder than I'd thought to find Juan. We had a daring rescue planned. It involved Will holding them off with his pistol and Juan setting fire to the Bull Inn as a distraction while I grabbed you. But in the end, we didn't need to do anything.'

'The princess's letter,' I reminded him in a mutter, telling myself not to behave like a fool over him.

Alejandro drew a deep breath. 'The princess's letter,' he agreed, his look suddenly very grim. 'Did Marcus Dent take it away from you when you were arrested?'

For a moment I could not remember. It seemed so long ago since we were in the woods together, playing a dangerous game of cat and mouse with Marcus Dent and his men. Yet it could only be a few short hours. Then my head cleared and I saw in my mind's eye the black stallion drinking from the stream, his wet muzzle and resentful glance. Then the fallen branch in the undergrowth, its hollow end now stuffed with mud and leaves . . . and something rather bulkier.

'I hid it,' I gasped, and grabbed at his arm. 'It's still in the woods.'

Alejandro led me to the cart and helped me up onto the seat beside a wildly grinning Juan. 'We'd better hurry, then.'

TWENTY-ONE

Summons

Riding in through the gates at Woodstock Lodge just after dusk, we found the place in uproar. Torches had been lit in the courtyards, candles burned in all the windows, and there was the sound of shouting from inside the house. Two guards stood at the gate, their expressions uncertain in the thickening dusk.

'Who goes there?' one of them demanded, lowering his pike as Alejandro tried to ride through.

'Alejandro de Castillo,' he replied in some surprise, and reined in his horse. 'John, is that you? Let us pass, I've brought Meg Lytton back to the Lady Elizabeth. Her brother's with us too, Will Lytton. I'm sure Sir Henry Bedingfield will not begrudge him a bed for a few nights, the man's been badly hurt.'

'I'm sorry, sir, I didn't recognize you at first.'

Alejandro stared up at the brightly lit building. His eyes narrowed, and I saw his hands clench compulsively on the bridle. 'What's happened here? What's to do?'

'I shouldn't really say . . .'

'Come, man, I'm one of the Lady Elizabeth's priests,' Alejandro said persuasively. I had never heard him sound so warm, so approachable. Perhaps he was the one with the gift after all, I thought bitterly. 'I was sent here by Queen Mary herself. What cannot be said to me?'

The guard glanced at me and Will on the cart behind Alejandro's, then nodded reluctantly. 'Very well, sir. The Lady Elizabeth has been summoned to court. An urgent letter arrived this afternoon, along with some of the Queen's men. She is to leave at first light, under heavy guard.'

Suddenly I could not breathe. The Lady Elizabeth, ordered urgently to court? This could only mean one thing. Proof of her treason had at last been found and she was indeed to be questioned again, just as the princess had feared. I only hoped no word of her incriminating letter had reached the Queen during our absence.

Alejandro caught my eye and shook his head minutely. 'Thank you, John,' he told the guard, and nudged his horse forward through the gates. 'I had best get Meg Lytton back to her duties as quickly as possible then. The Lady Elizabeth will be needing her.'

As Alejandro dismounted in the courtyard, I jumped down from the cart and ran to him. 'Could they know of the letter? Do you still have it safe?'

He patted his cloak reassuringly. 'Safe enough, and so it will remain until the Lady Elizabeth destroys it herself. Now hush, no more until we can be private. They may be listening.'

He insisted I went up to reassure the Lady Elizabeth while he helped my poor brother inside. Following them into the narrow hallway, I could see there was nothing I could do to help Will, and knowing how terrified Elizabeth must be at this latest blow, I gathered my somewhat soiled and torn skirts and ran up the stairs.

The guard outside Elizabeth's door was a man I did not recognize. One of the newcomers from London, perhaps? I explained who I was and he shrugged, not seeming to take much notice of me.

I knocked, but there was no reply. Since the door was slightly ajar, I pushed it open and entered the princess's candlelit bedchamber on tiptoe.

Elizabeth was on her knees by the window, hands clasped fervently together as though in prayer. She gasped at the sight of me and lurched to her feet. Blanche Parry, who had been packing the princess's travelling chests, turned to see who had come in and cried out in shock.

'Meg!' The princess was pale, her dark eyes wide, her lips trembling. 'We thought you were dead.'

'I nearly was,' I replied drily, and threw back the hood of my cloak.

Elizabeth stared at my shorn hair. 'Your hair!'

'The witchfinder Master Dent felt I was too vain. So he cut off my hair.'

'Yes, we heard about the charges. Thomas Parry sent word from the Bull that you had been arrested and condemned to die this very afternoon.' Elizabeth looked horrified. 'How is it possible that you have escaped with your life?'

'Master Dent withdrew the charges of witchcraft at the last minute,' I told her loudly, for the benefit of the guard in the hallway. 'He declared it a malicious accusation and allowed me to go free.'

I pushed the door shut and sank into a curtsey that almost killed me. My body was aching as though I had been kicked by a mule.

'Lady Elizabeth,' I began carefully, not sure if my whisper might be overheard by the new guard outside, 'we have done that which you required us to do.'

Colour rushed back into the princess's cheeks. 'Get up,' Elizabeth insisted, helping me to my feet. 'Please get up. This is excellent news. It is what we have been praying for. I don't know how to thank you.'

I looked at her, then at Blanche Parry, who had turned back to her packing with a smile.

'I heard you had been summoned to court,' I murmured. 'Do you think . . . ?'

Elizabeth laid a warning finger on my lips and shook her head. 'My dear sister the Queen has kindly sent a small troop of guards to protect me on my return to court,' she explained cautiously, again in case the guard was listening. 'It seems the Queen desires to speak with me at once. I am glad you have returned. You can help Blanche to pack for me. Nothing must be left behind at Woodstock, for I . . . I do not think I will ever come back here again.'

I suddenly realized what she meant. The princess was

leaving Oxfordshire for good. And that meant I must leave too.

'I cannot go home,' I whispered. 'You cannot send me home, my lady. My father . . .'

'I cannot afford to keep you at court,' Elizabeth told me, and shook her head. 'I'm sorry, Meg, truly I am.'

'Then I will serve you unpaid.'

'Meg, dearest, do not be foolish. How will you eat? And clothe yourself? Life at court is hard enough for a wealthy noble, let alone a penniless servant with a mistress in disgrace.' She knitted her fingers together, her eyes suddenly tortured. Her voice dropped to a whisper. 'Besides, I may not be at court for long. If I am found guilty of whatever accusation has been brought against me this time, my sister will have me removed to the Tower again. And thence . . .' The Lady Elizabeth broke down and turned away to hide her tears.

'She cannot do that,' I said, not knowing how to comfort her.

But I very much feared Elizabeth was right, and this urgent summons to court was in truth a warrant for her arrest. Men had come to escort her back to London under armed guard, to face more questions at court. What else could that mean but another accusation of treason?

'The people love you too much to allow any such unjust treatment, my lady,' I said more firmly, and tried to cheer her up with a carefully worded message. 'Alejandro has . . .

what you lost, and will bring it back to you soon. You will see with your own eyes that no one can use that against you.'

She nodded, and dried her eyes with a white lace handkerchief. 'Thank you.'

There was a quiet knock at her door. I opened it at Elizabeth's command and felt a warm sense of relief when I saw Alejandro in the corridor.

'Come in,' I murmured, noting that the guard outside Elizabeth's door was watching us suspiciously. 'Her ladyship is expecting you.'

He slipped inside the room, and I closed the door behind him. Let the man listen if he would. I knew Alejandro's natural caution too well. The guard would hear nothing he could use against Elizabeth.

Alejandro strode straight to the window and drew the shutters across it. Then he dropped to one knee before the princess and withdrew the letter from within his cloak, handing it to her without a word.

She took the letter with trembling hands, opened it and read it through to the end, her lips working. She gave a little gasp as she saw what had been added after her signature, and I saw her brows contract with sudden fury. The princess would have spoken then, but Alejandro cautioned her to silence with an abrupt gesture and pointed instead to the candle.

Elizabeth nodded, seemingly not offended by this impolite behaviour, and took the letter to the candle.

Holding the edge in the flame, she waited for the parchment to be well alight, then cast it into the cold hearth.

We stood and watched the letter burn until there was nothing left but a pile of papery ashes.

'Thank you,' she said simply, and gestured Alejandro to rise.

He bowed. 'It was my pleasure to serve you in this, my lady.'

'Even against your mistress's wishes?' she asked in a whisper, her eyes lingering curiously on his face.

'I am a Spaniard and I serve King Philip,' he commented drily. 'Not your royal sister.'

Elizabeth's brows rose. 'You think the King would approve of your actions here?'

Alejandro hesitated. 'His Majesty is a man, my lady,' he replied carefully, and his gaze flicked to my face and away. 'He would understand that when a woman asks him for help, an honourable man must act as he sees fit – even if that involves breaking a few rules.'

Elizabeth glanced from him to me. A knowing look crept across her face. 'I see,' was all she said.

Blanche coughed behind her. 'We leave at first light, my lady,' she reminded Elizabeth, and scattered another handful of dried herbs into the chest to keep the clothes dry and sweet-smelling until they arrived at court. 'And there is still much to be done.'

'I will help you, my lady,' I said at once, and took up a

petticoat that needed to be folded. 'Then I must go and pack my own things for the journey home.'

Alejandro frowned, and looked at Elizabeth, who bit her lip.

'Oh, very well,' the princess exclaimed, a little scarlet point burning in each cheek. 'You can come with us to court, Meg. You have certainly earned my thanks and I would be churlish indeed to turn you away. But I do not know how I will be able to afford your board and lodging.'

'Leave that business to me, my lady,' Alejandro said mysteriously, and bowed low over her hand. 'Now I too must go and prepare for our removal to court. Father Vasco's health has improved these past few weeks. He should make the journey well enough.'

'My brother!' I had clean forgotten about Will. Now he would have to go home after all, for he was too weak to remain here alone.

'Don't fret,' Alejandro told me. He had a twinkle in his eye. 'Your brother can travel with Father Vasco as an additional guard against thieves and sturdy beggars. My master King Philip provides plentifully for our expenses, so there should be enough in my purse to cover the cost of his food and lodgings on the way. The roads are so dangerous these days, don't you agree?'

When he had gone, Elizabeth turned to me with a teasing little smile.

'Now, let me see. You were away two days and one night,'

the princess murmured, and helped herself to a sweetmeat. There was mock disapproval in her tone. 'So where did you sleep that night, I wonder? Not in the arms of the soon-to-be-ordained Alejandro de Castillo, I trust?'

'No, of course not!' I gasped, but felt myself blush deep scarlet, much to the two women's amusement.

I folded one of the princess's second-best gowns very roughly, then had to stop and refold it more carefully, trying to ignore Blanche's sniggering laughter.

Alejandro was coming with us to court too, of course. I had forgotten that in my rush of fear for the Lady Elizabeth. But it did not matter if he came with us or not, I reminded myself sternly. In a few days' time, I would be at court, and surrounded by dozens of young men who would not soon be priests and who knew nothing of the charges of witchcraft laid against me. Besides, my duty lay with the Lady Elizabeth, whatever dreadful trials she might face in the coming weeks and months. I would forget Alejandro de Castillo, and he would go back to Spain and take holy orders.

Later that night, while the princess slept, I sat cross-legged on the warm hearthstones with my charm-stone before me, and heated a tallow candle in the dying flames. Once the stinking tallow was warm and pliant enough, I fashioned a rough doll from it. Using the blackened tip of a half-burned stick, I drew Marcus Dent's thin features on the wax doll as best I could, murmuring his name as I did so. The spell would have been stronger if I had possessed something that belonged to the witchfinder, but in the absence of some shred of clothing or hair from his head, I would have to make do with a crude representation of his body. The power of the charm-stone, which Dent had kept close for so many months, should do the rest.

When the doll was finished, I scratched the slanting initials M.D. on its belly, just to make sure the spell found its rightful target.

I laid the Marcus doll carefully on the hearth and passed the charm-stone over it three times. Then I broke the burned stick into splinters to represent his men and those villagers who had been present at the pond, and held out my hands above the magickal heap.

'Let Marcus Dent's tongue be silenced against me, and his men's tongues too. Let the villagers believe their memories a dream not to be trusted. Let forgetfulness fill their minds if they should ever speak of me, and the drowsiness of sleep overtake them like death. Bind up the skin of their fingertips and dry all the ink in their wells. Make my name a bird's cry on the wind. From this night, Meg Lytton shall be nothing to them but the sound of ice cracking underfoot in the forest. Blessed be.'

The spell must have drained the last of my waning strength. I woke on my back in the chill dawn light, lying stiff and uncomfortable on the stones of the hearth. Hearing the household beginning to stir downstairs, I stood and stretched, then peered in through the threadbare curtains that hung around the bed. But the Lady Elizabeth was still asleep on her pillows, her sleeping cap askew, her narrow face flushed.

I kneeled and searched in vain for the tallow doll amongst the ashes in the hearth. I found nothing but shreds of softened sticky tallow. The doll had melted while I lay exhausted, unable to keep vigil over it as I should have done. But had my spell worked first? Had I managed to silence Marcus Dent and his men?

I rubbed my charm-stone clean and hid it in the pocket hanging from my belt. There was no way to know for sure that the spell had worked. All I could do now was wait and see if we were taken to the Tower on reaching London.

The weather had changed overnight, bringing a spring tempest from the east, and although the sunshine soon returned, the journey south was violently windy. We had to keep stopping for fear that the litter in which Elizabeth was travelling would be blown completely away. The curtains of the litter flapped open and shut like vast wings, affording little glimpses of her cross red cheeks to those country folk who came out from their cottages to see her pass. Every now and then, an angry exclamation would be heard from within, and a white, jewelled hand would appear, struggling to hold the curtains together.

It was exactly like the vision I had seen in the scrying

mirror: the horses and carts, Elizabeth in her litter, the strong winds gusting about our procession, and me struggling to hide my short hair under a cap which kept threatening to blow away.

Yet what of the terrible dark shadow that my vision had shown creeping behind me?

I glanced nervously over my shoulder a few times on the road to London, but only ever saw a cloudy blue sky and green fields behind us.

At last we reached Hampton Court, which was where the Queen had chosen to reside for the birth of her child, expected within the next few months. The vast red-brick towers and twisting, fluted chimneys could be seen from quite a distance along the bank of the River Thames, whose waters lapped just below the walls. I could see now why Elizabeth had been so downcast by the decaying ruins of Woodstock Palace. It must have seemed like a prison indeed to a princess more accustomed to such stately magnificence as this.

Commoners who had heard we were on the road came out to cheer their princess as we approached Hampton Court. Several even kneeled in the road as Elizabeth's litter passed, a gesture of defiance which made Sir Henry Bedingfield curse and order the outriders to move more quickly. When we finally reached Hampton Court itself, he ushered Elizabeth and her entourage through the massive arched gateway with a look of relief on his face.

Even before we arrived, we'd heard reports that Queen Mary was quite swollen up with this pregnancy, and rarely stirred beyond the royal chambers. We were told her ladies were hard at work preparing a comfortable room for her lying-in, shut off from the outside world. Even the windows would be kept permanently closed and shuttered, so Queen Mary could await the birth of her child in darkness and tranquillity.

Elizabeth heard this news with a sympathetic smile, always expressing in public her heartfelt wish that the Queen would be delivered safely of a son. In private though, she would chew her lip after these conversations, or stare furiously at nothing, as though imagining a rather more violent outcome to her sister's pregnancy.

Shocking though this anger seemed, I couldn't help feeling a little sorry for Elizabeth. If her sister produced a healthy child, Elizabeth's hopes of becoming Queen herself would be dashed for ever. Indeed, she might then find herself spending the rest of her life in a series of dank and miserable prisons like Woodstock, or simply executed on some fresh trumped-up charge of treason or witchcraft, to safeguard against any threat to the new heir's life. Nor was it hard to see why those who wished for an end to Catholic rule in England awaited this birth with as much trepidation as Elizabeth herself.

On arrival at Hampton Court, Elizabeth was escorted under guard to one of the private apartments at the rear of the palace. Blanche Parry and I followed respectfully in her wake, while the men of the household were led away to separate quarters.

'Am I still Her Majesty's prisoner?' Elizabeth demanded of the Lord Chamberlain, her face very pale. She studied the gorgeous antechamber in which we stood, as though expecting to find chains on the wall and instruments of torture. 'No new charges have yet been brought against me. Am I to expect that?'

The Lord Chamberlain looked uneasy. 'The Queen asks that you should remain here for your own safety, madam, until such time as she may send for you. She is at present closeted with her ladies for her lying-in, and so is not able to receive you. I heartily suggest you do not attempt to leave these rooms, nor talk to any courtier without the Queen's permission.'

Elizabeth curtseyed, her eyes lowered, and said nothing in response. But as soon as the Lord Chamberlain had left the apartments, Elizabeth tore off her neat white cap and cast it to the floor.

'I am still a prisoner!'

Blanche Parry, who had been exploring the lavish and expensively furnished suite of rooms, smiled at her placatingly. 'But a more comfortable one than at Woodstock, my lady.'

Elizabeth went to the window and stared out gloomily over the broad expanse of the River Thames below. Bars had been newly set across the window as if the princess might be tempted to climb out, even though the apartment was several storeys high. She glanced at me over her shoulder, her small eyes brooding.

'Meg, what do you say? You have some talent to know what the future holds, or so John Dee said.' She pulled on one of the iron bars across the window. 'Will I ever be more than a prisoner in my own father's palaces?'

'Hush!' Blanche warned her, and went to check the door was properly shut. 'We are no longer in the country, my lady, but at court. Walls have ears here.'

I did not know how to reply. 'If I have any such talent, my lady,' I began cautiously, 'then it has not yet been made clear to me. But I agree with Mistress Parry. This is a far better place than Woodstock to be held under guard. Perhaps the Queen will be ready to receive you once . . .'

I hesitated, seeing Elizabeth's delicate brows knit together. I had been going to say 'once the child is born' but suddenly I did not dare to.

'Once Her Majesty is feeling stronger,' I finished, and knew I had not convinced her.

Elizabeth threw herself onto a heap of velvet cushions that had been scattered on the floor. She lay there on her back, arms outstretched, staring up at the ornate golden ceiling.

'The Queen has brought me here to humiliate me in front of the whole court.' Her eyes flashed and her small lips pursed tightly. 'Well, I am back at court as she desired. But if my sister thinks to send me to the Tower on yet another false charge of treason, she will find me more my father's daughter than she has bargained for!'

TWENTY-TWO

Queen of Shadows

Days passed in our gilded prison at Hampton Court, and slowly turned into weeks. Still there was no summons from Queen Mary, nor was she any nearer to giving birth – or so the gossip went. But Elizabeth must have been allowed some money from the royal coffers, for all of us received costly new gowns, more suited to court life. And, on Elizabeth's orders, Blanche Parry found me a selection of hoods with veils to conceal my shorn hair, so I no longer had to put up with whispers when I accompanied the princess into the privy garden below.

Elizabeth's apartments were forbidden territory for the courtiers, her door guarded at all times. Yet they came to see her, nonetheless. Noblemen with pearl earrings and jewelled doublets would slip past the guards in the sultry afternoons, always claiming they had the Queen's permission to pay their respects to the Lady Elizabeth. One evening, King Philip himself came to speak privately with Elizabeth, though I had gone to bed early with a stomach pain that night and missed seeing him. Even Blanche Parry enjoyed a few visits from her cheerful husband Thomas, who had come to Hampton Court in our wake, along with a number of other gentlemen and yeomen who had been part of Elizabeth's household before her arrest.

Yet neither my brother nor Alejandro de Castillo came to visit us. Nor was I able to discover any news of them from the lofty, tight-lipped servants who brought us our meals.

The sedate glory of Hampton Court seemed a very long way from the green valleys and ramshackle villages of Oxfordshire. Soon, it was hard to believe that I had recently been tied up and nearly drowned there, accused of witchcraft and heresy, and had watched my poor aunt burn for the same crimes.

Elizabeth and Blanche discreetly never mentioned my brush with death, and with no sign of Alejandro to remind me of that other life, my ordeal at Marcus Dent's hands became like a dream to me. Still frightening, living on in shadowy nightmares, but no longer quite real.

When three long weeks of silence had passed, I decided that Alejandro must have gone home to Spain to take holy orders, and that this was entirely the best thing for both of us. I could not spend my life pretending to be something I was not. The longer I sat sewing my sampler or dressing the princess's hair instead of following the witch's path as my aunt had done before me, the sooner I would run mad with frustration.

I gave a simpler version of this explanation to Blanche Parry when she asked what had happened to 'the young Spaniard', and then made her stare by bursting into violent, scalding tears.

'There, there,' Blanche murmured in surprise, and drew me against her comforting chest. 'That young man will come back for you one day, you'll see. And if he doesn't, there are plenty more fish in the sea.'

'Don't . . . want . . . a . . . fish,' I choked.

'Of course you don't,' she agreed soothingly. 'Nasty smelly things. Now, don't cry too hard. You'll only make your nose red, and then if he does come to see you, he'll think you as ugly as can be.'

I laughed through my tears at this, though Blanche was clearly being serious. 'Very well.' I fumbled for my handkerchief and blew my nose. 'Better?'

'Much better.' She pointed to my embroidery sampler, which I had tried to hide earlier behind a beautiful room screen decorated with elaborate carvings of mermaids and mermen. 'Head down now. A little hard work will soon cheer you up.'

Late that same afternoon, there was a discreet knock at the door to the apartments and I looked up idly from my needlework to see Alejandro de Castillo standing there. I had been sitting alone, waiting for Blanche and the princess to return from their daily walk about the privy garden below, which was the only outing Elizabeth was allowed. The words of apology at the princess's absence died on my lips as I realized who it was in the doorway, and I stood, dropping my sampler.

At first I had not recognized him. I was used to seeing

Alejandro in the plain robes of a novice, or in his workaday clothes when we had walked out at Woodstock to gather berries or accompany Elizabeth around the old palace grounds. But here at Hampton Court, Alejandro de Castillo looked very much the Spanish noble in an expensive black doublet, sleeves fashionably slashed to reveal crimson silk beneath, his shoes of the finest red leather.

He stared at me for a moment, then swept off his velvet cap with its jaunty feather and bowed very low, meeting my gaze as he rose.

'Mistress Lytton.' He addressed me formally, as though we were barely acquainted. 'I had not thought to find you alone.'

'Señor de Castillo,' I replied in a murmur, sinking into a curtsey low enough for the King of Spain himself.

At first sight of him in the doorway, I had felt faint and almost sick with pleasure. But then my head rebelled. Where had Alejandro been all this time? Why had he sent no word to us of his safety or whereabouts? My teeth ground together, and suddenly I wanted to punish him for staying away so long.

Alejandro glanced about the empty apartment. 'The Lady Elizabeth is not here?'

'As you see, sir,' I agreed coolly, and took up my hated sampler again. 'Though she may return shortly . . . if you care to wait.'

I sat and put an odd lopsided stitch into the sampler

without really looking, then another, pretending to be utterly absorbed while secretly watching him through my lashes.

Alejandro walked to the window and looked down at the river for a long while. When he eventually spoke, his voice sounded strained. 'I am sorry I didn't come before to visit you,' he muttered. 'First I was intent on finding your brother some clerical employment in London. Then Father Vasco was taken seriously ill, and I have barely left his side since then.'

'I'm glad my brother is settled in London, though I'm very sorry to hear that Father Vasco has not been well,' I said, rather too quickly. 'I trust he may return to full health soon, for I know he intends to return to Spain by the end of this summer. I suppose you will be going back with your master, won't you?'

Alejandro turned to stare at me. I could hear the frustration in his voice. 'Meg, are you angry with me?'

I bent my head to my sampler again. 'No,' I muttered indistinctly. 'Why should I be? You have already explained that you were at Father Vasco's bedside for the past few weeks. And Hampton Court is a very *large* palace. It is not surprising you were unable to find the Lady Elizabeth's apartment before today. I only hope you will find your way back to Spain more easily.'

The sharp irony in my voice seemed to have done the

trick of bursting his dignified exterior. Alejandro came back towards me, his tread purposeful, and I looked up from my untidy embroidery in anticipation, half hoping he would seize me.

But Alejandro stopped before he reached me, his eyes very dark, his mouth a thin hard line. He stood a moment, crushing his fashionable velvet cap between his hands until it must have been quite mangled. Then he bowed, and replaced the cap on his head. Astonishingly, it still looked perfect.

'Madam,' he said stiffly, his gaze fixed on the carved legs of the high-backed, silk-covered seat on which I was sitting, 'would you be so kind as to convey my greetings to the Lady Elizabeth on her return? I have today written to the Queen on behalf of my master, whose sickness prohibits him from making his report in person. In this letter, I have described the Lady Elizabeth's most pious and fervent Catholicism over the past year, and her absence of contact with the outside world. I have explained to the Queen that there can be no doubting her sister's faith, nor the chastity and honesty of her person. I have also described your service to her, and begged that some provision might be made for your upkeep at court.'

Alejandro paused, and his voice became colder and even more distant as he realized I was not going to reply.

'I believe Her Majesty has not yet granted an audience to the Lady Elizabeth, nor set her free from this too-long imprisonment. Hopefully my letter will help to heal the breach between these two sisters.'

He muttered some farewell and then was gone, closing the door quietly behind him. I felt a sudden desperate urge to run after him and throw myself at his feet, to tell Alejandro I was sorry, that I had not meant to speak so coldly to him, that it had all been a terrible mistake.

But some tiny spark of pride still left in me refused to go out. I sat in awful silence instead, and stared at the closed door until my eyes ached.

Alejandro de Castillo's letter of testimony would make it very difficult for anyone to prove Elizabeth either a traitor or a heretic. And I had repaid him for this loyalty by suggesting he got back on a boat to Spain as soon as possible.

That evening, as we were preparing the princess for bed, there was a knock at the door to the apartments. Blanche went to answer it, irritable and perplexed, and came back into the bedchamber with a tall, stately woman in tow. She was swathed in a cloak of soft dove-grey, her lined face partially concealed beneath her hood, but Elizabeth seemed to recognize her at once as one of the Queen's ladies-in-waiting.

'Mistress Clarencieux,' she said faintly, and curtseyed. Her face was suddenly very pale. 'Have you come from the Queen?'

The woman nodded. 'Her Majesty wishes to see you.'

'Now?'

Elizabeth's eyes widened, though she sounded more alarmed than surprised. She was probably afraid they might take this chance to convey the princess to the Tower of London under cover of darkness. She was still so popular with the common people that I imagined the government must fear sparking a riot if they tried to take her to the Tower by daylight.

'Are you ready?' Mistress Clarencieux replied, a little haughtily, and I sensed that she did not like Elizabeth.

Elizabeth hesitated, then nodded. No doubt she felt this might be her only chance to clear her name.

Her face composed, Elizabeth allowed Blanche to fasten a cloak about her shoulders and bring her outdoor shoes. Then we set off down the stairs to the privy garden, with Mistress Clarencieux leading the way. Blanche and I followed the princess, both of us unwilling to let her face the Queen alone. Behind us came half a dozen of Elizabeth's guards, their faces stern, and several gentlemen ushers with torches.

We crossed the privy garden in silence under a gentle moonlight, and came to the base of the Queen's lodgings.

The door swung open on a narrow winding stair lit by flaming torches in brackets. My heart beating hard, I glanced at Blanche. She was trembling, her lips moving in a silent prayer. It seemed that neither of us expected this night to end well.

Indeed, it was hard not to be frightened when all the time we could hear the gentle lapping of the River Thames behind us. It was only a short barge trip along the river to the Tower of London, the grim prison where Elizabeth's mother had been lodged before her execution.

'No one but the Lady Elizabeth,' the Queen's lady-in-waiting told us, barring our way.

Elizabeth turned, and there was naked fear in her eyes. 'I will not go up alone,' she insisted, and a mulish look crept over her face. I thought she had never looked younger. 'Mistress Parry must accompany me.'

But Mistress Clarencieux shook her head. 'Not Blanche Parry,' she said cruelly, then her gaze flicked contemptuously to me. 'You may take the girl instead.'

Gathering my full skirts, I stepped into the base of the tower after Elizabeth. They did not want the princess to feel safe or comfortable with her old servants about her. That was why I had been chosen. But I saw relief in Elizabeth's face and wondered if she was hoping my gift might help sway the Queen to forgive her.

My palms began to sweat as I followed Elizabeth up the winding stair. Did she expect me to influence the Queen herself? I could lose my head for such a dangerous act, and this time there would be no one to save me.

To my surprise, the Queen's apartments lay in silence and almost complete darkness. I did not entirely know what I had expected, but this sombre, unlit maze of rooms seemed more suited to a mole under the earth than a queen. Certainly I could never envisage Elizabeth living in such humble conditions once she was on the throne. Mistress Clarencieux seemed unperturbed by the darkness, leading us without faltering down a narrow, low-ceilinged corridor that opened into a vast, palatial apartment dominated by a magnificent bed hung with heavy curtains in some dark material. This room was lit only by a small fire that burned fitfully in the enormous hearth, its light barely reaching the creeping shadows beside the bed.

Coming to the centre of this strange room, Elizabeth sank at once to her knees and appeared to be praying fervently. I followed her example, kneeling a few feet behind her. I too bowed my head over my clasped hands as if in prayer, though all my senses were alive, listening to each tiny sound in the room.

Then Elizabeth raised her head and spoke, seeming to address the deep shadows beside the drape-hung bed. I feared to stare too hard, but listened instead. Earnestness trembled behind every word, a slight catch to Elizabeth's voice as though she was on the point of tears.

'Your Majesty,' she breathed, 'please believe that I am your humble and most loyal subject. Whatever you may have heard to the contrary, I protest these to be lies and wicked falsehoods. This I swear by Almighty God. You know my heart, for it is unchanged. I have remained true to Your Majesty from the beginning and shall be for ever.'

There was a movement from the shadows, a pale hand raised to an even paler face. The fire flared behind me, and I saw the slumped figure of the Queen, seated on a high-backed chair near the bed.

'Still you cling so stoutly to the same tale and refuse to confess your offence.' A hoarse voice spoke out of the shadows near the bed. 'Take caution, Elizabeth, that your immortal soul be not perjured in this.'

'I cannot confess an offence of which I am innocent, Your Majesty.'

'I pray to God it may fall out so.'

'If it does not,' Elizabeth said, her voice tremulous, her hands still clasped together, 'I request neither Your Majesty's favour nor your pardon.'

'Be that as it may,' the Queen replied sharply, and straightened in her chair. The heaped folds of her gown fell away to reveal a large, rounded belly. I remembered the horoscope John Dee had cast, and wondered if there was indeed a child growing in there, or whether my own reading of the chart had been right, that the child was nothing but a phantom conjured up by a Queen desperate for an heir. 'I daresay you will claim now that you have been unjustly punished at my hands.'

'I should never say so to you, Your Majesty.'

The Queen snorted. 'To others, then. Once you are safely away from here.'

'No indeed, Your Majesty,' Elizabeth persisted, and her

voice grew more gentle. 'For my long imprisonment is a burden which only I must bear. I have borne it now for more than a year. What I have told you here is nothing but God's own truth. I humbly beg and pray Your Majesty to have a good opinion of me and to consider me still your true subject.'

There was a long silence. I felt the heat of the fire at my back, sweat on my forehead, and heard the rustle of Queen Mary's gown as she shifted heavily in her chair. She was breathing erratically now, as though torn between two equally painful courses of action. The princess had never stood in sharper danger, I realized.

I stilled my own breathing to concentrate on the Queen's instead. My fingers tingled with power, suddenly hot, almost unbearably so. If I could not influence her to show mercy, there was nothing to prevent Mary from sending her half-sister to the Tower, and from there to the block. After all, why not? Elizabeth, with her red-gold hair and flawless skin, must remind the ageing Mary of that wicked young beauty who had stolen King Henry away from her mother.

If Anne Boleyn could die a traitor's death on the scaffold, so too could her daughter.

In, out. In, out. In, out.

I raised my eyes to that shadowy face, just the faintest gleam of eyes in the firelight, and fought the Queen's frantic and almost hysterical desire to condemn her sister to death. Sweat crept down my neck, my body ached, and my mind warred with hers in terrible silence. Never before had I attempted something so grindingly difficult, to use my gift without speaking, to influence someone's will with just the power of my mind. Yet somehow I had to do it. I could not fail Elizabeth again.

The Queen's breath caught in her throat. Mary was about to speak.

'*Sí*,' Mary whispered, her head turned aside. '*Sí, sí, entiendo*.'

My gaze widened on the Queen's face. She had spoken under her breath in Spanish, but to whom?

Rapidly, I searched the room with my eyes whilst trying not to draw attention to myself, still on my knees behind the princess. Perhaps there, in the shadows behind the bed, where the curtains hung most darkly . . .

Queen Mary stirred. She gestured Elizabeth to rise and held out her hand.

'Come, sister, let us be comfortable together and argue no longer. I had a most favourable report from the priests who were with you at Woodstock, and I know you have taken the Catholic faith to your heart.'

Elizabeth stepped forward and kissed Mary's hand, then drew back, swaying slightly as though ill.

'Perhaps I have been too harsh with you,' the Queen muttered, seeming genuinely contrite. 'Your cheeks seem very flushed. The palace at Woodstock was very damp, I am told. The air there does not seem to have agreed with you.'

'I am not as well as Your Majesty,' Elizabeth replied, lying smoothly. I saw her head turn as though her gaze was lingering on those deep shadows behind the curtained bed. 'But now that I have come to court again, Your Majesty, perhaps my health will improve.'

Was it possible that Elizabeth knew who was hiding there, and was addressing that person – and not the Queen?

The two sisters spoke quietly together, mostly of the pleasures of country living compared to the smells and hardships of court. Then the Queen professed herself tired and dismissed us with a wave of her stubby-fingered hand. I followed Elizabeth out of the apartments, my head bowed discreetly. Had my magick arts had any effect on Queen Mary, or had she been influenced by whoever had been hiding in the shadows?

Whichever, the outcome was the same. All charges against the Lady Elizabeth had been dropped and she was not to be taken to the Tower again. I was overjoyed for the princess, and more than a little relieved for my own sake. If Marcus Dent had survived the hellish storm into which I had cast him, he had not yet sent word to the court that the Lady Elizabeth had a witch for a maidservant. So perhaps my spell that night had held true, binding the witchfinder's tongue and hands against betraying us. It was an exhilarating thought.

Back in the safety of her private apartments, Elizabeth hid her face in her hands and stood speechless for a moment, her whole body shaking. I thought at first that she was weeping. Then she raised her reddish-gold head and burst out laughing, her eyes alight with it.

'I am free!' Elizabeth told Blanche Parry, clapping her hands in delight. 'It is over. I am free!'

EPILOGUE

Promises, Promises

Following her late-night interview with the Queen, the door to Elizabeth's apartments stood constantly open to a stream of well-wishers and courtiers curious to see the newly-pardoned princess. She kept discreetly to her rooms for a few more days, then began to venture out into the court itself. Then Elizabeth was invited to dine in the banqueting hall, and went thankfully, delighted with her new prominence. Even King Philip came to see her on several occasions, his blue eyes appreciative of her youth and beauty. His priests and Spanish courtiers often accompanied him, no less admiring, though I never saw Alejandro de Castillo among them.

Indeed, it was almost June before I saw Alejandro again. That morning, Elizabeth had insisted on a game of bowls in the privy garden, and was playing barefoot in the warm sunshine, surrounded by her newly gathered entourage.

Feeling a little low, I begged leave of Blanche Parry to be excused from my duties for an hour or two. Blanche did not seem to mind. Her eyes glowed as she watched Elizabeth enjoying herself in company once more, free of taint and wearing a newly refitted court gown with a gold foreskirt and peach satin sleeves.

I slipped away from their laughter and games, ducked under the low arch of the waterside gate and took a walk along the gently rolling river.

Even alone, I could not seem to shake off my mood, which felt like a heavy grey cloud hanging over me. Perhaps, I thought dismally, I should have stayed with Elizabeth and hoped to catch the eye of some young man who would offer me marriage and a good home. That was how I had always imagined I would spend my days at court, after all.

Yet now that I was here, and Elizabeth was out of disgrace, I found myself constantly unhappy and on edge. As though there was something else I should have been doing, but I had forgotten what it was.

Suddenly I shrieked in horror. A vast, long-tailed rat had darted out of a muddy hole in the river bank and was scuttling towards me, its black eyes gleaming. There was something horrible about the way the rat stopped a few feet away from me, standing on its hind legs like a man, and with such an air of purpose . . .

I stared. It was as though the rat knew me, as though it had been waiting for me and was now about to attack, its eyes as mad and determined as those of Marcus Dent.

I began to back away, my heart shuddering with panic, and cried aloud as a pair of strong arms seized me.

Looking up with a shocked reprimand on my lips, I fell silent. It was Alejandro de Castillo.

'Why did you scream?' he demanded.

'There was a rat.'

In vain, I looked round, up and down the stinking, muddy bank of the Thames. The black rat had disappeared. I felt myself flush with embarrassment. Standing on its hind legs, indeed. It had been nothing but my stupid imagination running away with me again.

His brows had risen at my explanation. His tone became sardonic. 'This is a river, Meg. There are always rats on a river.'

Now my heart was beating hard for quite another reason. Alejandro was quite infuriatingly handsome, I thought, trying not to stare at his chin, his mouth, the broad forehead or sweeping dark hair.

Was I in love with the Spaniard?

It didn't matter even if I loved him to Hell and back, I told myself fiercely. I turned and fixed my little-girl-in-love gaze on the dirtily flowing river instead of him. This thing bursting in my heart was an impossibility. Alejandro and I could never fit together in this dangerous England that Queen Mary had made. That was something I had to accept, and the sooner the better.

Alejandro set me back on my feet and bowed low, one hand on his sword hilt. I curtseyed in return, unsure why he had come out here after me.

When I looked at him again, his face was as sombre as it had been on the day we parted. I knew then that Alejandro had not forgiven me.

'I hear that Elizabeth is no longer under guard,' he said, watching me steadily.

'Yes, the Queen finally agreed to see her, and after that meeting the guards disappeared.' I felt my cheeks grow hot under his gaze. 'I think we may have you to thank for that courtesy, Señor de Castillo. Her Majesty mentioned your letter.'

His brows rose again at that. '*Señor de Castillo?*' he echoed softly.

My flush deepened. 'Alejandro.'

Alejandro took my hand and raised it to his lips. 'Meg,' he said, pronouncing my name with obvious satisfaction, and there was something in his tone that made my toes curl and my body shiver.

'Anyway, thank you for helping,' I whispered.

'It is King Philip you should thank for the Lady Elizabeth's release,' he told me quietly. Although he was still not smiling, the taut lines about his mouth seemed to have melted away.

'So the King *was* there!' I exclaimed, and he hushed me. I dropped my voice. 'I knew there was someone else in the chamber with us, hiding behind the bed curtains. The Queen spoke in Spanish. So it was the King?'

At last he smiled, and gave a little nod. 'But that is not to be told to Elizabeth.'

I searched his face. 'Very well.'

A stately barge of courtiers on a pleasure trip floated

slowly past on the Thames. Some of the richly dressed lords and ladies on board stared at us, much to my annoyance. I stared back until they averted their eyes.

Frowning, Alejandro touched my hood with its trailing veil. 'Is your hair growing back under this?'

Damn my blush!

'A little every day,' I agreed. 'The Lady Elizabeth thinks it best if I keep my hair hidden while it grows, so the courtiers don't stare.'

Alejandro nodded. 'Of course,' he interrupted bluntly. 'She wants you to marry.'

'No.' I laughed at his misunderstanding. 'Quite the opposite. I do not think Elizabeth wants me to marry at all. Now she is back at court, it suits her better to have other unmarried women about her. This hood is so severe, I think she's hoping no man will look twice at me.'

'A court of virgins,' he mused, 'to set against an ageing Queen, still undelivered of her child?'

I looked away. I had been wrong. He had understood perfectly.

'There is a whisper,' I said cautiously, 'that the Queen is not pregnant at all. That she was never pregnant.'

Alejandro looked sombre again. 'Time will tell,' was all he would say on that score, though he took my hand again. This time I could feel his heart beat through the rapid thud of warm blood. His thumb caressed the inside of my palm. 'Meg, I am glad to have found you alone at last. There is something I wish to ask you. That is, I was wondering . . .'

My mouth was suddenly dry. I stared up at him, terrified of what he was going to say. If I was honest, I had dreamed of this moment a thousand times, staring out of the window or lying in my bed at night. I had imagined Alejandro's voice, how he would take me in his arms afterwards . . .

For a few precious seconds, I met his beautiful eyes and my heart sang with joy. And then reality flooded back into my heart, cold and cruel as the water they had tried to drown me in. Alejandro was soon to be a priest. I was a witch, or would be one day, if I could find a way to complete my apprenticeship now that my aunt was dead.

Such a marriage would be like hitching a cart to a cat. Fur would fly from the beginning.

'My family back in Spain is very wealthy,' he began, as though this would reassure me. His smile was awkward. 'I have my own large and gracious home in the country, and lands too, with a marvellous vineyard. I even have a title that I will inherit in time, for only a nobleman may become a priest in the Order of Santiago. I would be honoured if you would share those things with me, Meg Lytton.'

The blood had drained from my face. I had heard little of what he had said. I knew only too well though what I must say in return.

I shook my head vehemently. 'Alejandro, no.'

He frowned at my refusal. 'But you don't understand. I am asking you to marry me.'

I felt as though my heart had been torn from my body and tossed into the swiftly flowing River Thames beside us. 'I know,' I whispered, and looked down at my hand, the hand he was still holding, his thumb still moving slowly across my skin. 'Please don't.'

Alejandro released my hand at once. He stood there in silence, his brows knitted fiercely together, his dark eyes fixed on mine. He looked like a man who had just heard his own death sentence pronounced, and yet could still not take it in.

He shook his head. 'This answer,' he said slowly, his voice raw, 'I cannot accept. I refuse to accept it.'

'You must, for I will not marry you.'

'Give me a reason why not!'

I sought for one which would satisfy him. 'Because I do not love you.'

'Yes, you do,' he said tautly, and his lips pulled back from his teeth in a mirthless smile. 'That is a lie.'

'I am not noble. We would not suit.'

'Your father is a landowner. He could afford to buy a coat of arms for his family if he chose. You have served a royal princess at the Queen's court. That will be enough to satisfy my family.'

I stared at him, fragments of my broken heart falling about us like black relentless rain, burning wherever they fell.

He nodded grimly at my silence. 'You have no reason to

refuse me. Now give me your answer, and this time make it "Yes".'

'You can't bully me into marrying you!' I cried furiously.

'Can I not?' Alejandro demanded, and grabbed my arm, dragging me ruthlessly towards him.

His mouth met mine and we kissed, my whole body leaning instinctively into his. Compulsively, my hands touched his dark hair, his strong neck, the flat expanse of his chest. Ah, I truly loved him! Alejandro laughed under his breath and drew me closer. I was giving myself away with every ragged breath I took, and I knew it.

He drew back and looked down at me triumphantly, his eyes glittering. 'So you do love me. Why pretend not to?'

'I'm a witch,' I moaned. 'And you . . . you still intend to become a priest, don't you?'

His hands tightened on my shoulders, and he nodded. 'As soon as we get back to Spain, yes. Priests in my order are permitted to marry, so long as they observe certain strict rules of chastity. But that will not be too hard to do, for I cannot risk your life.'

It was my turn to frown. 'Risk my life?'

'The curse,' Alejandro reminded me grimly. 'Julia's dying curse on me for betraying her. She swore that the woman I love will die in childbirth, and my child along with her. I cannot risk your death. So I will not be tempted to break the chastity vows of my order.'

'I cannot live like that, Alejandro.'

He lowered his gaze to the ground and seemed to consider this for a moment. 'You think it would be too hard for you to abstain?' he asked at last. There was a dark colour in his cheeks. 'For me too. You are very beautiful, Meg. But I will control myself to save your life.'

'I didn't mean it like that.' I tried to explain myself, painstakingly. 'I can't live with you if you become a priest, Alejandro, because I will not give up being a witch. It is in my blood. It is what makes me special. But unless I give it up, we cannot marry.'

Alejandro let me go and took a step backwards. 'I had not realized how much witchcraft meant to you,' he muttered.

I saw the hurt in his face and longed to comfort him. But it would be cruel to make him think I might change my mind.

'I'm sorry,' I whispered. 'It has always been hard for the Canley women to marry, for that reason. My aunt never married. But my mother did, and she had to give up the craft to do so. She knew it was impossible to live as a mother and a wife, and still be a witch.'

He turned away for a moment, staring with dull eyes at the river water. Then Alejandro raised his head and looked back at me. 'I need time to think, Meg, and so do you. But I don't want to lose you. Will you at least agree to a period of betrothal and give me your final answer in a year?'

'My final answer?' I was perplexed.

Alejandro nodded and came back, taking my hands in his. There was a new and burning light in his face.

'Sometimes in my country, a couple will agree to a betrothal for a year and a day. More than a year sometimes, if need be. A young man may have to go off to war, or to make his fortune. So the woman agrees not to give her promise to any other man until the year is up. Then the man returns and asks her again.'

'In a year's time?'

His smile was brilliant. 'Say yes to me now, Meg, and our marriage will not be binding until I ask you again in a year and a day.'

I stared at him. Everything in my body tingled with the excitement of this crazy idea, that all I had to do was say 'Yes' now, and in a year and a day, I could take it back and say 'No'. Meanwhile, we would be as good as betrothed to each other.

'Well, *mi querida*?' Alejandro prompted me, his eyes on mine.

I thought of my aunt's prophecy that a traveller would bring danger. Marcus Dent had just returned from Germany at the time, and Alejandro would have been on his way from Spain. If the prophecy had meant Marcus, the danger was now past. But if it *was* Alejandro my aunt had seen in her vision, that danger might yet lie ahead for me. *Beware a traveller who comes over water, over land.*

I stared at him, torn between love and prophecy. I could not make my mind up which man it had indicated. Meanwhile, I had a more urgent question to answer.

I took a deep breath and gave myself up to the danger. 'Yes.'

Acknowledgements

I owe my thanks to my marvellous agent Luigi Bonomi and his talented wife Alison for their inspiration and support during the writing of this novel; to my editor Lauren Buckland, whose helpful and perceptive suggestions greatly improved *Witchstruck*; and also to Annie Eaton, Natalie Doherty, Emily Banyard, Lisa Mahoney and all the team at Random House Children's Books for their infectious enthusiasm and encouragement; to my husband Steve and my children Becki, Dylan, Morris and Indigo, who have had much to put up with by way of crazed moods, lengthy absences and towering stacks of books in every room; and to all my writerly friends on Twitter, Facebook, and at the Romantic Novelists' Association, without whose ongoing friendship and support I would have struggled not only to start but to finish this novel.